Lucy Ashford studied Englis
Nottingham University, and the Regency era is her favourite period. She lives with her husband in an old stone cottage in the Derbyshire Peak District, close to beautiful Chatsworth House, and she loves to walk in the surrounding hills while letting her imagination go to work on her latest story.

Also by Lucy Ashford

'Twelfth Night Proposal'
in *Snowbound Wedding Wishes*
The Outrageous Belle Marchmain
The Return of Lord Conistone
The Rake's Bargain
The Captain and His Innocent
The Master of Calverley Hall
Unbuttoning Miss Mathilda
The Widow's Scandalous Affair
The Viscount's New Housekeeper
Challenging the Brooding Earl
Lord Lambourne's Forbidden Debutante

COMPROMISED INTO MARRYING THE DUKE

Lucy Ashford

MILLS & BOON

First published in Great Britain 2025
by Mills & Boon, an imprint of HarperCollins*Publishers* Ltd,
1 London Bridge Street, London, SE1 9GF

www.harpercollins.co.uk

HarperCollins*Publishers*, Macken House, 39/40 Mayor Street Upper,
Dublin 1, D01 C9W8, Ireland

ISBN: 978-0-263-34515-5

04/25

This book contains FSC™ certified paper
and other controlled sources to ensure responsible forest management.

For more information visit www.harpercollins.co.uk/green.

Printed and Bound in the UK using 100% Renewable Electricity
at CPI Group (UK) Ltd, Croydon, CR0 4YY

Prologue

Oakfields, Kent—
June, four years ago

When Marianne Blake woke up on that sunny summer morning, her first thought was: *Today I will see Anthony, for the first time in almost a year.*

She was seventeen now, nearly eighteen, but she still felt as excited as a child on Christmas morning. Jumping out of bed, she ran to peep out of the window and saw that the grooms were busy sweeping the courtyard and the local dairyman's cart was trundling up the drive with supplies of milk and cheese. There was to be a party here at Oakfields tonight, to celebrate her older brother Simon's twenty-first birthday—and Anthony had promised to come, all the way from London.

Anthony's father was a duke and she knew that some day Anthony would inherit the title and all the family's wealth. But he had been Simon's best friend for years, ever since they were at Eton together, and she liked to believe he was her friend too.

She went over to her dressing table to brush her long hair, remembering how Anthony teased her about it. 'Copper top', he used to call her, pointing to her long and rather unruly chestnut locks which always wanted to escape from the ribbons that were meant to tame them. Anthony's hair was black, his eyes were a kind of silvery grey and whenever he smiled at her she felt herself glowing inside.

He usually spent most of the summer at his father's vast house in Kent, Cleveland Hall. But since the Hall was less than a mile away from Oakfields, he rode over here often and when Marianne once asked him why, he had thought a moment then replied, 'Because your house feels like a home.'

She had been puzzled. Had he meant that his father's wonderful house didn't? She hadn't asked him any more, but later Simon reminded her that Anthony's mother had died long ago and his father, the Duke of Cleveland, much preferred to live in their grand London home. Gazing at herself in the mirror, she sighed a little. Perhaps Anthony too had learned to prefer London, because he'd not visited them since last August—and that had only been to say goodbye.

'My father wants me to live with him in Mayfair,' Anthony had told her. 'He says it's my duty as his heir, and of course he is right.'

What could she say? Anthony was already a marquis, the Marquis of Kelham. Some day he would be the Duke of Cleveland. Their lives were diverging, the way they were always destined to. Coming to Simon's birthday party was an act of loyalty to an old friend, that was all.

Feeling rather despondent now, she tied back her hair, put on a plain print dress then went downstairs—and for the rest of the morning she didn't get a chance to fret about tonight, or Anthony, or her hair. For she quickly realised that her mother, Lady Hermione, was driving their poor staff to distraction with her instructions for the party and it wasn't long before Mrs Thurlby the housekeeper came rushing up to Marianne.

'Please, Miss Marianne, I beg you. Can you tell Lady Hermione that Cook and I really do have everything under control?'

'I'm sorry, Mrs Thurlby,' said Marianne earnestly. 'My mother is very excited about tonight, but I'll see what I can do.'

She rather feared she could do little. Her mother's ambitions for this party had escalated day by day and Marianne was worried because Simon, who'd been at the races in Newmarket all week, was travelling home with absolutely no idea of what lay in store for him.

'Remember, Simon doesn't like too much fuss,' she had tried to warn her mother, but Lady Hermione had blithely waved her daughter's doubts aside. What could Marianne do to distract her? Inspiration struck when she spotted that a delivery of extravagant hot-house flowers had just arrived. Off she went to find her mother, who was inspecting the silverware in the dining room.

'Mother,' she said, 'those flowers you ordered are here. Don't you think that you, as the hostess, should arrange them yourself rather than leaving it to the housemaids?'

'What an excellent idea,' declared Lady Hermione. 'I believe I always did have an artistic flair.'

'Indeed. You'll make a wonderful job of it,' said Marianne, 'and tonight everyone will look at them and say, "That must be Lady Hermione's work!"'

Marianne left her happily absorbed in her task and escaped out to the stables to chat with the grooms. After lunch she sought refuge from the general bustle by retreating to the parlour, where her mother's cat Cuthbert was dozing on the sofa. With a small sigh she sat beside him and tried not to keep thinking, over and over again, that later Anthony would be here.

She attempted to read a book. She even tried to read an old copy of *The Lady's Magazine*, until at two o'clock precisely she heard her mother calling, 'Marianne! Your brother has arrived!'

She ran to the window to see that indeed, her brother was riding into the yard looking exceedingly grand in his caped riding coat. But she also registered his astonishment as he took in all the activity in the courtyard and soon enough the whole house rang with the sound of his voice in the hallway.

'Mother,' he was calling. 'Mother, what on earth is going on?'

Within moments Lady Hermione was leading him into the parlour. 'What is going on?' their mother echoed. 'Why, Simon, we're having a party tonight, darling! For your very special day!'

Simon glanced at his younger sister then rubbed his forehead in disbelief. 'Marianne. Didn't I tell you weeks ago that I did *not* want any fuss?'

Before Marianne could utter a word, Lady Hermione replied with soothing words. 'Now, no grumpiness, Simon, please. It's only fitting that we mark the occasion, surely?'

'Really, Mother, is there a need for such a grand affair? We're not that sort of family.'

'What sort of family is that, Simon? Your dear father was very highly regarded in the neighbourhood, while I am, after all, the daughter of an earl.'

Marianne nearly giggled then and her brother rolled his eyes. 'Mother, you've been saying that for as long as I can remember,' said Simon. 'But you must remember that we never actually met your father, because he was disappointed that you married someone without a title.'

'That was highly foolish of him,' said Lady Hermione. 'And do stop being so tetchy, dear!'

Simon let out a loud sigh then grinned at Marianne. 'Well, obviously the party can't be cancelled at this late stage, so I suppose I'd better make the best of it.' He was shrugging off his coat. 'Is there a guest list? Who have you invited?'

Lady Hermione brightened. 'Oh, just about *everybody!* Our neighbours the Critchlows are coming, and all your father's old friends with whom he used to play bridge, and several of our acquaintances from Sevenoaks—'

'Yes, yes.' Simon nodded. 'But have you invited Anthony?'

'Naturally. He was the first on my list—and he wrote *immediately* from London, to say that he would be coming.'

'That's good, at any rate.' Simon looked at his sister. 'A party just wouldn't be right without Anthony, would it, Marianne? Marianne, are you listening?'

Marianne had suddenly busied herself stroking Cuthbert, but now she looked up at him and said, 'Good heavens, we simply had to invite Anthony. It will be rather nice to see him.'

'Rather nice?' Simon widened his eyes in surprise. 'I thought you would be delighted. You were always fond of him.'

'Of course she is fond of him,' declared Lady Hermione. 'We all are. Dear Anthony. Even though he's a marquis, he's promised to arrive early—isn't that good of him?'

But Marianne was glancing down in dismay at her shabby dress. 'How early, exactly?'

'Didn't I tell you, dear? I received a letter from him just this morning, saying that he hoped to be here by four.'

Marianne gasped. Simon looked at her with a grin on his face. 'That gives you less than two hours to prepare for him, then.'

'Indeed,' said Lady Hermione. She pointed to her daughter. 'Marianne, wherever did you find that odd dress? And you have bits of hay caught in your hem. Anyone would think you'd been out in the stables!'

'That's because I have been out in the stables, Mother,' said Marianne.

'Well, you must certainly go and change before Anthony arrives. He is our chief guest, and a very important one at that. Off you go, and I'll send one of the maids up to help you.'

'There's no need to fuss,' said Simon. 'Anthony has seen Marianne looking far worse than she does now. Like the day when she jumped into the pigpen for a bet, but then she couldn't get out so Anthony and I had to—'

'Stop!' Lady Hermione had her hands over her ears. 'Stop, Simon. I cannot bear it.'

'I'm just pointing it out. Anyway, I'm starving, so I'll get something to eat in the kitchen then keep a lookout for Anthony. If he's early, like you said, then he can give me a hand shifting furniture, that sort of thing. I assume there'll be dancing?'

'Of course,' said Lady Hermione loftily. 'But you cannot ask Anthony to do such menial work. And another thing, Simon—*Simon?*'

Whatever she was about to say went unanswered, because Simon had already vanished in the direction of the savoury smells coming from the kitchen. Marianne also took the opportunity to escape and swiftly climbed the stairs to her bedroom, where she sat on her bed and frowned.

Her mother had such grand ambitions for her, but by the standards of the London *ton*, the Blakes of

Oakfields were minor players indeed. Her father had been a well-respected gentleman and landowner, while Lady Hermione herself was one of the several daughters of an earl. But unfortunately, this earl had no sons, with the result that his estate, wealth and title had gone to some distant relative who wanted nothing at all to do with the rest of the family. Yes, it was generous of Anthony to come here today, but his future lay elsewhere.

She supposed she'd always known it really, but her spirits sank anew as she gazed down at herself. Her mother was right, she looked a mess: this old dress was patched and faded, and she knew without looking that her hair must be in a tangle, for however much she tried to tame it, it always ended up falling in disarray around her shoulders.

Slowly she rose to her feet. Some day, Anthony would be the Duke of Cleveland and would choose a bride from amongst the elite of Society's debutantes. She, on the other hand, was expected to marry a country gentleman and be very happy. Or so everyone kept telling her.

'Just think, Miss Marianne,' Mrs Hinchcliffe the cook had said to her only the other day. 'It won't be long before you're collecting admirers. You're almost eighteen, and plenty of girls have sweethearts or even husbands by then.'

Yes. She knew that. But she really couldn't imagine marrying anyone from their current circle of acquaintances, who were mostly farmers with a conversation that often revolved around whether to grow turnips or cabbages in the coming season. She wasn't ready for such a life. It wasn't what she wanted.

So what *did* she want?

She went over to her dressing table and reached to the back of her drawer for a little velvet purse she'd sewn herself. From it she drew out a slender gold ring set with pink garnets that sparkled as she slipped it on her finger.

She wanted the impossible. She wanted Anthony.

That was the moment when a tall, gaunt-looking maid came bustling in. 'Dreaming again, Miss Marianne?'

'Oh Alice, it's you! Mother said she would send someone up to me.' Alice had been a servant here for as long as anyone could remember and Marianne was fond of her. She added, 'Mother is rather agitated, I'm afraid.'

'Agitated? Her Ladyship's in a right old flap if you ask me. She warned me that at the moment you look like a farm girl and she wasn't far wrong, was she?'

'I've been in the stables,' Marianne explained. 'I was helping the grooms.'

'So that's why you've got bits of hay in your hair?'

'Oh, my goodness. Have I?'

'You certainly have. We'd best start tidying you up.'

With that, Alice set to work and Marianne submitted patiently. Her long hair was braided and coiled on the crown of her head; her old dress was cast aside and a new one, made of pale green silk, was eased on and carefully adjusted until finally Alice stepped back.

'There now.' The maid spoke with an air of satisfaction. 'Take a look at yourself, why don't you? You know, you're turning into quite a beauty.'

What? Marianne was so surprised at this unexpected compliment that she almost laughed. This dress was pretty, she had to admit, but her red-gold hair had a tendency to curl, which was not at all fashionable. Madame Gertrude, her mother's hairdresser, often commented on it during her visits here. 'Marianne's hair,' she had once declared, 'is an unusual colour. It is also rather wayward, but if suitably styled it can look quite charming!'

That, thought Marianne, was lukewarm praise indeed. As for her eyes, they were brown. Brown! They should have been forget-me-not blue or sea-green if she wanted to be admired as a beauty—which, she reminded herself, she definitely did not.

She looked hopefully at Alice and said, 'Have we finished? Please?'

'For now.' Alice wagged a finger in warning. 'But don't you go doing anything to spoil that lovely dress, will you?'

'I'll try. And thank you!'

Once Alice had gone Marianne flopped down on her bed, only to jump up again as she realised she had crumpled her new dress already. She sighed. Honestly, this was ridiculous; here she was all dressed up, and it would be hours before the party began.

But, a little voice whispered inside her, *Anthony might be here soon.*

She left her room and tiptoed to the landing at the top of the staircase. In the distance she could hear the rattle of pots and pans in the kitchen where Mrs Hinchcliffe was rallying her troops, and there was also the sound of heavy furniture being shifted around in the drawing room. All the staff would be buzzing with excitement at the news that Anthony was coming, for they had all been fond of him. Would he be amused by her efforts today to dress like a young lady of the *ton*, or—even worse—would he perhaps feel sorry for her?

For heaven's sake, she told herself sternly. *Get*

busy with something—anything—rather than standing around muttering to yourself like this.

'I know!' she said aloud. 'I shall go into the garden and gather some flowers.'

She hesitated, because there were a lot already in the house. But those exotic orchids and lilies weren't the kind of flowers that she loved. She liked the ones that grew in abundance in their own garden, so back she went to her bedroom, where she changed her flimsy satin shoes for some laced leather boots and put on a long and shapeless cotton jacket to protect her gown. After collecting a wicker basket from a storeroom, she slipped out through a side door into the garden and began picking sweet peas. But the sun was warm, the sparrows were twittering in the apple trees and before long she came to a halt and closed her eyes in sheer pleasure at all the delightful scents and sounds.

Your complexion, Marianne! her mother would scold. *Where is your bonnet? You must remember, at all times, that as a lady you have to avoid the sun!*

But she loved the sun. Humming under her breath, she pushed some pale blue flowers into her braided hair and carried on happily filling her basket, when suddenly she stopped. She had heard some very purposeful, very male footsteps coming from the house in her direction and she whirled round to see… Anthony.

He had taken off his coat and loosened his cravat. His riding boots were still dusty from his journey and his dark hair was falling untidily over his forehead, just as it always did. With the sun shining down on him, he looked so handsome that for a moment she couldn't speak and when she did, she was quite sure that her voice came out as a squeak.

'Anthony…' she said. 'I didn't realise you were here!'

He smiled that slightly teasing smile of his. 'I arrived rather early. I hope I haven't startled you too much?'

'No. Of course not!' She felt she was stumbling over every word. 'Simon must have been very glad to see you. I'm afraid he wasn't warned about the party and when he realised what was in store for him, I feared he might turn round and head off to rejoin his friends at the Newmarket races.'

Oh, dear. Now she was talking far too quickly, babbling almost. But Anthony was merely nodding with sympathy.

'I think,' he mused, 'that your brother has resigned himself to the inevitable. I asked Lady Hermione where you were and she told me you were upstairs, getting yourself ready for the party, but I guessed you might have escaped.'

Heavens. Was he saying that he'd come outside to look for her?

She quickly reminded herself that he was only here because he was Simon's friend and he would always see her as Simon's lively if often annoying little sister.

'Yes,' she said lightly, 'my mother was worried that I would leave everything too late, so I did get changed into my party dress. But then I didn't know what to do and so I decided to come out here for some flowers.'

He raised his eyebrows. 'Even though there are already quite a number of exotic and very expensive floral arrangements throughout your house?'

'I know! My mother ordered all those bouquets from her favourite florist in Sevenoaks. But I decided to gather some sweet peas to put in the entrance hall, because…because…'

She stopped. She looked down at her brown boots—goodness, they were ugly.

'Because,' Anthony said softly, 'your father loved them?'

She gazed up at him. *He remembered.* 'Yes,' she said. 'Yes, sweet peas were always his favourite flowers.' She would never forget that Anthony had come to join the bereaved family at her father's funeral three years ago, when they were all reeling from the shock of his sudden death.

'I think—' and Anthony spoke gravely now '—that your father would approve of your choice.' He added, 'Your mother would too.'

'I'm not sure about that.' Marianne sighed a little. 'I think she will be imagining that I'm still up in my bedchamber, doing whatever young ladies are supposed to do before a party.' She pointed to her jacket. 'I knew my mother would be worried about my dress, so I put this on to protect it.'

'I remember the jacket,' he said. 'You often wore it when we went for walks.'

'Indeed, and I've changed into these old boots so I don't ruin my party shoes. You see, I honestly did want to make an effort for tonight. Everyone is always saying I should act like a lady, and of course they are quite right to scold me, because sometimes my behaviour is ridiculous!'

He held up his hand. 'Marianne,' he said, 'I've never known you to be ridiculous. And please don't change, ever.'

She was speechless. He had often stood close to her like this, often smiled down at her like this, but she had never noticed before how his grey eyes glinted with golden lights in the sun, or how a faint shadow of stubble already darkened his jaw. She had never noticed either how his lips looked as though they might be silky and soft to the touch…

The sun still shone overhead. White fluffy clouds continued to sail across the blue sky and the bees buzzed happily around the fragrant flowerbeds. But Marianne's heart was beating fast, and it was because of what he'd said. *Don't change, ever.*

Anthony had been her friend for years and she had never been shy with him before. But this time she could think of nothing to say and, uncertain of what to do next, she reached for more flowers but stupidly dropped her basket. Inwardly cursing her clumsiness, she stooped to pick up the scattered blooms but somehow, she tripped over a raised paving stone.

She was still off-balance when Anthony reached to steady her, his hands firm and warm on her waist.

He had rolled up his shirtsleeves and once more she noticed things she'd never noticed before, like the way that his forearms were tanned and muscular, and covered with fine dark hairs. She gazed up at him to see that his jaw was set hard, his eyes had darkened and she realised that a low and unfamiliar pulse was fluttering through her body.

Her female friends were always gossiping about men and whispering secrets to one another. 'Marianne isn't interested,' they liked to declare. 'She doesn't want to flirt and have fun. She'll end up a spinster, most likely.'

Marianne pretended not to care what they said and anyway they couldn't be more wrong, because she did have her dreams. When she was younger, she had loved to read tales of adventure and romance, and whenever she'd pictured her storybook heroes they always had thick dark hair like Anthony and grey eyes like Anthony. Who was looking down at her now in a way that made her think of…

Of what?

Of his kisses, she suddenly realised. Of his lips, on hers.

He was four years older than her, and some day he would marry someone who was worthy to be his future duchess: someone beautiful and sophisticated, of a rank to match his own. She was the daughter of a country gentleman, nothing more.

But Anthony's hands still rested on her waist, warm and strong and wonderful, and she realised she had held her breath for so long that she was starting to feel lightheaded. *He* was the reason why she wasn't interested in the bashful young men who approached her at the village dances. *He* was the reason why she didn't join the groups of girls who gathered at parties and giggled over which of their suitors was the most dashing. Anthony already possessed her heart.

She backed away from him, clutching her basket of flowers. 'It was good of you to come today, Anthony. But I am afraid you will find the entertainment here at Oakfields very dull after the fun you must have in London. All those balls and parties and nights at the theatre—how exciting it must be!'

'Marianne,' he said, 'often I don't care much for London's so-called pleasures.' He was looking back now at the old half-timbered house. 'In fact, I believe that some of the happiest times I've ever spent in my life have been here at Oakfields, with you and your family.'

For a moment she couldn't speak. Then she shook her head, trying to laugh. 'No,' she declared. 'Surely not!'

'I mean it.' He added lightly, 'Unlike Oakfields, my father's house is exceptionally cold and draughty.'

She knew he was referring to his father's mansion close by and she nodded fervently. 'Cleveland Hall is rather large, but we had fun there. When your father was away, we used to play hide and seek, didn't we?'

'You and I and Simon, yes. There are so many rooms that sometimes even I get lost.' He had been smiling but suddenly his expression changed and he pointed at her hand. 'That little ring. We found it one wet afternoon when the three of us were exploring the attics, didn't we? So you still wear it?'

'I like it,' she said, almost in a whisper. *And you gave it to me, Anthony.*

He had lifted her hand to inspect the ring, but now his eyes were searching her face. 'While I've been in London,' he said at last, 'I've realised a lot of things. I've realised that the city can be ugly in all kinds of ways, and London life can be shallow and cruel. I've missed the countryside—and I've missed you, Marianne.'

He had *missed* her? Her heart was thudding so hard that she was sure he must hear it.

'No.' She shook her head in disbelief.

'It's true,' he said. 'At every party I go to, at every ball, I find myself remembering the happy times we've shared together. There are girls in London who imagine they are beautiful, but they aren't. Not compared to you.'

At his words, at the look in his eyes, her heart stuttered to a halt then began to thump again, this time slowly and painfully. She felt herself on the verge of saying something stupidly flippant, like, *No, that's ridiculous. Look at me, with my pitiful attempts to dress like a lady. To behave like a lady.*

But she didn't say another word and neither did he, because they had both become aware that a horse was galloping along the road to the house. On seeing them, the horse's rider hauled his steed to a halt and leaned forward in his saddle.

'I have a message from London,' he called. 'For the Duke of Cleveland's son, the Marquis of Kelham. It's urgent!'

Anthony strode swiftly up to the man. 'I am the Marquis,' Marianne heard him command. 'Give me the letter.'

It didn't take him long to read it. After folding it up, he came back to her, looking tense and pale. He said, in a voice devoid of emotion, 'I'm sorry, Marianne. But I have to return to London.'

No. No, this could not be. Her heart was thumping again, but this time she felt as cold as ice.

'Now?' she whispered.

'Yes. Now.' He lifted her hand and she could see he was looking at the ring.

'You'll want it back,' she said. 'After all, it's not really mine, is it?'

'Keep it,' he said. 'Keep it and remember me, will you?' He pressed her hand then let go. 'And now I must go to make my apologies to your brother and Lady Hermione.'

She stood there after he'd gone, unable to speak or even think. She wanted to call out, *Anthony. Please don't leave.* But the words wouldn't come.

She realised that the sun had gone behind a cloud and the heady scent of the flowers seemed suddenly cloying. Finally, she too went inside and put the sweet peas she'd gathered into a small vase in the parlour. Then she climbed to her bedchamber, where she took off the little ring and replaced it in its velvet purse at the back of the drawer. By the time she returned downstairs she found that Anthony had gone, and he had given no reason for his sudden departure.

Lady Hermione was upset and Simon immediately drew Marianne aside to say in a low voice, 'I saw you and Anthony out in the garden, and he was holding you. What happened, Marianne? What did he say?'

'Nothing.' She tried to speak lightly. 'Nothing of any importance, Simon.'

'Have you any idea why he left so suddenly?'

'A letter arrived for him, that's all.'

Anthony was frowning. 'Perhaps his father wanted him to return. Anthony has always had a strong sense of duty.'

Lady Hermione joined them. 'His departure is a disappointment,' she said. Clearly, she was trying to make the best of things. 'But doubtless we shall see Anthony again very soon.'

Marianne didn't say another word. Instead, she

went back upstairs, to take off her boots and her shabby coat. *Will I see him again soon? Did I imagine everything he just said? Or perhaps I mistook his gallantry for interest*, she told herself. *Naïve, unsophisticated and foolish, that's what I am. He would hardly have left like that if he'd meant any of it, would he? Foolish, foolish Marianne.*

By the time Anthony arrived at the Cleveland family's mansion in Mayfair that evening, his father was pacing the drawing room and there was another person there—a rough-looking man Anthony had never seen before.

'Who is this?' Anthony demanded. 'What is going on?'

His father's voice was hoarse. 'I've been gambling, Anthony,' he said.

Most men gambled. Anthony himself did from time to time. He said, 'Is that a problem?'

The stranger stepped forward then. 'My name, my lord marquis,' he said, 'is Ned Gibson and I run a gambling house that's not usually visited by men of your standing. But a while ago your father began to call in and he got himself into a spot of bother.'

Anthony felt a growing sense of apprehension. 'So you've come for money,' he said. 'How much?'

Ned Gibson pursed his lips. 'Oh, I want rather

more than money, my lord. You see, I've a fancy to have my daughter made a duchess.'

Anthony was so astonished that he almost laughed. He glanced at his father then back at Gibson. 'What? Surely you don't expect...'

Gibson was shaking his head. 'I'm not thinking of your father for my daughter, oh, no. I'm thinking, my lord, of your fine self.'

'No. Oh, no.' Anthony was angry now. Coldly angry. 'State what money you need, Gibson, and get out of here. Your demand is laughable.'

'Really? Perhaps not when I tell you the worst of it. You see, your father cheated.'

Anthony looked in disbelief at his father, who had sunk into a chair with his head bowed. Gambling, even heavy gambling, was acceptable amongst the *ton*. Cheating was not. Cheating was beyond the pale.

Gibson was saying, 'He cheated all right. One of my men warned me and I caught him at it. Take my daughter as your bride, my lord—no one will know she's mine. Then I'll cancel all that your father owes me, I'll even give you a handsome sum to pay off his gambling debts elsewhere—at least the ones we know about—and I'll keep silent about the cheating business. Otherwise...'

His meaning was obvious. *Otherwise, your fa-*

ther's name—your family's name—will be dragged through the mud.

Anthony's reply was swift. 'If I do what you say, Gibson, then people will think I married to settle gaming house debts of my own. Otherwise, why the hell would someone of my rank marry a complete unknown?'

'Proud, aren't you?' Gibson responded. 'But what's your alternative? Are you going to let your own father be denounced as a cheat? Either your father will face universal scorn for his weaknesses, or you marry my daughter. The girl is nineteen and she's really quite pretty. She speaks and behaves well enough and I can guarantee she's a virgin. No one will know she's mine, and as for me, I'll keep well out of your way, I swear.'

Anthony looked at his father's distraught figure. Then his gaze fastened on the historic crest of the Cleveland family that adorned the wall above the fireplace, with the motto that had been drummed into him since he was an infant. *Honora familia tua semper.*

Honour your family, always.

Chapter One

London 1817

One evening in May, almost four years later, Anthony, the Duke of Cleveland, climbed into the magnificent carriage that waited outside his home in Grosvenor Square and set off for the Earl of Ware's annual ball. It would be his first formal appearance in Society for some time and he wondered just how long it would be before he heard the whispers that circulated about him.

Just fancy, the Duke of Cleveland is showing his face at last! He married an unknown girl for her money, doubtless to pay off gambling debts, then he packed her off to his house in Kent, poor thing, while he enjoyed himself in London. She's dead now and his father died soon afterwards, probably broken-hearted by his son's scandalous behaviour...

Yes, Anthony knew what to expect.

It was a short journey to the Earl of Ware's house in Berkeley Square and once there he only had to take one step inside the Earl's vast ballroom for all eyes to turn on him. Even the musicians faltered and for a moment the silence was acute. But Anthony guessed that at any moment he would be surrounded by sycophants and greeted, outwardly at least, with nothing but profuse words of welcome.

He was, after all, a duke, and his hosts were already heading in his direction.

'Your Grace!' exclaimed the Countess of Ware. 'How marvellous to see you. We are truly honoured you have chosen to re-enter Society at our humble abode!'

The huge diamond on her purple silk turban bobbed up and down as she nudged her husband. 'My dear,' she said to him, 'Isn't it wonderful to have Anthony back in our midst, after his time of tragic mourning?'

'Wonderful,' echoed the Earl heartily. 'Wonderful.'

Anthony bowed his head. 'You are too kind.'

'Not at all,' said the Countess. 'Your poor wife, she was so young! And then, only months later, your dear father died. "The Glorious Duke", we all called him. Such a distinguished man.'

'Yes,' said Anthony. 'Indeed.'

The Countess was already looking around. 'Well,' she said breezily, 'we must allow you to circulate. Your many friends will be anxious to welcome you.'

Anthony gave his usual cool smile and they left.

Did he have any friends? Of course there were many who claimed they were because he was back once more in Society, he was now a duke and he was also, at the age of twenty-five, a widower. Gentlemen with unmarried sisters or daughters were always eager for his company, but there were only a very few that he trusted—and the best friend of his youth, Simon Blake, was no longer one of them.

Simon had confronted Anthony days after his wedding and made it all too clear what he thought of him. 'Marrying for money,' Simon had said. 'I would never, ever have thought it of you.' Perhaps he was thinking of his poor sister's heart too, as Anthony often had, though fate had now thrown that ship impossibly far off course.

Then, as now, unbidden memories flashed through Anthony's mind of carefree days in the Kent countryside long ago. But he forced them aside. Those days were over, so he braced his broad shoulders for more offers of condolence from London's foremost families. But already he felt oppressed by the heavy smells of perfumes and candlewax in here and he found himself glancing far too often at his watch.

He bore it with patience, the abundance of greetings, the outpouring of sympathy, though few dared to mention the name of his dead wife Cynthia. There were some sins, he supposed, for which not even a duke could be forgiven. He promised himself that as soon as the clock struck eleven he would leave, and indeed he was about to do so. He was even excusing himself from those who surrounded him, when he saw… Marianne Blake.

She was at the far side of the crowded ballroom talking to a slim, fair-haired man whose name, he recalled, was Moseley. He knew that Moseley was a smooth-faced wretch—and as for Marianne, the last time he'd seen her, she certainly hadn't looked like this.

She was wearing a rather unique turquoise ballgown, the likes of which he had never seen in a Society ballroom. She carried a large sequined fan and her red-gold hair was piled up in a sophisticated *chignon*. It was also plain that she and Moseley were definitely not in a state of mutual harmony.

One of his few friends, Tom Duxbury, had mentioned to him the other day that Marianne Blake was now living in London. 'You knew her in the past, Anthony, didn't you? She's engaged again, for the second time in twelve months,' Tom had told him, imparting the news rather carefully, Anthony thought.

'The second time?' Anthony kept his tone indifferent. 'What happened to her first fiancé?'

'He was an army officer, but all that ended abruptly, no one knows why. Later the fellow died in some foreign battle. This time Marianne has agreed to marry Jonathan Moseley.' Tom had glanced a little warily at Anthony. 'I'm not acquainted with him, but I believe Moseley's fairly wealthy and I hope it works out for her. She's regarded as a beauty, but I'm afraid she has acquired a certain reputation since she entered Society last year. You'll maybe have heard that her mother married Sir Edgar Radlett and they all moved to London?'

Anthony had heard. He knew that Oakfields had passed to Lady Hermione after her first husband's death, thanks to a legal settlement drawn up in her favour before their marriage. But now that she had married again everything she owned, including Oakfields, had gone to Sir Edgar.

And Marianne was engaged to Jonathan Moseley. *She has acquired a certain reputation.*

His spirits were low; maybe it was because of the heat and the noise. He could no longer see Marianne and anyway his chance to escape had gone because he was distracted by yet another group of near-strangers clustering around him, so he continued his efforts at polite conversation. But all the time he was remembering an afternoon in a country garden almost four years ago, when he'd realised he could easily fall in love with a beautiful and innocent girl with flowers in her hair.

For Marianne, the evening had begun badly three hours ago when she, her stepfather and her two stepsisters set off to the ball in Sir Edgar Radlett's ancient coach. Sir Edgar had reminded her once more that she was extremely lucky to have received a proposal from Jonathan Moseley.

'You were fortunate to attract his attention, Marianne,' Sir Edgar said. 'I really was a little anxious for your future.'

Always, the man tried to sound concerned and caring, but his comment grated because he had said almost exactly the same thing when she'd ended her brief engagement to Captain Max Weatherbrook of the Queen's Dragoons last year. Sir Edgar liked to declare that he valued her as one of his own, but secretly she suspected he could not wait for her to marry and leave his household.

It was partly her own fault, she knew. She made very little effort these days to get on with him, for she felt he had taken advantage of her mother's vulnerabilities and sometimes she told him so. It was no wonder, then, that Sir Edgar had expressed great pleasure when she became betrothed to Jonathan Moseley three months ago, and Jonathan was outwardly a suitable choice. He was fairly rich and he was civil. He wasn't handsome exactly, but his fair colouring and expensive tailoring gave him a certain distinction amongst the London elite. What was more, he had appeared, at the beginning at least, to be fond of her dear mother.

Unfortunately, Marianne had quickly found there was another side to him. His polite manners could vanish in an instant if he was displeased, his pale blue eyes could become icy-cold and it was soon apparent that many aspects of Marianne's character displeased him very much indeed.

Especially the way she dressed.

Tonight, she was wearing a gown that was in startling contrast to those worn by the fashionable young ladies of the *ton*. Jonathan didn't like it one bit and he'd told her so as they danced the gavotte.

'Well, I like this gown very much,' she had answered. 'I don't care to be like everybody else. I dress to please myself, as should anyone.'

'I've told you before,' said Jonathan curtly, 'that as my fiancée, I expect you to dress—and behave—

with more delicacy. Incidentally, how many glasses of champagne have you drunk tonight?'

'Oh, three or four,' she said. Actually, she was exaggerating to annoy him. 'Who cares?'

Jonathan was silent for a moment. 'Why,' he said at last, 'are you so determined to make a fool of me?'

She looked at him steadfastly and said, 'Have you ever thought that you made a bad mistake in asking me to marry you?'

'I certainly know now that you are a foolish, dangerous flirt. Your dress sense is ridiculous, you drink too much and you think of nothing but your own silly pleasures—'

'Stop,' she said.

'What?'

'I said, *Stop.* There is no need for you to say any more. I am ending our engagement now, Jonathan, and let me tell you, I do so with a feeling of great relief.'

His mouth had fallen open. He really did look rather ridiculous. Then he retaliated by saying, 'Very well. I am actually most grateful to you, because I've been thinking of doing the same thing for weeks.'

'You *have?*'

'Most definitely.'

She nodded thoughtfully. 'You began to regret

your proposal when I asked you if my mother could stay with us once we were married. Didn't you?'

'Yes.' Jonathan's voice was grim. 'Lady Hermione is simply dreadful.'

'Really? Most people find her extremely sweet.'

'She's silly, more like. Is she here tonight?'

'No. She doesn't enjoy parties very much these days.'

'Well,' Jonathan had replied, 'I don't want her and her ridiculous cat under my roof, or you either. You can take your silly, flirting ways and use them on someone else—if they'll have you!'

It was surprising, Marianne had decided, how ugly Jonathan could look when he lost his temper. A footman was passing by with a tray of champagne, so she reached for a glass and raised it high. 'I consider,' she declared, 'that I've had a lucky escape. To freedom!' She drank it all down. 'And now that's over with, I think I shall go home.'

'To Bloomsbury?' Jonathan sneered. 'Not exactly the height of fashion, is it?'

'It was my stepfather's choice to lease a house there. Not because he's poor, but because he is almost as mean with his money as you are. And now if you'll excuse me, I shall go.'

She stalked off. She stopped, realising that her

head was spinning from drinking that champagne too quickly.

How on earth was she going to get to Bloomsbury? Sir Edgar would stay till the bitter end, anxious to prove himself part of the elite, and she had no money for a cab. Looking around a little desperately, she saw her stepfather at the far end of the room with his daughters: Eleanor, who was into her second Season with no sign of a suitor, and Sybil, who had just commenced her first.

If only her mother had come. But Marianne guessed that she would be enjoying a game of cribbage with Alice, while relishing a supper of sherry and cake. 'What's done is done. We must make the best of things, darling!' her mother often said to Marianne.

But it was hard to see how anything good could be made of her marriage to Sir Edgar two years ago, when everything her mother possessed, including Oakfields, had gone to her new husband.

'Edgar seemed so kind,' Lady Hermione had said to Marianne two months after the wedding. 'Because he was a widower, he appeared to understand how I felt after your dear father died. He took on certain burdens for me…so naturally I believed him when he raised concerns about the financial state of Oakfields. Of course, I see now that he always planned to sell it. It is my fault we have lost our home!'

Marianne had tried to console her. But Sir Edgar's strict morals and dislike of extravagance had brought little comfort to her mother and even less to herself. In fact, at this very moment her dismay was mounting because she'd seen that Eleanor was advancing in her direction.

'Marianne,' said her stepsister, issuing an insincere smile. 'We thought you would be with Jonathan, your fiancé.'

Marianne summoned a cool smile in return. 'Mmm, yes. I think he's gone to fetch me another drink.'

'Not more champagne?' Eleanor raised her eyebrows.

Marianne shrugged. 'Oh, you know me. I like to enjoy myself.'

'Indeed,' Eleanor said earnestly. 'And I hope you like the fan I lent you. It goes wonderfully with your gown.' She glanced at Marianne's dress. 'What an eye-catching garment it is!'

'Eleanor,' said Marianne. 'Do you have something special to say to me?' Eleanor usually tried her hardest to ignore her at these events.

'I just wanted to warn you,' said Eleanor, in her

very best effort at a caring voice, 'that the Duke of Cleveland is here. Oh, dear. Did I startle you?'

For a moment Marianne felt unsteady. The music and the chatter all around her confused her senses. *Anthony* was here? Dear God, she had to get out. This minute.

'Of course I knew he was here,' she lied blithely. 'I saw him as soon as he came in.'

'He is hard to miss, isn't he? He's not appeared in public for months, but goodness, he looks as deliciously elegant as ever. He's over by the main door surrounded by lots of people, and I did think it best to warn you, my dear stepsister, because I've gathered that you and he were good friends for many years.'

Marianne adopted an expression of slight boredom. 'That,' she said, 'was a long time ago.'

Meanwhile, Eleanor was still prattling on. 'Of course,' she was saying cheerfully, 'the Duke is a widower now, so who knows? But oh!—I was forgetting.' She clapped her hand to her mouth. 'You will be marrying Jonathan soon, won't you?'

Enough. She'd had enough. Marianne gathered up her flouncy skirts and set off across that crowded room, brushing aside any eager gentleman who tried to approach her. She was heading for—

Where was she going, exactly? She knew now that

she couldn't leave the ballroom by the main doors because Anthony was there, Eleanor had just told her so. Neither could she face staying here, not for a single minute.

She suddenly saw that nearby was a narrow staircase. It was for the use of the servants, she guessed, and she had no idea where it led, but at the moment it offered her only chance of reprieve. Looking round swiftly to make sure no one was watching, she hurried up those stairs and along the landing into the nearest room. It was unlit, but as luck would have it the full moon was shining in through a window, breaking up the darkness with its silvery glow. The room was empty apart from several wooden chairs pushed into the far corner so she sat on one of them, hugging her arms across her chest to stop herself shivering.

Anthony's name would be on everyone's lips tonight. Indeed, there had been talk about him for years, ever since his marriage to a rich girl from the Midlands—an orphan, apparently—whom no one knew. Simon had been amazed and furious.

'Gambling debts,' he'd said to Marianne. 'That's what I've heard. He's amassed huge gambling debts and that's why he's been forced to marry so hastily.'

Marianne had said nothing. But now she couldn't help remembering how there had been even more talk about the sudden death of his wife early last year, and talk also when his father had died after months of isolation in his huge London house. She would never, ever have come tonight if she'd known he would be here. He was no longer the Anthony she'd once known. She wasn't a part of his world and never could be.

That was when she heard footsteps. She leapt from her chair with her heart thudding wildly. Could Jonathan be after her? Or someone else? Oh God, she was vulnerable up here, stupidly so, and when those footsteps came to a halt by the open door, she pressed herself back against the nearest wall as if sheer willpower could make her invisible.

But she couldn't hide from the husky male voice that haunted her dreams. 'Marianne. Are you in there?'

She couldn't speak. She couldn't move. Because it was—Anthony.

Marianne is none of my business, Anthony had kept repeating to himself when he'd seen her arguing with Moseley. *Absolutely none of my business.*

Neither was it any of his business when he observed her marching away from Moseley with her head held high and her cheeks burning. He even tried to ignore the fact that he'd seen her moments later hastening up a dark and narrow staircase.

He had done his duty tonight by making his appearance here so now he was free to go home. But instead he stayed and kept his eye on that staircase, seeing no one else go up there and no one come down.

He knew he was wrong, he knew he was in fact being unbelievably foolish, but he made some excuse to those around him and he headed up there himself.

He spotted her in the first room he came to, dark though it was, because of the sheen of her dress and the sparkle of her fan. Clearly, her first instinct when she saw him was to flee, but she had sense enough to realise she would never get past him if he chose to stop her.

'Marianne,' he said. His voice was sharper than he'd intended. 'What in God's name do you think you're doing? Are you hiding from someone?'

'Goodness, Anthony,' she said. 'I'm not hiding, as it happens. I merely came up here for a brief rest from all the fun downstairs—although I suppose I really should be returning now to the ballroom. So if you'll excuse me—'

This time she made a truly determined effort to reach the door, but by stepping sideways he easily blocked her way. 'Not,' he said, 'before you've told me exactly why you came up here. Because you weren't having fun down there. Were you?'

She gazed steadily up at him. 'Am I to understand, Your Grace, that you are physically preventing me from leaving?'

Her use of his title reminded him just how much everything had changed. He said, 'You told me you came up here to rest. Surely, if you are tired, you should have asked your fiancé to take you home?'

'Oh, he won't miss me.' She waved her fan in dismissal, sending several of its turquoise sequins drifting to the floor.

'All the same, you should not be up here alone.' He spoke abruptly. 'It's most unwise of you.'

'Goodness,' she said, 'you actually do sound like a duke now, Anthony. Very stern. Very pompous. The Duke of Cleveland, my, how grand!'

He stood very still. 'I think you've had too much champagne.'

'Who cares?'

'I do. And you should care too, about your safety and about your reputation.'

'My reputation? Perhaps. But I feel quite sure that I'm safe with you, because you're only attracted by women with money, aren't you? And I haven't got any. Not a penny to my name.'

'You are, I suspect, a little inebriated, Marianne.'

He said it quietly. 'I repeat: you should go back to your fiancé and allow him to take you home.'

'No,' she said.

'No?' Then he suddenly realised she was shivering; it was indeed cold up here, in this unlit and unheated room. For God's sake, she needed someone to look after her—with her reckless spirit, she always had.

But then she spoke once more. 'I cannot go down there again.' This time her voice was barely audible and her defiance had vanished. 'I just can't.'

For the last four years he had been trying to dismiss Marianne from his memory. She would no doubt have been shocked and possibly even rather hurt to learn of his marriage so soon after they'd last parted at Oakfields. He knew she would have heard all the rumours about him, as had her brother. Simon Blake had collared him a few days after his wedding to express his disgust that Anthony had married for money, so how could he expect Marianne to treat him any differently?

He ought to go downstairs again, now. He should find Moseley and tell him where she was, but something was wrong and there was no way on earth that he could abandon her now, alone and afraid. Instead, he guided her to a chair, pulled up another so he could sit beside her and said, 'Marianne. Will you tell me what's the matter?'

'Why?' Her voice was still very low. 'Why should you care?'

'Perhaps because once we were friends, you and I?'

For a moment he thought she wasn't going to answer, but at last she said, 'You've probably heard that my mother decided to get married again. To Sir Edgar Radlett. It has not worked out well for her.'

'Or for you?'

She shrugged, still not looking at him. 'He was a neighbour of ours in Kent, and a widower. She found some comfort in his company and eventually—two years ago now—she agreed to marry him. But in doing so, she lost both Oakfields and all her financial independence, for good.'

Anthony nodded. He knew already that Lady Hermione had lost her beloved home, as had Simon and Marianne. He said, 'What is Simon doing now?'

'He joined the army. He has been posted to India and of course we miss him badly.' He heard the catch in her voice, but then she managed to lift her head and added, after a moment, 'I really cannot get over my utter exasperation that my mother married Sir Edgar. And of course, I annoy him terribly.'

'Why?'

She waved a hand in dismissal. 'I resent his dominant attitude towards my mother. Also, he decided last year that since his older daughter Eleanor was to make her debut, I should join her in the events of London's spring Season. Some might say that was generous of him, but I knew his plan was to get me off his hands. Unfortunately, though, he became even more exasperated with me because I was the one who was attracting attention, not his daughters.'

'Attracting attention,' he repeated. 'I gather you've succeeded, not least because of your rather shocking attire. You were, I've heard, betrothed to someone before Moseley.'

Her expression changed. She said very steadily, 'So you are judging me too, are you? Along with everyone else. Then let me tell you that as a matter of fact, Jonathan is no longer my fiancé.'

'You mean he has ended your engagement? Tonight, here at the ball?'

'I ended it.' She was looking at him defiantly now. 'He didn't take it well. He made several comments I didn't like, so I resisted the rather strong temptation to slap him and I escaped up here.'

Two broken engagements, Anthony was thinking. Two was not good. Not good at all. At last, he said, 'Why did you agree to marry him in the first place?'

She looked up at him. She said, 'I would have

thought you'd be able to work that out for yourself. After all, I'd have been neither the first nor the last to marry for an improved situation, would I?'

For a moment he was silent. Then he said at last, 'I'm just surprised by your behaviour, that's all. I always thought you didn't care about wealth.'

'You remember me as a naïve young girl, Anthony,' she said wearily as she rose from her seat. 'Foolish and naïve. And now, if you will excuse me, I intend to make an inconspicuous exit and return home before either Sir Edgar or my stepsisters see me.'

'The Radlett sisters,' he murmured as he got up. 'Eleanor and Sybil.'

She looked at him sharply. 'You've heard of them?'

'Who hasn't?' He let a half-smile lighten his expression. 'Between them, I believe they've sent just about every eligible male in London running for cover.'

She gave a gasp of surprised laughter. Then, all of a sudden, he saw the glint of tears in her eyes and suddenly he moved closer. 'Marianne. Are you crying?'

She dashed a hand across her face and shook her head almost fiercely. 'Of course I'm not! So would you please move aside and let me get past, for heaven's sake?'

'No,' he said, and he took her in his arms.

Who was the foolish one now?

Marianne couldn't move. She had no desire to move either, because her cheek was pressed against his chest and she could hear the steady beat of his heart. She knew this ought to be wrong but it all felt so right, to be close to him like this and feel his warmth and the faint scent of…was it cinnamon?… that clung to his skin. Every single part of her was yearning for more of his touch. More of *him*.

Oh, how could this man still have such a hold over her?

Dear God, she warned herself. *Don't let him break your heart again.*

Most likely he had no idea what he had done to her that afternoon four years ago, when he had left her life so suddenly. Tonight he was trying to comfort her, that was all, as he might a younger sister.

But then, something else was happening. The moon no longer offered its silvery light, but she didn't need to see him to know that one of his hands was brushing her cheekbone almost wonderingly and then—then, as he bent his head over hers, she felt him press a gentle kiss to her forehead.

It was at that very moment that a harsh voice rang out from the corridor.

'Are you hiding up here, Marianne? Answer me, damn you!'

Jonathan was out there. She wanted to run, but already Anthony's strong arms were tightening around her. 'Do not move,' he ordered in a low voice.

As if she could. Meanwhile, those lurching footsteps had come to a halt and she heard Jonathan's words—his *drunken* words—piercing the darkness. 'Marianne! If you think you can treat me like this in public, you can damn well think again, because I will not stand for it. Do you understand? I swear, I shall—'

He broke off. There was an ominous silence, disturbed only by the faint sounds of music and laughter that drifted up from the ballroom. Had he already seen them? Might he come in? She was still enfolded in Anthony's arms and she held her breath for so long that her lungs almost hurt, but then she heard his footsteps and muttered oaths retreating along the corridor. He must have headed back for the stairs, but dear God, what kind of mess was she in now?

She should have insisted that Anthony leave the moment he'd arrived. She had said too much, confided too much—and then she'd let him hold her, kiss her even. How he must despise her. It was time, she knew, to get out of here and away from the danger that lurked on all sides.

She pulled herself away, but Anthony's harsh voice jarred her. 'Do not go yet. We can't be sure that he did not see us.'

'We can't?'

'No. And our immediate problem is, what next? There's no way you can go down to the ballroom again.'

'I had no intention of doing so. I shall make arrangements for my departure without anyone seeing me.' She spoke with spirit, but in truth she was exhausted.

'And get home—how? You came with your stepfather, I assume?'

'I did, but I shall find a cab.'

His expression was one of incredulity. 'On your own? At this time of night?'

She knew it was a stupid idea. She didn't even have any money. Anthony clearly thought it was stupid too, because already he was saying, 'You must stay here and I shall ask our host if one of his coachmen will take you home—to Bloomsbury, isn't it? I'll tell him you're tired and I'll also get the fact conveyed to your stepfather. Stay here and I'll inform you when the coach is ready. I think,' he added, 'that once the news is known that you've broken off your second engagement, no one will be in the least surprised that you decided to disappear.'

'Indeed.' She looked up at him defiantly. 'My vanishing act should keep everyone amused for several days, don't you think?'

His brow darkened. 'Is that your purpose in life? To keep people amused? Oh, Marianne. Whatever happened to the girl I used to know?'

'She vanished,' she said quietly, 'a long time ago.'

He gave her one final, lingering look and left, taking the remnants of her dreams with him. As she waited up there in the dark, she softly repeated to herself, *I do not care in the least what Anthony thinks of me. Not now.*

Why should she care? Everyone said that Anthony had married to pay off his gambling debts and—what was far, far worse—had proceeded to isolate his poor wife in the countryside until she'd died a lonely death. Surely, Marianne was able to resist his power to hurt her now?

But the answer was no, because Anthony's scorn hurt, as badly as anything had hurt in her whole life.

Anthony found the Earl of Ware and asked him if he could arrange for one of his coachmen to drive Miss Blake home to her stepfather's house. 'She is rather tired,' he explained. 'And she does not want to spoil her stepfather's evening by asking him to leave just yet.'

The Earl was a diplomatic fellow and he agreed instantly. In fact, he even escorted Marianne to the carriage. 'I am extremely sorry to hear you are unwell, Miss Blake,' he said. 'I'm glad to be of assistance.'

Anthony knew the Earl would know the true reason for Marianne's departure as soon as he heard that she had ended her engagement. He stayed on a little longer out of politeness but then he left too, his thoughts weighed down by this meeting that no doubt both of them would have cause to regret.

Especially that kiss.

Chapter Two

Marianne's spirits were already low and they sank even further as the carriage approached Sir Edgar's house in Marchmont Street. Even by the dim light of the street lamps it was clear that all the neighbouring houses had window boxes to brighten their facades and shutters that were smartly painted. But Sir Edgar's house looked so dreary and so unloved that even the humble London sparrows avoided it.

As the Earl's coachman helped her down, she remembered how the bustle of everyday life at Oakfields had often meant that the house was in a state of mild chaos. But everyone was happy and the servants had been distraught when Marianne's mother told them she was remarrying and leaving Oakfields for London.

Edgar had dismissed every single one of their staff, all except for Alice, who in her usual fashion had stated that she was coming with them whether

Sir Edgar liked it or not. Yes, Alice was their true ally and tonight, as Marianne entered the house, desperate to avoid any of Edgar's footmen, she was relieved to see Alice emerging from the parlour at the far end of the hallway.

'So you didn't last out the night, Miss Marianne,' said Alice as she took her cloak. 'Was it awful?'

'Truly awful, I'm afraid, so I decided to come home on my own. How is my mother?'

'She's missing the old days, as usual. So I was keeping her company and trying to cheer her up.'

'Bless you, Alice. I'll go to her now.'

In any normal household the notion of a maid taking tea in the parlour with her mistress was unthinkable, but Alice made up her own rules. She also frightened Sir Edgar's servants half to death, which amused Marianne hugely, especially as even the pompous butler, Perkins, was scared of her. Marianne made her way to the parlour, where her mother rose from the sofa so quickly that Cuthbert, who'd been curled up beside her, made a sound of protest.

'Marianne!' exclaimed Lady Hermione. 'You're home early.' Then she added more hesitantly, 'I hope you enjoyed the ball?'

Enjoyed it? She'd scarcely spent a worse evening in her life. She'd had to put up with Jonathan acting like a boor, and with Eleanor being even more sweetly vicious than usual. Then there was Anthony. Oh, God. *Anthony.* Altogether the ball had been a disaster.

But she led her mother back to the sofa and sat next to her. 'It was a splendid affair,' she said. 'The house was magnificent, and the ballroom was packed with guests. How has your evening been? I gather you've had company?'

'Indeed. Alice joined me soon after you'd gone out, so we had tea and cake and played cribbage. It was perfectly delightful!'

But Lady Hermione looked far from happy and Marianne longed to say, *Why did you marry again? Why?*

She knew the answer, though. Her mother had felt lonely and vulnerable after her widowhood. When Sir Edgar had warned her—wrongly—that the finances of Oakfields were not in a healthy state, she'd believed he would solve their problems. None of them had realised he intended to sell their family home.

Perhaps Lady Hermione was thinking the same thoughts because she sighed a little, but then her expression brightened. 'Darling, your dress looks absolutely lovely. Is that the one we found in Madame Minette's?'

Madame Minette had a shop at the less established

end of Oxford Street, where she sold second-hand ladies' gowns. Marianne and her mother often bought clothes there and enjoyed customising them to make them unique after their own fashion. But Anthony had clearly not approved. Her heart sank again as she remembered his scathing look when he'd mentioned her attire.

'My gown certainly attracted plenty of attention tonight,' she said.

'Oh, good! But where is the pretty fan Eleanor lent you? I was pleased to see her doing something kind for once. Darling, you've not lost it somewhere, have you?'

'It was falling to bits, which I'm sure Eleanor realised. So I pushed it into an umbrella stand before I left the party.'

'Oh, dear. And I thought she was being generous.' Lady Hermione frowned then asked rather cautiously, 'Jonathan was there, I suppose? Did you discuss any dates for your wedding?'

When Marianne failed to reply Lady Hermione peered at her and said, 'You've come home early. Was Jonathan there at all? Was he unkind to you, my darling?'

'Not really.' At least, Marianne thought, no more than usual. She took her mother's hand. 'Now listen, I have something important to tell you. Tonight,

I ended our betrothal. That's why I've come home early.'

She waited, expecting shock, tears even. But instead, her mother let out a cry of joy.

'Thank goodness!' she exclaimed. 'Darling, I never could stand that starchy young man. Come and let me hug you.' She looked around. 'That tea Alice brought in will be stone cold by now. But let's have something stronger to celebrate!'

Marianne returned her embrace and laughed. 'That means summoning Perkins. And you know, don't you, that Edgar dislikes anyone going into his drinks cabinet?'

'Bother Edgar,' declared Lady Hermione. 'Bother pompous Perkins too.' She went to ring the bell and, just as Marianne expected, Edgar's butler not only took his time in arriving but looked highly affronted at Lady Hermione's request for two glasses of her husband's best Madeira wine.

He also, however, glanced around warily to see if Alice was still there, which amused Marianne hugely.

'You will bring the Madeira instantly, Perkins,' declared Lady Hermione. Marianne and her mother shared a conspiratorial smile as he left, and his sour look when he returned with the two glasses of Madeira amused them even more. Marianne took only a sip of hers, but Lady Hermione did rather better and it wasn't long before the two of them were listing Jonathan's less appealing qualities.

'He takes himself and his clothes so seriously,' sighed Lady Hermione.

'He certainly can't stand the way I dress,' said Marianne. 'Mother, I was afraid you might be horribly disappointed by my news.'

'Why on earth should I be, my darling?'

'Well, partly because we hoped—didn't we?—that when I married and left this house, Edgar would be in a much better mood, because I know I annoy him. I also thought you might enjoy the prospect of coming to stay with me whenever you wished.'

Lady Hermione's reply was staunch. 'Me, staying at Jonathan's house? Can you imagine it? I think I would rather stay here. Better thc devil you know, as they say.' She added rather wistfully, 'You realise, I suppose, that one of the reasons I married Edgar was because he promised to give you a London Season?'

'I know it,' said Marianne.

'And you have had some success, haven't you? Someone far nicer than Jonathan is bound to turn up!'

Mother, Marianne wanted to say, *my time in London has been a disaster.* But she didn't because her mother, as usual, was trying to cheer them both up.

'Now,' Lady Hermione was saying, 'I see you've left your wine, which I suppose I will have to dispatch myself, but do have some of this gorgeous cake.' She pointed to the tea tray. 'Alice and I didn't manage to finish it all.'

Lady Hermione cut them both a generous slice and took an appreciative nibble. 'At least,' she said after a moment, 'Edgar is out most of the time, either at his charity meetings or parading those unpleasant daughters of his around town. He really is desperate to find them both husbands.'

She looked at Marianne with a gleam in her eyes. 'Is there the slightest chance, do you think, that Jonathan might propose to Eleanor? I've always thought they would suit each other perfectly.'

Marianne put down her cake and thought a moment. 'They both have faces that remind me of a wet Sunday,' she said at last.

'Yes! And they both have utterly *dreadful* taste in clothes. Eleanor has no sense of style, and though Jonathan likes to think he is a man of fashion, those high cravats he wears are ridiculous. As for his tight evening coats, they are quite appalling. Oh, Marianne, just think what he might have worn on your wedding day!'

'Just think what *I* could have chosen to wear,' said Marianne. 'I was rather looking forward to appearing in a shocking gown from Madame Minette. Can you imagine the expression on his face?'

They both finished the cake and Lady Hermione drank Marianne's glass of Madeira as well as her own, but their merriment came swiftly to an end when they heard the front door opening.

Edgar and his daughters were back from the ball. Was there time to hide the empty wine glasses? Quite simply, no, and moments later Edgar came into the parlour, followed closely by Eleanor. He looked at the remnants of wine and cake, he looked at Marianne, then he said, 'I heard some disturbing news about you tonight, Marianne. I heard that you've broken off your betrothal with Jonathan Moseley. Is it true?'

'Edgar,' said Lady Hermione, 'she would not have been happy with him. She has a right to make her own decisions—'

'Mother.' Marianne put her hand on her arm. 'Mother, it's all right. Leave us, will you? I shall deal with this.'

Lady Hermione hesitated, then left the room. Marianne faced Sir Edgar defiantly. 'It's true. I've ended my engagement.'

'Then I'm very concerned,' her stepfather said, 'that you have thrown away yet another opportunity of marriage to an honourable man. I really have tried my best for you, Marianne—bringing you to

London, gaining you entry to Society alongside my own daughters. But you appear intent on damaging your chances.'

Eleanor had a smug smile on her face while Sybil, just behind her, listened eagerly.

'I don't happen to care much for what people think,' said Marianne. 'In fact, I ended my engagement with Jonathan because I could see that he intended to take away what little freedom I have, just as you do.'

Eleanor gasped with indignation. 'Papa! Really, you must not stand for this!'

Edgar had put on his sad, serious look. Then he said, 'It is fortunate for you, Marianne, that I am a man of honour. I fear for your reputation and I think it best—for your own sake—if you consider yourself confined to the house for a week until the gossip about you dies down.'

He spoke a little more about the need for a young female to be obedient and demure, until at last Marianne managed to escape to her bedroom. She sat on her bed in the darkness, burning with fury and an appalling sense of helplessness.

If only she could leave. But where could she go? *Where?*

She had hoped that marriage to Jonathan might bring her a measure of independence, but the man was indeed a detestable prig, just like Edgar. In fact, he was so much like Edgar that it was almost laughable, except that at the moment she didn't feel like laughing in the least.

She had tried to tell herself when she came to London that this was her chance to forget Anthony completely. After all, wouldn't she meet plenty of handsome men? Max had been handsome. Max had been fun at first—but he was also a rogue. One night soon after their betrothal she had sneaked out of Sir Edgar's house because Max had persuaded her to come to a party held nearby by one of his army friends.

'You'll love it, Marianne,' he'd told her.

She hadn't loved it. The other women there were older than her and she'd even wondered if some of them had been paid. The army officers were drinking heavily and they had laughed when Max introduced her. 'You've found yourself a young innocent there,' they'd said.

She had told Max she wanted to go home, but instead he'd tricked her into going upstairs, where he'd attempted to kiss her and more. When she'd fought him off, he'd snarled as she ran, 'You're nothing but a tease. You asked for it.'

She hadn't. She really hadn't. She had managed to get back into Sir Edgar's house without being seen and when Alice found her weeping in her bedroom she had guessed instantly what had happened. 'You poor love,' she had said, her gruff voice amazingly kind. 'Men. *Men.*'

Marianne still had nightmares about Max's cruel fingers pawing at her, his lips greedily exploring hers. She was remembering it now and was still sitting in darkness when the door opened and Alice came in.

'I thought I'd find you up here,' she declared, depositing the candlestick she was carrying on a side table. 'What have you been up to? Battling Sir Edgar again?'

Marianne tried to smile. 'Yes. He's very disappointed in me. As usual.'

Then, without warning, her voice broke and she found Alice's arm wrapped around her. 'Now, then,' Alice soothed in her gruff voice. 'You've been very brave, putting up with Lord knows what through no fault of your own. But don't give up, will you? Things will get better, you'll see.'

Alice helped her out of her dress and into her nightrobe and once she had gone Marianne went over to the window to part the curtains. Outside, she saw that a murky London fog had descended so thickly that she could barely see the street lamps or hear the carriages rattling by below.

Things will get better, Alice had said. But how?

She closed the curtains and went to sit at her dressing table, where she slowly brushed her hair. 'Your hair suits you,' Anthony had once said. 'When the sun catches it, it's like sparks of fire.'

But he couldn't have meant anything by it. He had got engaged to that unknown girl so swiftly that all the *ton* had been taken aback and rumours about gambling debts had spread far and wide. After the marriage, it didn't take long for further whispers to be heard.

Simon was still based in England then, and it was he who had told Marianne all this. 'I'm afraid they say she was desperately unhappy,' he'd told her grimly. 'Apparently, she longed for a divorce but Anthony wouldn't grant her one. So she set off from Kent to London one winter's day to plead with him to rethink, but she was flung from the carriage when it skidded on ice and she was killed.'

'Is there proof of this awful story?' Marianne had cried to her brother.

Simon had shrugged. 'Anthony makes no effort to deny it. What more proof could you want?'

On the morning after the Earl's ball, Marianne was late going down to breakfast. When she reached the dining parlour only her mother was there, sipping weak tea and nibbling half-heartedly at a piece of cold toast.

She looks ill and tired, Marianne thought.

Lady Hermione looked up as she entered and attempted a smile. 'Good morning, darling. There's a letter for you.' She pointed.

Marianne's heart sank, because instantly she recognised the handwriting. It was Jonathan's, and her heart sank even further when she read the contents.

'Is it anything special?' asked her mother.

Marianne did her best to sound cheerful. 'No,' she answered, 'not at all.' She put it to one side and helped herself to tea and toast. But she had lied, because the note from Jonathan was short yet lethal.

Last night, I followed the trail of sequins that had dropped from your ridiculous fan—and I saw you in the Duke of Cleveland's arms. He was kissing you. Is he the reason why you ended our betrothal? I could ruin you, you know. Quite easily.

Her mother was still watching her so she tried to force down a piece of buttered toast, but her throat was tight with panic. After making a feeble excuse, she took the letter up to her room to read it again but the words danced before her eyes like teasing demons. She couldn't deny it because Anthony had held her and kissed her. Why, God alone knew—but gossip, she knew, ran like poison through the veins of this city.

Why on earth had Anthony done what he did? She had no idea, nor did she know how she could deal with Jonathan's threat, for he could indeed ruin her. After a moment she drew a deep breath, sat down at her desk then reached for paper and a quill pen.

'I am not,' she said aloud, 'the only one to blame for this.'

With those defiant words, she began writing a letter to Anthony.

At around the same time in the Cleveland mansion in Grosvenor Square, the servants were scratching their heads in puzzlement. Why, they asked one another, had their master gone out riding before even taking his breakfast?

They were concerned. Many of them had worked here since he was a boy and knew that His Grace had never been one to lie in bed till midday like some of his idle contemporaries. But this morning he hadn't even wanted some strong coffee before setting out.

Did he have an urgent appointment? Was there fresh trouble brewing for their master? The servants continued to anxiously speculate until Travers, the Duke's elderly valet and the most loyal of them all, came up with a suggestion. 'I think,' said Travers, 'that His Grace is missing the countryside.'

He was partly right, for as Anthony set off on his fine bay mare towards the grassy acres of Hyde Park, he was hoping that a brisk ride in the morning air might lower the tension that gripped his mind and his body. Unfortunately, it would have taken a plunge in the Serpentine to do that, for last night Marianne Blake had come back into his life.

In his youth, she had always defended him like a miniature Fury if anyone criticized him. But he doubted very much that she had made any attempt to protect his name when she'd heard he was marrying an unknown girl possessed of a fortune. She also appeared to be set on a fairly steady course of self-destruction herself.

He had been a damned fool to follow her up those stairs last night. Even more of a fool to take her in his arms and kiss her. He tried to tell himself it was merely to comfort her, but that was a lie, because he had relished the softness of her body and delighted in the fragrance of her skin and hair as he'd pressed his lips to her forehead. While asleep in his bed last night he had dreamed of making love to her and he'd woken hard with longing.

He hadn't forgotten that fateful day years ago when he'd arrived at Oakfields for Simon's party, only to be summoned back to London and a choice of either accepting a forced marriage, or letting his father's name be ruined. He'd seen Marianne there with flowers in her hair and his heart had soared. *There are girls in London who imagine they are beautiful, but they aren't. Not compared to you.*

It was true, but if he had known what was coming for him he would never have uttered it aloud. She must think him a rogue, the Rogue Duke everyone said he was. Cursing under his breath, he turned his horse around and set off for home. But he had hardly got through the door when his butler, Simmons, presented him with a sealed letter on a silver tray. 'This was delivered while you were out, Your Grace.'

He could hardly believe it, because the letter was from Marianne.

Less than an hour later, Anthony arrived in Marchmont Street and rapped the knocker sharply. Sir Edgar's butler opened the door and gaped at the fine carriage that had pulled up outside.

'I'm here to see Miss Blake,' Anthony said. 'Tell her it's Cleveland. The Duke of Cleveland.'

The butler stuttered and bowed. 'Yes, my lord. I mean, yes, Your Grace. I will just—'

But the butler was unable to finish, because already he was being swept out of the way by Lady Hermione.

'Dear, dear Anthony! How good to see you.' She turned round to call, 'Marianne, come quickly. We have a visitor. Perkins, please don't stand there gaping. I assure you that you're no longer required. Anthony, come this way to the parlour; I'm sure that Marianne will be here any minute. My husband is out with his daughters.'

Her comment about her husband was said, felt Anthony, with some relief. She pointed the way into the parlour, where he had to smile to see her elderly cat dozing on the hearthrug. At least Cuthbert had happily survived the transfer from Oakfields. Then he looked round, because Marianne had appeared in the doorway.

He saw that today she was wearing a high-necked dress with long sleeves, nothing like the one she'd worn last night, and her hair was tied into a simple knot at the nape of her neck. The dress was grey and without adornments, but he felt his heart tighten because, with her lustrous brown eyes and her gorgeous red-gold hair, she somehow cast a glow of light around this cold, drab room.

He wondered again about that rather startling gown she'd worn last night. Maybe it was her own form of defiance against convention, just like her youthful adventures when she was a girl and as determined to be every bit as bold as her brother and himself.

He clamped down hard against the stirring-up of old memories because now Lady Hermione was urging her daughter, 'Do come in, Marianne. Isn't it delightful to see Anthony again, after all this time?'

Anthony saw Marianne hesitate. Then she said, 'Actually, Anthony and I did happen to meet last night, at the Earl of Ware's ball.'

So she had said nothing of it to her mother. Anthony saw that Lady Hermione's eyes had widened. 'Darling. Whyever didn't you tell me?'

'Because it was a very brief encounter,' answered Marianne. 'Nothing of consequence.' At the same time she was giving Anthony a swift but meaningful glance that meant, *Please. Say nothing.* 'But as it happens, Mother, Anthony and I have a very minor matter to discuss, so would you mind if we have a few moments together? Just the two of us?'

'Just the two of you. Of course!' Lady Hermione stooped to gather up her cat in her arms. 'Come, Cuthbert. You and I shall go upstairs to my room.'

And she left, casting one last conspiratorial glance at them both.

Anthony went to close the door. 'Well?' he said

to Marianne. 'Why exactly did you wish to see me so urgently?'

He hadn't meant to sound so curt. He thought she flinched, but when she spoke her words were calm.

'I assure you,' she began, 'that I had no desire to involve you in my personal business. But it appears that Jonathan recognised both of us last night, and this morning I received a message from him. It's a threat, I fear. I felt I ought to warn you of it.'

She reached into the pocket of her gown and handed him a letter. He studied it, then looked up. 'This is bad,' he said. 'I'm sorry. I have to hold my-self responsible for this, since I was foolish enough to follow you upstairs last night.'

She ought to have looked puritanical in that grey dress. Anyone else would, but not her. *Remember her two broken betrothals*, he reminded himself. *Her self-confessed flirtations and fondness for cham-pagne.*

She was meeting his gaze steadily. 'You did, at the time, blame me for going up there in the first place. I merely wanted to get away from the crowded ballroom, but as you see from his note, Jonathan has mistakenly concluded that you were the reason why I broke off my engagement to him. Of course, he is absolutely wrong.'

What emphasis she put on that word, *absolutely*.

'Of course,' he agreed.

She sighed. 'I'm afraid that when I read it this morning I foolishly panicked. Since then I've had a change of heart, and I now consider it would be a grave mistake to draw you into the matter further. So I've decided the best thing I can do is to visit Jonathan myself—'

'What?'

She lifted her eyebrows a little. 'I have decided I must visit him myself, and explain that you and I are merely old friends.'

'You certainly will not visit him! Marianne, you must stop rushing headlong into trouble. Don't you realise this can only end badly? I will go.'

'But I've just told you. I do not want you to!'

'Going yourself,' he said, this time with strained patience, 'would be a disaster, believe me. And I don't think you have anyone else who could speak to Moseley on your behalf. Do you?'

'Certainly not Sir Edgar.' She looked rather weary now. 'He is furious with me for breaking off the engagement.'

'What about Simon? Do you have any idea at all when your brother will return from India?'

She shook her head. 'We think his regiment might

have already set sail for England. But we have no idea exactly when he will arrive home.'

'Then I shall deal with Moseley myself and you must not object. It is inconceivable for you to visit him the day after you've ended your betrothal. Apart from anything else, the man is a preening fool. Why on earth did you agree to his proposal?'

He thought he saw her flinch, but her voice was calm as she said, 'A young woman has to marry, you know. Isn't that the purpose of having a Season?'

He looked at her. He said, 'Oh, Marianne. Were you really so desperate?'

It took Marianne a moment to recover from that. *Desperate.* It was a low blow and maybe it was as well she was spared from having to answer, for at that very moment her mother came back into the room.

'Now,' said Lady Hermione, 'I have asked Alice to bring you some refreshments, because I hope you are staying for a while, Anthony?'

But Anthony was already shaking his head. 'Reluctantly, Lady Hermione, I have to leave. But it has been a great pleasure seeing you again.'

'I will show you out,' said Marianne. She followed him into the hallway, after closing the door so her mother wouldn't follow. 'Anthony. Please think about this. I repeat: when I wrote to you, I was only thinking of asking for your advice, and warning you too. I was worried that your reputation could suffer because of last night.'

He gave a grim smile. 'Do you really think that Jonathan Moseley could harm me? And whatever he says, Marianne, do you think I care? Believe me, I've grown well-accustomed to rooms suddenly falling silent whenever I appear. Don't worry. I can deal with him.'

Perhaps he was right. He so outranked Jonathan that he could warn him off instantly, whereas she had no power at all. She bowed her head.

'Very well,' she said.

He was heading for the door, but he hesitated a moment. 'Though there is something I must ask you, before I confront him. Marianne, is there anything I ought to know about your relationship with the man?'

She was puzzled. 'I don't quite understand what you're saying. I accepted his proposal and I ended it—preposterous of me, I know, but that is all.'

She could see he was searching for the right words. 'What I mean is, was there anything at all that happened between the two of you which he could use to malign you? Have you perhaps accepted inappropriate gifts, or at times been more intimate with him than you should?'

She spoke resolutely. 'Never. I swear it.'

He looked at her for a moment then he nodded and left. She closed the heavy door herself, leaning her back against it and almost fighting for breath. Because she had suddenly remembered there was something she should have told him. Something truly awful.

Jonathan knew about Max—and what was to stop him telling Anthony?

Chapter Three

Yes, someone, somewhere, had once told Jonathan she had gone to the party. Jonathan had been kind about it at first. 'You're my fiancée,' he had said, 'I will protect you and besides, Max is dead.'

No other rumours had appeared to spread and she had thought she was safe. But lately Jonathan had begun to use the nasty tale almost like a weapon against her. 'A woman's reputation,' he liked to muse, 'is a precious and fragile thing.' Jonathan was her enemy now. If he was confronted by Anthony, he could very well tell him the awful story and even embellish it.

Oh, God. Just the thought of it wrapped itself around her, dragging her down and down.

Her mother was waiting for her in the parlour. 'How delightful,' began Lady Hermione, 'to see Anthony again—' She broke off on seeing Marianne's expression. 'Is anything wrong?' she asked hesitantly. 'Anthony was pleasant to you, I hope?'

Marianne closed the door. 'Mother,' she said, 'let me warn you now that there is no chance whatsoever of Anthony proposing to me.'

'Oh. Well, I didn't expect *that*, exactly—'

'I think you did.'

Lady Hermione sat down. 'I do hope you weren't cold towards him, were you? Simon, I fear, speaks rather ill of him, but I cannot believe the rumours that fly around. There is always so much gossip in London. Why, only the other day my friend Lady Anne Marwell was telling me…'

Marianne sat there, barely hearing a word. But suddenly she realised that her mother had stopped talking and was watching her anxiously. Then she said, 'Should we perhaps go out for a little walk, dear? Maybe visit a shop or two?'

Marianne hesitated. Sir Edgar had confined her to the house, but Edgar was out—and besides, what could he do? Things couldn't really get much worse and she felt desperately in need of some fresh air. But before she and her mother could get as far as the hallway, they heard the front door opening.

Edgar and his daughters were home.

Like a pair of conspirators, Marianne and Lady Hermione dived back into the parlour, hoping to wait until the coast was clear. But within minutes Eleanor came in.

'Marianne!' Eleanor could hardly get her words out quickly enough. 'Perkins told us that the Duke of Cleveland has called. He didn't come to see *you*, did he? Why didn't you ask him to wait? You must have known that we would be home soon!'

'He was in a hurry,' said Marianne. 'He—actually, Eleanor, he came to see my mother. Yes, my mother. To ask her advice on…' Floundering a little, she looked around for inspiration and spotted Cuthbert.

'On buying a cat,' Marianne continued. 'He has always been very fond of cats.'

Lady Hermione stifled a gasp of amusement, but Eleanor's face creased in a scowl. 'I don't believe that for one minute. I think that you—' and she pointed at Marianne '—are trying to use your flirtatious ways to entice the Duke, now that you've broken off your latest engagement.'

Marianne almost had to laugh. 'I assure you, Eleanor, that you could not be more mistaken—'

She didn't get any further, because that was the moment when Cuthbert decided to inspect Eleanor's mohair shawl. It had long tassels trailing almost to the ground and he began to pat at them one by one. Eleanor let out a shriek. 'That cat! This is my very best shawl!'

Cuthbert glanced up at her and strolled disdainfully out of the room. Eleanor was desperately examining her shawl for damage and Marianne took advantage of the diversion to say, 'Actually, Eleanor, my mother and I were just about to go for a walk. So do excuse us, will you?'

'But my father ordered you not to leave the house!'

True. But Marianne was suddenly inspired. 'The Duke of Cleveland,' she said casually, 'would certainly be interested to hear of that. And rather displeased, I imagine.' She beckoned to Lady Hermione. 'Shall we get ready to go out, Mother?'

Eleanor, however, had one more weapon in her armoury. As they left, she called out, 'Do you know the name people have given him? They say he's the Rogue Duke! They say his poor wife actually *died* because of his coldness to her!'

Marianne pretended not to hear. Instead, she swiftly helped her mother into her pelisse and fanciest bonnet, then she put on her own outdoor attire and together they set off along Marchmont Street.

'That's better,' she said, taking her mother's arm. 'Isn't it lovely to be out in the fresh air? We shall go and look in the windows of that vastly expensive hat shop in Soho, shall we?'

Her mother's pace quickened. 'Indeed. You always have such clever ideas, Marianne.'

But after that Lady Hermione was unusually quiet as they walked. At last, she said, 'It cannot be true, can it? That Anthony treated his wife badly? Because if so, he is not the person I once knew.'

'Eleanor is addicted to gossip,' was Marianne's only reply. 'The nastier the better.'

As was most of Society, it appeared, and she feared that by asking for Anthony's help, she had made everything far worse for herself. She could only pray that he would forget about that note and forget about her.

So it was as well she had no idea that Anthony had in fact gone straight to Jonathan Moseley's house, and was at that very moment knocking on his front door.

A footman showed Anthony promptly to Moseley's drawing room and within moments Moseley himself appeared. He was elegantly, almost foppishly dressed as usual and his fair hair was trimmed to perfection.

'Your Grace,' said Moseley with a slight bow. 'To what do I owe this honour?' The greeting was deferential, but there was still the hint of a sneer in the man's voice.

Anthony refused the offer of a seat. He also refused the offer of a drink. 'You'll know very well,' he said, 'that I'm here about Miss Blake.'

'Ah. My former fiancée.' Moseley strolled to the sideboard and lifted up a decanter of whisky. 'I think I'll take a drink, even if you won't.' He poured an inch or so into a crystal glass and sipped from it. 'So, what exactly has been going on between the two of you? Are you the reason why she ended our engagement?' Swiftly he added, 'Not that I care.'

Anthony walked steadily up to him. Taking the glass from his hand, he slammed it back on the sideboard and saw Moseley flinch. He said, 'I had nothing to do with the fact that Miss Blake ended your engagement. She made that decision by herself, for which I applaud her thoroughly. As for anything going on between us, in fact I hadn't seen her for years until we met by chance last night.'

'And you met her *by chance* in an unlit upstairs room?' Moseley appeared to have gathered his courage now. 'Tell me, Your Grace. Can you deny that I saw you making rather intimate advances to her? But wait, maybe I've got this wrong. Maybe it was Marianne who lured you into that embrace, having already calculated that you were a far better catch than me. After all, what girl doesn't dream of marrying a duke?'

Anthony said softly, 'I'm warning you, Moseley.

If you say another despicable word about her, either to me or to anyone else, you will be sorry.'

Moseley gave a shrug. 'Does your gallantry mean you're going to make her your mistress? It's a tempting enough notion, but maybe I should warn you about her. She was engaged before, you know, to an army fellow—and her behaviour with him was quite scandalous. She let him take her to a wild bachelor party, then she went upstairs with him. And once up there she—'

Anthony punched him on the chin.

Moseley staggered back against the sideboard, causing all the bottles to rattle wildly. Anthony waited until he had pulled himself upright and said, 'You are lying.'

'I swear it's the truth!' Moseley's voice was barely decipherable because he was still rubbing at his bruised jaw. 'She admitted as much herself. If you attempt to defend her virtue, no one will listen to you because they'll know—from me—that you were caught embracing her last night. And remember that people have not forgotten your own history. How you kept your ailing father virtually a prisoner in his London home, while your wife died many miles away in the country because of your neglect. Your cruelty.'

Somehow Anthony managed to restrain himself from further physical force. 'I think I had better leave,' he said, 'before I do you some serious damage. But I'm warning you, Moseley. I could get you blackballed from every single London club if I wished. So keep your foul mouth shut about Miss Blake, or you'll regret it.'

Once outside, he saw that dark clouds had gathered and a flurry of rain was making the roads and pavements glisten. But instead of heading straight for his carriage, he stood there thinking hard. Moseley was a blasted wretch. But what if the tale about Marianne and that army captain was true? And why the hell hadn't Marianne warned him about this lurking disaster of a story?

At last, he returned to his carriage and spoke to the driver. 'Chancery Lane next,' he said.

All the way there, his mind seethed with dark thoughts. Could his sweet Marianne really have become the lady of easy virtue Moseley claimed her to be? *We were young then*, he reminded himself. *People change. Things change.* Since everything had changed for him, he had tried to consign his feelings for her to the inaccurate memories of youth, when the sun was always shining and the days were filled with promise.

But he just couldn't forget last night, when he had

found Marianne alone and frightened in that shadowy upstairs room. All Moseley's foul insinuations became irrelevant because she was still the girl he remembered—yes, with the same habit of hurtling into disastrous situations, but also with the same eagerness for life and, God help him, the same disarming loveliness.

She heralded danger.

His carriage came to a halt in busy Chancery Lane, alongside a building whose brass nameplate bore the inscription *Tild and Palgrave, Attorneys*. Inside, the high-ceilinged reception area resembled a church with its dark furniture and polished brass candlesticks, and everywhere smelled of parchment and ink.

One by one the black-suited clerks rose from their desks with bows and murmurs of greeting as he, the son of the much-revered Glorious Duke, followed the chief clerk into the office of Mr Palgrave, who had been the family's lawyer for decades. Two young clerks who were busy filing paperwork made their bows then left. Mr Palgrave closed the door firmly after them and waited for Anthony to take a chair before sitting down himself behind his enormous desk.

'Your Grace,' Palgrave said. 'It is a pleasure, as always, to welcome you here.'

Anthony nodded. 'Your letter arrived this morning, Palgrave. I gather you have news for me?'

'I have indeed,' said the lawyer earnestly. 'Good news, I'm glad to say. I can now tell you that every penny that your father owed has been paid off, despite the fact that many of his debts were only gradually uncovered.'

'My father gambled widely,' said Anthony.

'Indeed. Claims have drifted in from as far afield as Paris and Brussels, but the Cleveland estate is at last completely free of his debts.' Palgrave reached for some papers. 'Here are the precise statements relating to your investments and income, Your Grace. The whole process has been a lengthy one, but you can finally rest assured that all is dealt with.'

Anthony took the papers. 'Just a reminder, Palgrave. No one else must know of my father's weakness, ever. You understand that, don't you?'

'I do. But as I've pointed out before, you have borne a heavy burden these last few years in keeping your father's disastrous habit a secret. I fear the speculation about your marriage did great damage to your own reputation.'

Anthony allowed not one flicker of emotion to cross his impassive features. 'I never complained about my marriage. Not once.'

'Yes, but you must have been hoping to choose a

bride who could bring you happiness!' The elderly lawyer spoke with sympathy. 'Instead, you were obliged to marry a complete unknown, thus causing a scandal that must have pained you greatly. Why, Your Grace, should I and your personal bankers be the only ones to know why you married as you did? Why should you continue to sacrifice your own reputation for the sake of your dead father's misdeeds?'

Honour your family, always. Anthony could almost hear the family motto that had been a part of his childhood. He looked at Palgrave steadily. 'I take it you understand the concept of filial duty?'

'Of course. Of course! But there are other obnoxious rumours. People still whisper that you deliberately had your wife shut away in your country home so that you could enjoy yourself in London. That she died in a carriage accident in the snow because she was heading for London, desperate to beg you for a release from the marriage! Why will you not tell the world the truth?'

'The same reason as before, I suppose, Palgrave.' Anthony's voice was expressionless. 'I don't wish for my father's name to be blackened. I suppose you could also say that I have my own kind of pride.'

'I see that,' said the lawyer, 'and I respect you for it. But I wish I could make you change your mind.' Palgrave sighed a little and handed over a sheaf of papers. 'Here, Your Grace, is everything you require for your records.'

Anthony picked up the documents and returned to his carriage. All the way back to Grosvenor Square, the lawyer's words were ringing in his ears. *Why should you continue to sacrifice your own reputation for the sake of your dead father's misdeeds?*

It was because he had been unable to see any other way out of the situation he'd found himself in.

His upbringing had been strict. His mother had died when he was four, and even as a child he was forever being told by his tutors of the responsibilities that lay ahead of him. He was coached also on the importance of alliances with his equals, and at Eton he'd had the opportunity to mix with the sons of the highest in the land.

But whenever the vacations came, he was at his happiest spending time with Simon and Marianne Blake. His father had preferred London life and made no objection to Anthony staying at Cleveland Hall in Kent, under the care of his personal manservant Travers and the kindly housekeeper there, Mrs Manville. Anthony had realised from an early age that his father was content to live his life unencumbered by the presence of his young son.

By the time Anthony was eighteen, he was noticing whenever he was in London that his father would often be out till dawn, but Anthony had ignored the warning signs, because he was inevitably being drawn into the life he was born into and he would be a liar to say he hadn't enjoyed it. But all of it came to an end when that horseman arrived at Oakfields like a messenger of doom, bearing a letter from his lawyer. *You must,* Palgrave had written, *make haste to London. I fear that your father's business affairs require your urgent attention.*

Which was how Anthony had learned that the Glorious Duke had been steadily building up mountainous gambling debts—and worse. That evening, after Ned Gibson had left the family's house in Grosvenor Square, Anthony had endured a confrontation that he could never have imagined. His father, who had been drinking heavily, blustered excuse after excuse; they even had an excruciating row until the older man finally sank into a chair, looking broken and exhausted. 'Help me, my son,' he had whispered.

Anthony had pressed his hand. 'I will,' he vowed.

The next afternoon Anthony had gone to Gibson's office in Holborn, next to his gambling hell, known as the Clover Club. Gibson had presented Anthony with a bundle of promissory notes signed by Anthony's father, all referring to debts owed.

'Of course,' Gibson had told him, 'your father

has other debts elsewhere. And more will no doubt emerge over time.'

Anthony had absorbed the news in silence. The debts to Gibson alone amounted to a sum that Anthony knew could not be paid without selling off land in Kent and maybe even the house there too.

'A tricky situation, eh, my lord?' said Gibson. 'But you seem like a sensible young man and you'll have realised my solution is the only one available to you. Like I said, my daughter Cynthia is nineteen and a sweet girl, if a little shy. I'm a rough man whose father was an Essex brickmaker. But I've brought her up properly, well away from London, and she's been educated as a lady should be. As long as you do your duty by her, no one will know she's mine. Like I said, as well as cancelling all these debts—' and he patted the heap of promissory notes '—my Cynthia's generous dowry will help you pay off everything else we know your father owes. Most important of all, I'll keep quiet about your father's cheating. But mark my words, I want a grand wedding for my girl—and very soon!'

Anthony's marriage to Cynthia had taken place three months later. Ned Gibson had attended the service and sat at the back of the church, a man nobody knew or noticed. By then the whispers about Anthony's marriage had proliferated—some said his wife was an orphan, while others wondered if she was maybe some lordling's illegitimate daughter. Whatever the story, everyone knew she was a nobody from the Midlands with no known connections. Why on earth, they all wondered, had Anthony married her?

The whispers had grown worse when it was realised that although Cynthia lived at Cleveland Hall in Kent, Anthony spent most of his time in London. He had to, in order to watch his father constantly for any signs of lapses into his secret and disastrous habit. He'd also endured hours on end with Palgrave and the family banker as between them they'd gradually untangled his father's extensive debts. No one dared speak their thoughts to him directly for, after all, some day he would be a duke. But he knew what people said. *He married the poor girl for her money, then banished her to Kent. Yes, he shut her out of his life quite shamelessly.*

Anthony had shouldered his burden in silence but when his wife died in that notorious carriage accident in the snow, the whispers grew truly malicious. He knew there was even a rumour that he had planned the accident in order to get rid of her.

Then, a mere few months after his wife's funeral, Anthony's ailing father had died and the *ton* glossed over the new Duke's supposed sins, for wasn't he now the most desirable male on the marriage market? London's hosts waited with scarcely concealed impatience for him to observe the necessary months of mourning.

Anthony would have been happy to isolate himself for even longer, since his disillusionment with Society was almost total. But it was his duty to appear in public, so last night he had attended the Earl of Ware's ball—with almost disastrous consequences, for there he had met Marianne.

She had been betrothed twice and yet she was flippantly dismissive of her past. She seemed to enjoy defying propriety and drank champagne when young ladies were expected to drink only lemonade. Whether or not Moseley's story about Marianne and her now-deceased first fiancé was true, she was reckless, something he did not need in his life, not now, when all he wanted was peace.

Yet all his old feelings of loyalty towards her and the memory of their past friendship tugged hard at his conscience. She had turned to him in her hour of need and, for old times' sake if nothing else, he felt obliged to help her. She needed to get out of the path of Society's gossips, and out from under the thumb of that stuffy Sir Edgar Radlett. But how?

It was then that the answer came to him. It was her old home, Oakfields.

Chapter Four

Two days later Marianne sat in the parlour after lunch, helping her mother to decorate an old summer bonnet with pink ribbons. At least she was supposed to be helping, but the sewing box lay by her side, untouched.

She was still confined to the house. Sir Edgar had rebuked her solemnly when Eleanor and Sybil told him that Marianne had gone for a walk to the shops with her mother. He had been suspicious, too, about the reason for Anthony's visit and had told her she was now to stay in the house for two weeks, starting today. It was not a punishment, he explained. He was doing it out of concern for her reputation.

Marianne didn't really care, since she had nowhere in particular to go. She had heard nothing more from Anthony and knew she ought to be relieved, because it would be unbelievably awful if he had gone to see Jonathan and Jonathan had told him about that dreadful party with Max.

Her mother was in low spirits too. That was partly why Marianne had suggested the sewing, which her mother usually loved. But this afternoon Lady Hermione was very quiet, and at one point she put down her sewing and said, 'Darling, I've been thinking again about Anthony. Do you know, I always felt there was something *special* between the two of you.'

'Then I advise you to stop thinking about him,' said Marianne as gently as she could. 'He called the other day only because he was being polite to former friends, that's all.' She picked up the bonnet her mother had been working on. 'You really have done wonders with this! The violet silk petunias you've sewn on look lovely and all your friends will be jealous.'

Her efforts to be cheerful were in vain, because her mother said after a moment, 'I know you're trying hard to make the best of things. But you must hate living here with Edgar. I thought, when we came to London, that you might enjoy the parties and balls, but it hasn't worked out very well, has it?'

Marianne spoke dismissively. 'I might have fared better in this household if I'd made more of an effort to get on with everyone, Mother. Instead, I'm afraid I've alienated his daughters.'

'I'm not surprised. Who could get on with that pair?' Lady Hermione sighed. 'As for Edgar, I thought he would be a strong shoulder to lean on. He promised to make the Oakfields estate prosperous, but instead he sold it! He's driven Simon away, he is far too intolerant of your independent ways, and I have no money to call my own. Nothing has worked out as I'd hoped!'

Marianne thrust aside the flower-strewn bonnet and rushed to hold her mother tightly. 'Please, please don't fret. I've told you—a lot of it is my fault too, for being awkward and deliberately doing foolish things to annoy Sir Edgar!'

Lady Hermione tried to smile but then she whispered, 'I miss Oakfields so much.'

Marianne was silent. So did she, but there was nothing to be done. 'I know,' she said. 'But let's cheer ourselves up with some tea and cake, shall we?'

Marianne went to ring the bell for a maid. But as she was about to do so, she heard the sound of the brass knocker on the front door being firmly rapped. Perkins the butler must have opened it, but as she listened Marianne realised that Sir Edgar was in the hallway too, for she could hear his voice greeting someone.

A few minutes later Sir Edgar arrived in the parlour, looking rather tense. 'His Grace the Duke of Cleveland has arrived,' he said to them both. 'I understand he wishes to see you, Marianne, but of course your mother and I will be with you also. His reputation is unfortunately tarnished, but he holds a prestigious title and we will treat him accordingly. I have shown him into the drawing room, so please, both of you, follow me.'

Marianne and her mother looked at each other once he'd left the room. 'Marianne,' whispered Lady Hermione, 'what can this mean? Why has he come to see you again?'

She looked hopeful. Marianne, on the other hand, was in a state of panic. What if he had been to see Jonathan? What if Jonathan had told him about Max?

She felt quite ill. She set off after Sir Edgar, followed by her mother. But when they were about to enter the drawing room she halted again, because she realised her stepfather was talking to Anthony about his daughters.

'Both Eleanor and Sybil,' Sir Edgar was saying, 'are enjoying the new Season, and of course they are attracting a good deal of admiration. Perhaps you have met them?'

'I don't believe,' Anthony replied, 'that I've had the pleasure.' But then he broke off. 'Lady Hermione. Miss Blake.' He bowed to them. 'How delightful to see you both.'

Marianne gave a light curtsy. 'Likewise, Your Grace.'

Her heart was hammering. There was nothing to be detected in his expression, but her consternation was growing because he looked quite wonderful. His clothes were expertly tailored, of course, but it struck her that he could have worn a London cab driver's outfit and still set female hearts racing everywhere he went. She had to stay calm. There was no more use in her getting silly ideas in her head now than there had been when she was seventeen.

She guessed Anthony was about to say more, but her stepfather was speaking again. 'I understand, Your Grace,' said Sir Edgar, 'that you and my good wife, Lady Hermione, have been acquainted for some time?'

Anthony looked at him with an unreadable expression on his face. 'Of course. Miss Blake and her mother were neighbours of mine in Kent for many years, so you could say we're old friends. In fact, since the weather is fine, I have come to ask Miss Blake if she would like an outing with me in my carriage.'

Marianne gasped. Would Sir Edgar dare to tell Anthony that he had confined her to the house?

Clearly, Edgar was struggling. 'This is a generous invitation,' he managed at last, 'but I think it's hardly fitting that my stepdaughter should accompany you unchaperoned.' He forced a smile. 'You will know, I'm sure, what the London gossips are like.'

'Indeed I do. I was assuming, of course, that Lady Hermione would accompany us.'

Lady Hermione nodded. 'How delightful! I would love that.'

Anthony turned to Marianne. 'And you, Miss Blake? I've not had your answer yet.'

For a moment she couldn't speak, but it was wonderful to see Edgar's face because he was extremely annoyed.

'I would be happy to accept your invitation, Your Grace,' she answered politely. 'On a beautiful day such as this, what could be more pleasant?'

She saw Anthony arch his brows slightly as if to say, *Overdoing it rather, aren't you?* She enjoyed that almost as much as Edgar's fury. But she didn't have much else to be excited about, because after that he looked merely indifferent.

He bowed and said, 'I shall wait outside with my carriage for you, ladies.'

* * *

Marianne went upstairs and summoned Alice's help to get changed. All the time she was thinking, *Why?* Why did he want to see her this time? It must be about Jonathan. Or Max. *Oh, heavens.* It was as well Alice was there to aid her, because her fingers fumbled hopelessly over every dratted button.

She had decided to put on a riding habit recently acquired in Madame Minette's second-hand shop, made of royal blue velour with gold braid trimmings. She guessed its previous owner had decided they weren't quite bold enough for its rather startling style and colour, but she loved it and after examining herself in the mirror, she decided to add a tall blue hat adorned with a gold cockade.

Alice nodded her approval. 'Outrageous,' she declared.

'Exactly what I intended,' said Marianne, who almost glided down the staircase to where Lady Hermione was waiting for her. Then she realised Eleanor was there also, and she was holding out a dainty white parasol.

'It's my best one,' she said in a simpering voice. 'Do take it, Marianne. You will wish to protect your complexion from the sun, won't you?'

Rather startled, Marianne accepted the furled parasol then went with her mother out to where

Anthony waited by his open barouche. He seemed completely unmoved by her flamboyant costume but merely helped them inside, climbed in himself then instructed his groom to drive on.

'I thought,' Anthony said to them both, 'that we might visit Montagu House.'

Lady Hermione's face fell. 'I thought we would be going to Hyde Park. But… Montagu House! That's a museum, isn't it?'

'It is,' agreed Anthony, 'and I can assure you it will be a fascinating experience. Besides, it's not far from here, and I imagine you haven't been there yet, Lady Hermione?'

'I certainly haven't. Isn't it full of skeletons and old vases?'

'Indeed. There are vases from ancient Egypt and Greece, there are stuffed animals and prehistoric skeletons and even some rarities such as a unicorn horn, if you can believe that.'

'I should be quite happy to go there,' said Marianne. In fact she'd felt a rush of relief, because with her mother for company and the museum staff all around, she would be safe from having to face any more of Anthony's intrusive questions.

But then she realised that Lady Hermione had begun to look around her and as the carriage entered Tavistock Square she suddenly said, 'Oh, Anthony,

I have just remembered that my good friend Anne, Lady Marwell, lives here and I've been promising to visit her for days. Could you drop me off and collect me after you've been to the museum?'

Marianne was aghast. Leaving her alone with Anthony? She hissed, 'No, Mother. No.'

Lady Hermione patted her hand. 'Now, darling. You know how I love to see Lady Anne.'

No, you don't, thought Marianne desperately. *She was rude about one of your hats and you haven't spoken to her since.*

But Anthony had already called out to his driver to halt the barouche. 'An excellent idea, Lady Hermione,' he said as he helped her down. 'We shall pick you up from here in around an hour or so, if that will suit.'

'Perfectly. Goodbye, my dears!' Her mother gave Marianne a cheerful wave before heading towards Lady Anne's house and Anthony, after settling himself comfortably again, told the driver to proceed. 'What a pleasant thing it is,' he mused as the carriage moved off, 'to keep up with one's old friends.'

Marianne was silent a moment. Then she said, 'You did that deliberately, didn't you? Suggesting the museum so my mother would take fright and flee?'

'I did.'

She summoned a deep breath. 'Anthony, I've realised I was completely wrong to drag you into the problem of Jonathan's letter. I have decided that if he does make a nuisance of himself I'm perfectly capable of dealing with him on my own.'

He said nothing at first but merely appeared to be taking in their surroundings. Then he looked at her and said mildly, 'How, exactly?'

She could think of no answer and she felt a little desperate. Had he spoken with Jonathan, or not? Those poisonous words Jonathan had written kept seeping into her mind. *I could ruin you, you know. Quite easily.*

Just at that moment the driver called over his shoulder, 'We've arrived at Montagu House, Your Grace.'

'Go round the block again,' Anthony replied. Then he turned to Marianne. 'Tell me, are you just hoping Moseley will go away? I'm afraid you're dealing with a very bitter man.'

'So you've seen him, then?' She could barely whisper the words.

'Yes.'

She took a moment to steady herself. 'I suppose he's going to tell everyone about seeing us in that upstairs room at the ball the other night. But we both know it meant nothing, don't we? You can certainly survive any scandalous talk he tries to stir up, and as for me, I can simply laugh it off—'

'I'm not sure you can laugh this off, Marianne.'

'Why not?'

His grey eyes were sombre. 'Because he told me,' he said, 'that you allowed your first fiancé—Max, wasn't it?—inappropriate intimacies.'

She closed her eyes. *Oh, no.*

'Please.' Anthony was speaking more urgently now. 'Marianne, you must be honest with me. Was Moseley speaking the truth?'

This was horrific. Just as she'd feared, Jonathan had told him what he'd heard about that awful party—and he'd no doubt embellished it, as revenge against her for ending their betrothal. Now Anthony would be blaming her for it too. Men. *Men.*

She said at last, 'No. I did not allow Max *anything.* But I'm afraid I do have an unfortunate habit of getting myself into difficult situations, and that is what happened that night with Max. I suppose Jonathan is going to tell the story to everyone, is he?'

He shook his head. 'It's all right,' he said quietly. 'I silenced him. It's all right.'

For a moment she couldn't speak. Anthony's voice was grave but somehow so kind that it almost deceived her into believing that he was still her friend, still someone she could trust with any problem, any secret. But she had to remember that everything had changed.

Not for him, though. He was a duke, so he was safe from any indignity. He too had attracted malicious gossip, yet he was still welcome in the highest circles because of his rank. But Society despised women who had the slightest stain on their character, and now Anthony must believe the worst of her too.

He was still watching her. After a moment he said, 'That miserable excuse of a man will have to keep his malicious comments to himself from now on. I also told him that if he caused you any more trouble, I would get him blackballed from all of London's clubs.'

She knew she should have been relieved, but instead she was even more confused. Why had he done this? Was it because he felt sorry for her? Was it to acknowledge that he had let her down by abandoning their old friendship, which for her had been so much more?

At last, she said, 'Believe me, I am suitably grateful.'

'Are you?' he said in a different tone of voice. 'Then don't be. I don't want any gratitude, because you owe me nothing, Marianne. You've clearly been through hell these last few years and you don't deserve it.'

It was his sudden sympathy that weakened her. His apparent kindness, when at the ball he had seemed so judgemental. Her throat ached with suppressed emotion, and she was unable to speak.

But he appeared not to notice. In fact, he was looking around and saying, 'I do believe we are about to pass the entrance to the museum for the third time. Would you care to look around inside? I imagine unicorn horns and the like might provide some light relief for you.'

Ignoring her quaking heart, she checked that her jaunty hat was straight, she summoned a smile and she declared, 'Nothing, Your Grace, could be more delightful!'

Montagu House contained a bewildering array of musty relics and its elderly curator, Mr Ayscough, was determined they should get at least a glimpse of all the museum's treasures. He certainly knew a good deal, even if she couldn't understand quite all of it.

She could almost have said she was enjoying herself, but it was difficult to be with Anthony again like this. It was difficult to behave as if he was just an old family friend and to forget that once she had dreamed he could be something much more. She was proud of herself, though. She managed to chuckle at Anthony's droll asides to her about the various exhibits, many of which were extremely odd. Marianne was particularly startled by some ancient Greek vases that portrayed athletes both male and female getting up to activities that made her glance closer then blush. She gasped at the unicorn horn. She gazed in wonder at the Egyptian mummies.

But when they were asked by Mr Ayscough to admire a jar of preserved maggots—which, their guide told them proudly, were extracted from a living man's ear by a renowned British surgeon—Marianne whispered to Anthony, 'I think that I have had enough. I rather dread to imagine what the poor man will bring out for us next.'

'He's certainly making the most of having us as visitors, isn't he? Shall we leave?'

'Yes, pray let's.' She gave a little shudder, 'Otherwise I shall be thinking of those maggots for days.'

Anthony's carriage was waiting for them outside. 'What next, Your Grace?' asked his groom cheerfully.

Anthony glanced at Marianne. 'Do you think your mother will be ready for us yet?'

She fervently hoped so. 'I think,' she said lightly, 'that there is a limit to the time that she and Lady Anne can talk about gowns and bonnets.'

'Then we'll head to Tavistock Square for her,' replied Anthony. He reached to help her into the carriage and suddenly the touch of his hand on her arm, the strength of him, together with the faint scent that clung to him—*cinnamon,* she thought, *why cinnamon?*—made her trip on the step that the groom had lowered.

'Steady,' said Anthony softly as he held her.

She backed away quickly, annoyed with herself because it was the kind of trick that Eleanor employed to gain a gentleman's attention. 'I'm sorry,' she said in a low voice. 'That was clumsy of me. I'm quite all right now, thank you.'

But she wasn't. She was remembering the many times in the past that he had helped her out of various fixes, always with good humour and a smile. Foolishly, there had been a time when she had believed he would *always* be there to help her.

Of course, he had decided to put her through this fresh ordeal in order to tell her that he'd warned Jonathan to keep quiet about her supposed sins. He had maybe saved her from Jonathan, but in the process he had learned about Max, which was awful. *Please*, she was muttering to herself. *Please. Can't we just collect my mother and go home?*

No. Apparently there was more. She was looking around as the carriage progressed along the street, pretending to be engrossed in the shops and the people they passed, but gradually she realised that he wasn't showing the same interest in their surroundings. He was studying her outfit, from top to toe.

She did her best to ignore him until at last he said, 'Where on earth do you buy your clothes?'

That was it. He was amazed by her audacity in wearing such a bold outfit. She gazed back at him then smoothed down her bright blue jacket and patted the gold braid adornments. 'You disapprove, I suppose?'

He smiled, a slow, lazy smile that made her pulse jump. 'I don't object,' he said, 'to what you're wearing at the moment.'

She shrugged, implying that it was of no interest to her if he did. 'My mother and I frequently visit a small shop run by Madame Minette in Oxford Street. She sells second-hand clothes.'

'Second-hand? Really?'

'Indeed. They've only been worn once, maybe twice, by wealthy ladies who feel the need to have a new gown for every occasion. My mother and I alter them to fit and add our own choice of trimmings.' She flashed him a smile. 'I'm so glad you approve of my style!'

He looked at her in the questioning way he used to use when she had got herself into a fix. 'I always did,' he said. 'And the gown you wore at the Earl of Ware's ball. Was that from Madame Minette's shop too?'

'Of course.' She reached for Eleanor's furled parasol and began to fiddle with it. 'I'm fond of bright colours.'

She was pretending to be absorbed in watching a passing carriage when Anthony suddenly said, 'I'm gathering that you and Lady Hermione have very little money to spend. Surely Edgar gives you both an adequate allowance?'

'Most definitely not. My stepfather is careful with money and my mother has to ask him for every penny she spends. I feel he almost tricked her into marrying him. She has no freedom!' She shook her head. 'Enough. I realise there is nothing to be done and it is wrong of me to even speak to you of this.'

But he was listening intently. 'No. I'm glad you did.'

'You *are?*'

He nodded. 'I've heard of solicitors who occasionally succeed in fighting for the wife in cases such as this, but I'm afraid the law is firmly weighted on the husband's side and the costs are enormous.'

'It is so unfair!'

'I know. But Marianne, listen. You've told me very clearly that you don't want me to interfere. But I've been thinking about the problems that you and your mother face, and I have a suggestion. Your mother would love to have Oakfields back, wouldn't she?'

Just for a moment she couldn't speak. *Oakfields.* Yes, her mother would love it and so would Simon, so would she…

At last, she said, 'Sir Edgar sold it. The property is no longer his.'

'I know. But I happened to see it was on the market again and I was thinking that maybe I could buy it myself.'

She was staggered. 'Do you really think that we would accept your charity, Anthony?'

'I don't want you to think of it as charity. It would still be mine, but you and your family would be able to use it whenever you wished. You could maybe think of it as an acknowledgement of my years of friendship with your family.'

Paying me off, she thought bleakly. *I should have expected him to think in such a transactional way.*

'I told you,' she said, 'I have no desire for such a huge gift. And Anthony, please do not go behind my back and try to tempt my mother with it, because she might not have the strength to refuse. I will find my own way to cope with our future.'

'I'm sorry,' he said. 'Once I thought we understood one another, you and I.'

'Did you?' she said politely. 'Did you really?'

Inside, she was shaking. Four years ago, this man had disappeared from her life for good, she'd thought—but now he'd come back into it and once more thrown her emotions into chaos.

'Marianne,' he suddenly said. He pointed. 'What has happened to your gloves?'

She looked too, and almost dropped the parasol when she realised that her best cream gloves were stained with spots of yellowish grease. 'It's cooking fat!' She was horrified. 'And look what it's done! Eleanor lent this parasol to me. She must have smeared it on the stem, and now it's on my gloves. Oh, I should have *known*.' She could have wept.

'I'm afraid they are ruined,' he said. 'Let me help you.'

Very carefully, he took the parasol and laid it on the floor of the carriage. Then he eased off her gloves one by one and laid them down beside it. 'I shall dispose of the lot,' he said. 'And I suggest you say nothing at all about this incident to your stepsister.'

'Why?'

'Because she won't expect that. Eleanor will be mystified and also a little fearful. She won't know what's afoot and will be waiting for the trap to spring.' He smiled. 'It's a simple solution, but the best ones usually are.'

At his smile, she felt her heart lift, just a little. 'Yes! You're absolutely right. But this is typical of her. She is so mean.'

'The Radlett sisters.' He nodded. 'Every London bachelor's nightmare.'

But Marianne was silent now, because those were the only gloves she possessed that were fit for polite society. What a disaster of an afternoon. Soon they would reach Lady Marwell's house, then Anthony would take them home—which was a sanctuary of sorts, because at least there she could retreat to her bedroom. But then she realised Anthony was ordering his driver to take a diversion to nearby Soho.

Marianne was startled. 'Why are we going there?'

'You'll see,' he said.

Soon enough, they were pulling up outside the expensive milliner's shop that Marianne and her mother always gazed at longingly but never dared to go in. 'Anthony,' she began again, 'what…'

He stooped to pick up her ruined gloves and climbed out of the carriage. 'Stay there,' he said. 'I won't be long.'

Indeed, very soon he was rejoining her and telling the driver to proceed to Tavistock Square. Then he handed her a tissue-wrapped package. 'Open it.'

She was totally mystified, but she opened it and found that inside was a pair of gorgeous cream gloves. She didn't know what to say so instead she turned them over and over in her hands, shaking her head in disbelief.

'Try them on,' Anthony urged.

She did so very carefully. 'They are a perfect fit,' she said in wonder, still a little dazed.

'So they should be. I showed them your old gloves and they were able to find a pair that matched almost exactly. And don't you even think of refusing them, Marianne, or I shall give them to Eleanor.'

She was overwhelmed. She felt this was the Anthony she had once known, who had carved himself a place in her heart. There was such a lump in her throat that all she could whisper was, 'Thank you.'

Soon they were pulling up outside Lady Anne's house, where her mother was gazing out from a bay window. Within moments she was coming down the steps to the carriage and Anthony was helping her in.

'I hope you both enjoyed the museum?' she said as she settled in her seat. 'Anthony, I've been telling Lady Anne about the picnics we used to have with you in the countryside, and those games of croquet we played on our lawn, even though it was bumpy with molehills! Oh, dear me, I fear I am being silly because of course you will have forgotten it all entirely…'

'Lady Hermione,' Anthony said quietly, 'I have never forgotten those happy days, believe me.'

Her mother was furiously dabbing away some tears. 'Forgive my foolishness. You were always good to us all, and to see you now, with Marianne…'

'Mother,' Marianne said in a low voice. 'Mother, please stop.'

'Of course.' Lady Hermione took a deep breath. 'That's quite enough of my sentimental chatter. We must get back before Edgar becomes grumpy again and remembers that he has forbidden Marianne to leave the house.'

'Has he?' Anthony looked at Marianne. 'Marianne, is this true?'

'Indeed,' she said. 'He tends to do that when I displease him. Clearly, though, he made an exception for you.'

He nodded, but his expression was grim. 'If there are any repercussions because of this outing, let me know.'

Oh, she thought, the repercussions would be many. A sudden burst of longing for the friendship they had once shared almost toppled her and the brief remainder of their journey passed in silence. Even Lady Hermione said nothing. No doubt she was already oppressed by the thought of entering Sir Edgar's gloomy house.

Marianne remembered how in his youth Anthony had been full of ambition and optimism for the future, but now faint lines of fatigue had etched themselves too early around his mouth and she could see that in his grey eyes that once shone with laughter there was cynicism, even bitterness, as might be expected in a man who'd married purely for money.

She found herself suddenly remembering how, one summer day, she and Anthony had gone to look for wild strawberries and as they'd strolled together he had told her that he envied her happy family. She had said, with the earnestness of youth, 'It's your family too, Anthony. You will always be a part of it.'

She was wrong. Time and circumstance had separated them, and how very cruel life was, to have thrown her back in his path like this. How cruel to be faced with the bitterness of him offering to reclaim their beautiful old home for their use when she could not accept it. Her family could not afford to be in any way reliant on Anthony—and that was final.

All too soon the carriage was drawing up outside Sir Edgar's house and Lady Hermione was dabbing at her eyes with her lacy handkerchief. Marianne took her mother's hand and said gently, 'Now, this will not do. No more tears, Mama, and look, your lovely bonnet is all crooked. Here, let me straighten it.'

After bidding farewell to Anthony, she led her

mother inside, while resolving that she must leave all her stupid dreams behind her, for dreams did nothing but destroy you.

All the way home to Grosvenor Square, Anthony could not forget the look on Marianne's face when he had given her those gloves. She had been astonished, emotional even, and he had been consumed by the longing to pull her into his arms and…

And what, you fool? Kiss her in public and cause yet more problems for her, when she was in enough trouble already?

He knew that life had hurt her badly. She had lost her beloved home, her brother was far away and she had to endure living in the household of a man who treated her with no kindness. *I should have been there for her*, he told himself.

But what, exactly, could he have done?

He had been forced to marry, forced to lead a new life in which his efforts to keep his father from gambling once more and to take over the running of the vast Cleveland estate took up all his time. He could not deny that his memories of an enchanting girl with red-gold hair had always haunted him, but he guessed she despised him for his marriage, just as her brother Simon did. By mentioning Oakfields, he had only made matters worse. But she had done nothing to help herself lately, had she?

While he was still troubled by frustration and regret, he also had another worry.

He had felt for some time that he was being followed—nothing definite, just the odd sense that, as he went around town, some stranger would be looking at him a little too closely then vanishing down a side street. Maybe it was his imagination. But when he finally returned home that afternoon and noticed a man who'd been loitering close by hurry into nearby Brook Street, he was absolutely sure of it.

He was being watched. Who by—and why?

Marianne and her mother got home to find Sir Edgar standing in the hallway with his daughters lurking behind him.

'Sir Edgar,' said Marianne lightly as she removed her tall hat and handed it to a maid, 'you look displeased. I thought you might approve of my outing with the Duke.'

She took a brief moment of pleasure in the way Eleanor was staring in bewilderment at her gloves.

'Marianne,' said Sir Edgar, 'have you really no regard for your reputation?'

She found herself stiffening with rebellion. 'I beg your pardon?'

He looked at Lady Hermione. 'I'm disappointed with you, Hermione. You left Marianne and the Duke together at the earliest opportunity, didn't you?'

Poor Lady Hermione was unable to reply. How did he know? Marianne could only guess that her stepfather had sent one of his footmen to spy on them. The next minute, he was addressing her again. 'So Cleveland came to take you out on public display, but surely you realise that his attentions will do nothing for your reputation! I speak out of concern for you, and I must tell you that Jonathan Moseley is anxious about you too.'

She was aghast. 'You've spoken to him?'

'Indeed. I met him this morning and I apologised to him on your behalf.'

'No! How could you?'

'Because I was embarrassed that you, my stepdaughter, had broken off the betrothal. But Moseley was a true gentleman, Marianne. He explained that although he was sadly aware of your failings, he preferred not to speak any ill of you, since he feared it might damage your future prospects. Prospects which I fear are diminishing day by day.'

Eleanor and Sybil were listening, wide-eyed.

Marianne was absolutely furious. So Jonathan had resolved to dig the knife in her reputation by pretending to be concerned about her! How absolutely maddening—especially as there was nothing even Anthony could do about that. She wanted to walk out of the house for good, right this minute, but she knew she was trapped, and it was the most horrible feeling in the world.

Her mother was touching her arm. 'Marianne,' she murmured, 'don't get upset, please.'

Marianne nodded and took a deep breath. 'Is that all you wished to say, Sir Edgar? Because if you've finished your lecture, perhaps I can go upstairs to change my clothes.'

She was already leading her mother towards the staircase when Edgar called after them. 'Hermione, I am relying on you to guard your daughter more carefully. And Marianne, do not forget that for your own sake you are still confined to the house!'

The two of them found refuge in Lady Hermione's bedchamber, where Marianne shut the door firmly. 'Now,' she said to her mother, 'I'm afraid Edgar is in a particularly bad mood today, but it's not the end of the world.'

Judging by her mother's face, however, it probably was. 'Darling,' Lady Hermione said, 'I truly don't think I can stand much more of this. I know

I was misled by Edgar, but he seemed so kind! Despite having you and Simon, I was lonely without your lovely father. But now I have lost everything.'

Marianne hugged her because that, really, was all she could do.

Lady Hermione pulled away at last and said, 'It was wonderful to see Anthony again. You and he were always so close. I used to hope—'

'Hope that we would marry? Dear Mother, I'm afraid you pinned your hopes too high there. He is a duke and he married for money even then, remember?'

Lady Hermione sighed. 'Indeed, the marriage was not at all the thing for a duke's heir. Nobody could understand it.'

I did not understand it either, thought Marianne. As for his offer to buy Oakfields, it was an act of pity which she would not accept, for she had her pride too. If anyone was going to obtain a measure of freedom for herself and her mother, it would be her—and already she had an idea.

Chapter Five

The perfect opportunity to embark on her plan presented itself to Marianne the very next afternoon. Sir Edgar was at his club, hosting a luncheon for his charity committee, Eleanor and Sybil had gone to an afternoon tea party, while Lady Hermione was once more visiting Lady Anne Marwell, who was now, it seemed, her very best friend.

Marianne put on an old grey cloak and tucked her hair under a plain bonnet, then she went to find Alice, who was sitting in Sir Edgar's library reading Lady Hermione's latest copy of *The Lady's Magazine*.

Alice looked up. 'Before you ask,' she pronounced, 'I'm supposed to be dusting the bookshelves.'

Marianne had to laugh. 'Alice! If Sir Edgar's butler saw you…'

'Oh, I'm not scared of pompous Perkins.' She

stood up and squared her shoulders. 'I'm three inches taller than he is, for a start.'

'Well, I'll have to tear you away from your reading, because I need you now. You and I are going on an important expedition.'

'Important?' Alice looked her up and down. 'In that case, whyever are you wearing such dreary clothes?'

'I don't want to be conspicuous because I have a plan. You see, I'm going to visit a lawyer in Stukeley Street, because look—I found this advertisement in *The London Gazette!*'

Alice peered at the newspaper Marianne thrust at her and read aloud, *'Confidential advice given on marital issues. All cases considered. Call at Messrs Fawcett and Co, Attorneys, Stukeley Street.'* She looked at Marianne darkly. 'What are you up to this time? Stukeley Street—you do realise it's close to St Giles and the rookeries?'

'Maybe.' Marianne was getting impatient. 'But quite simply, Alice, I'm desperate to help my mother. She really is unhappy here and I know it's partly my fault, because I just can't stop myself from annoying Sir Edgar terribly.'

Alice sniffed. 'The man could do with more people standing up to him, if you ask me. He's only angry with you because you're so much prettier than his daughters. So you're thinking of seeing a lawyer, are you? I've a much better idea. You should present Sir Edgar with an obliging lady of the night, then with any luck she'd wear him out and give him a heart attack.'

Marianne had to laugh. 'No good, Alice! The man's a puritan. I do have a serious plan, though. That's why I'm going to see this lawyer.'

'Meddling again,' sighed Alice. 'Very well, then. I'll come with you.'

Alice still looked unhappy as they left the house and made their way to the nearest hackney stand, but very soon they arrived by cab outside the unimpressive office of Messrs Fawcett and Co. After paying their driver, Marianne looked around, already uncomfortably aware of a group of men outside an alehouse staring at them.

'Like I said, we're close to St Giles here,' murmured Alice. 'This area's a proper nest of thieves, so you'd better get on quickly with whatever you came to do, miss.'

Marianne nodded and entered the rather dingy premises of the lawyers with Alice at her heels. A grey-haired clerk approached her, looking none too friendly. 'May I assist you, madam?'

'Indeed, I hope so,' Marianne replied brightly. 'I wish to speak to Mr Fawcett.'

His expression did not improve. 'Your name? Your business?'

'I would prefer not to give my name at this point. But I can inform you that I need advice on a rather delicate matter.'

Maybe her confident manner won him over a little, for he said, 'I think Mr Fawcett is free. I'll take you through.'

She nodded then turned to Alice. 'Wait here for me, will you?'

Mr Fawcett rose from behind his desk as she entered. He was rather plump and his clothes were ill-fitting and untidy. In fact, she could see that the whole room was untidy, with stacks of papers piled high, and when she spotted a half-empty bottle of whisky and a used glass on top of a filing cabinet, her heart sank further.

'Young lady,' Mr Fawcett pronounced, 'am I to believe you have come here by yourself? No husband? No father?'

His words were slightly slurred. Goodness, the man indeed sounded as if he had been drinking. 'I have come by myself,' she said, 'because I am perfectly able to deal with my own business. May I take a seat?' She sat without waiting for his approval.

Mr Fawcett settled behind his desk once more, still frowning. 'Why exactly are you here?'

'My mother was widowed seven years ago,' Marianne began, 'and she lost all her assets to her new husband upon remarrying. I understand there are ways of getting these assets returned to her and I would like to explore them.'

His bored expression did nothing to raise her spirits. 'Presumably,' he said, 'she married of her own free will?'

'Yes, but let me make it clear! My mother was deceived into thinking that her new husband was caring and generous, but since their marriage he has tried to control every aspect of her life.'

'Perhaps your mother needs her husband's guidance. Many women do.'

Marianne felt her anger rise. She feared she would get little help here, but it was worth stating her case at least. 'My mother is unhappy,' she said. 'I wondered if you could help her because, you see, she owned a fine house in Kent and received income from its land and my dead father's investments. But she lost all of that when she married again.'

'It's the law,' said Mr Fawcett. But he was beginning to look slightly more interested. 'She was wealthy then, was she? The problem is, has she still got enough money to pay me for any investigation into her rights?'

'Not at present, no! But I assure you that once the

case is won, my mother will be perfectly able to pay you in full, and—'

'Oh no, no. Allow me to inform you,' Mr Fawcett said firmly, 'that I do not work for nothing. I need some form of security at the very least. So I suggest, young lady, that you be grateful for the care your stepfather presumably provides for you both and leave the matter there. Good day to you.'

He rose from his chair and pointed to the door.

'Please.' Marianne stood up too. She was desperate. 'I have no money with me, but I do have this.' Reaching into the pocket of her cloak, she pulled out a small velvet purse and extracted from it perhaps the most precious thing she had ever owned.

It was the ring Anthony had given to her years ago. As she placed it in the lawyer's fingers and remembered what it meant to her, she felt as if a little part of her had died.

Mr Fawcett stared at it a moment, then he found a magnifying glass from amidst the clutter on his desk and sat down to examine it. Looking up, he said, 'Where did you get this?'

'It was a gift.' She was anxious, she was upset at seeing her ring being pawed over by this stranger, but she was desperate too. She added, 'Might you take it as a guarantee of payment in the future? To be returned to me, of course, once you are successful?'

He didn't answer. At last, he said, 'I need someone else to value it. Wait here.'

So Marianne waited. She paced up and down the untidy room. She looked up at the big clock on the wall several times before realising it wasn't working. She thought she heard Mr Fawcett talking to someone outside and went to listen, but couldn't make out any of it so she sat down again, trying to reassure herself.

This is my only option, she reminded herself. Once all this was over she would get the ring back and have her mother's money to pay the lawyer's fee...

She jumped to her feet on hearing loud voices and footsteps. The door opened and Mr Fawcett came in, but this time he was followed by two burly-looking constables.

Marianne stared at them. What was going on? 'Mr Fawcett,' she said, 'I have changed my mind about employing you. I'm leaving now and I also want my ring back, this minute.'

One of the constables stepped sideways to block her escape. '*Your* ring?' He said it with a sneer in his voice that made her suddenly afraid. 'Are you sure about that?'

'Of course I am. It was a gift!'

'From whom?' said the lawyer. She was silent. He nodded. 'You're not very good at lying, are you?'

He turned to the constables. 'She babbled about a rich mother. But look at her—she's dressed as if she's not got a penny to her name. Then she produced this ring.' Holding it in his hand, he waved it at Marianne. 'Now, it might not be worth a fortune in itself. But young lady, haven't you seen the markings inside it?'

She was bewildered. 'Markings? No, I haven't.'

'Then you're not very observant, are you? This ring is inscribed with a family crest. Half of it is worn away, but an expert will decipher it quickly enough. Clearly, it belongs to some fine family—yet you still claim that it's yours?'

A family crest. Of course—the emblem of the Clevelands. Dear heaven, this was awful, to be trapped by the ring she loved so much. 'Please,' she said. 'It is mine, I swear it is!'

'You can swear as much as you like, missy,' said the constable gruffly. 'But we're still taking you and the ring to Bow Street magistrates' court. Come along quietly now.'

Already they were hustling her outside and Marianne looked round desperately for Alice, to tell her what was happening. But Alice had gone.

At around the same time in Mayfair, Anthony was preparing for an afternoon outing and Travers was helping him with his clothes. 'Perhaps you should try the new olive-green coat your tailor delivered the other day, Your Grace? It looks rather more… light-hearted, I would say, than the dark brown one.'

Light-hearted? That certainly wasn't Anthony's current mood. 'I'm fine with the brown,' he said. 'Thank you, Travers. I can manage the rest myself.'

He knew he spoke too curtly to his loyal old retainer. Sighing, he checked his image in the mirror and saw that in this formal coat, with a starched cravat and cream breeches, he looked exactly as a duke should—upright, regal, forbidding almost. But did he like himself for it? Not in the least. Turning his back on the mirror, he completed the finishing touches by putting on his boots and a pair of York tan gloves, then he went downstairs.

His friends were due to collect him at two, and on the exact hour a luxurious barouche drew up. Anthony had agreed to go with Tom Duxbury and others to a private viewing of some new paintings at the Royal Academy. It would, he thought resignedly, at least take his mind off Marianne, since he was struggling with his frustration that she would not accept his help, as well as the hateful feeling that he had let her down.

He had prepared himself for a typical high-society

afternoon: a brief tour of the paintings followed by a ride in the park. But as he approached the waiting carriage, Tom jumped down and drew him to one side to say in a low voice, 'Just a swift word of warning, my friend.'

Instantly, Anthony was on the alert. 'Yes, Tom? What is it?'

Tom was looking round as if even the paving stones had ears. 'It's like this. Unfortunately, there appear to be rumours going around that you're planning to set up Miss Blake as your mistress.'

Anthony's first reaction was one of disbelief, followed by pure anger. Would the continuous stream of gossip about him never stop? He said flatly, 'That's ridiculous, Tom. I took her for an outing yesterday, but she had her stepfather's full permission. We visited a *museum*, for heaven's sake!'

'Well, someone's spreading the story. I'm afraid you have an enemy.'

Moseley, thought Anthony. It had to be Jonathan Moseley. He remembered again his suspicion that he was being followed—was that Moseley's work too?

But he had no time to do anything about that now, because Tom was ushering him towards the carriage, where he noted that a space had been left for him between Kitty, the daughter of Viscount Cadogan, and Lady Sarah Duxbury, Tom's younger sister. Both girls were among the debutantes from whom he was expected to pick a new bride; they were pretty, well-mannered and untainted by scandal.

So why, then, was he only thinking of Marianne? Why were his damned dreams so persistently haunted by her, gazing up at him with those defiant brown eyes and declaring, 'Do you really think that we would accept your charity?'

Where was she now? he wondered. What was she doing? Then he realised that Kitty was leaning out of the open carriage to speak to him. 'Your Grace, I am so looking forward to seeing Sir Thomas Lawrence's latest portraits. What a treat! And afterwards we have made plans to—'

But he never found out what those plans were, because at that very moment he heard someone calling out from along the street, 'Stop! Your Grace, please stop!'

On turning round, he saw that a tall, thin woman in a black cloak was running desperately along the pavement towards him. He knew her. She was Alice, the former housemaid at Oakfields who had come to London with Lady Hermione and Marianne. *Dear God, what now?* He went swiftly to stop her drawing too close to Tom's barouche. 'What has happened, Alice?'

'It's Marianne, Your Grace!' The maid was out

of breath. 'She doesn't know I've come to you, but she's in trouble, bad trouble. You see, she's being held at Bow Street.'

For a moment Anthony was lost for words. 'For God's sake, why?'

'Your Grace, she went to see a lawyer and she took me with her. I waited outside, and I saw the constables arrive then lead her away. They're saying she's stolen something!'

He glanced back at his friends, who were practically hanging out of the carriage, desperate to hear what was being said. He addressed Alice once more. 'So she went to a lawyer,' he said harshly. 'And he decided she was a thief? Why?'

'It was something to do with a ring, that's all I know, and you're the only person I believe she can trust. Please, you must rescue her!'

'A ring…' he said slowly. Suddenly he remembered the ring he'd given to Marianne long ago, made of gold and set with pink garnets, but he quickly shook himself out of his reverie.

Whatever the source of her trouble, she was in Bow Street magistrates' court and, dear God, only she could get herself into such a fix. He went over to his waiting friends. 'Someone I know needs my help,' he said, 'so I'm forced to abandon the outing. I offer you all my apologies. Enjoy your afternoon.'

Tom's sister, Lady Sarah, looked ready to burst into tears. 'Oh, Anthony. You're not leaving us, are you?'

Tom was rather more sensible. 'Is there anything I can do to help?'

'Nothing at present, but thanks for the offer.' He returned to Alice and said to her, 'I shall take a cab to Bow Street, rather than use my carriage. It's too recognisable and the fewer people who know about this, the better. You must come with me and I'll drop you off at Sir Edgar's house on the way.'

Alice's expression became stubborn. 'I want to come too. I cannot leave Miss Marianne.'

'It's better if I deal with this myself, Alice. I'm taking you home to Bloomsbury, where you must tell Lady Hermione that you've left Marianne with friends.'

When he arrived at Bow Street, the entrance hall of the court house was busy but he marched straight up to the officer behind the desk. 'I believe a lady called Miss Blake is here. I need to see her, immediately.'

'She's been brought in for theft, sir. You can't just—'

'Take me to her. *Now.*'

His air of command did the trick. Anthony was instantly led to a cell-like little room with only one barred window and walls of rough stone. Marianne was sitting on a wooden bench beneath the window with her head bowed and he marvelled at the way that the sparse light in here still managed to pick out the red and gold tints of her hair.

She rose as the door opened. 'Anthony?' She looked very pale. 'Why on earth are you here?'

'I'm here,' he said, 'because Alice came to find me.'

'No,' she said emphatically. She was shaking her head. 'No, Alice had no business doing that…'

She broke off and Anthony became aware that the officer who'd led him here was directing a look of such outright lechery at her that he barely resisted the urge to floor him. 'Out,' he growled to the man. 'Get out, you wretch.' He slammed the door shut then he turned back to Marianne.

She folded her arms across her chest as if to protect herself. 'Of course you would feel you had to help, for old times' sake. But oh, Anthony. I wish you hadn't.'

He had never seen Marianne like this before. She was almost overwhelmed, he guessed, by her predicament, but damn it, she still managed to look as lovely as ever, even in that ugly old cloak, even though her brown eyes were shadowed with an anxiety she just couldn't hide. Certainly not from him, who knew her so well.

He suddenly remembered a crisp autumn day in Kent many years ago, when Marianne had insisted on riding her father's new bay gelding even though both Anthony and Simon had warned her it was too strong for her. Predictably, it threw her and she broke her wrist, but she kept protesting to them, 'I'm all right. I'm *fine*,' until she'd almost fainted from the pain.

Anthony had taken her home on his big horse while Simon followed with the bay gelding. He remembered how she'd kept whispering to him, 'Such a *fuss*, Anthony! And I know exactly what you're thinking.'

He had smiled down at her. 'What am I thinking?'

'That I'm nothing but a nuisance.'

'Oh, most certainly,' he'd said. 'But you are a very sweet nuisance, so I forgive you.'

They had been friends in those days. Now their relationship was marred by doubt and mistrust and it was clear she didn't want him here. But he still said to her, 'Well, I'm here now. So what exactly have you been up to this time?'

She looked around and then at him. 'I really would appreciate it,' she said, 'if you could get me out of this awful place.'

'To do that, I'll need to know a little more. You realise, I hope, that getting yourself arrested is quite a feat, even for you.'

He thought she flinched slightly, but then her gaze was defiant. 'Maybe it's all in a day's work for me. You once said I had a habit of stirring up trouble wherever I went, and I would hate to disappoint you.'

Oh, Marianne. He felt an almost overwhelming surge of emotion. He was aware of a longing again to hold her in his arms and comfort her, just as he had that night at the Earl of Ware's ball—but look where that had got them both.

So he stayed where he was and said, 'What exactly happened, Marianne? And no making light of it either.'

She spoke a little wearily now. 'You know already how concerned I am about my mother. Sir Edgar is wearing her down, Anthony! Yes, I know you offered a possible solution, but that would mean we were as indebted to you as much as we are at present to Sir Edgar.'

Right. So he was being compared to Sir Edgar now, was he? His mouth set in a grim line.

'So,' she was saying, 'I decided that the only way to get her away from Sir Edgar was to consult a lawyer.'

'*What?* But I warned you—'

'I know! I know you told me there was little chance of achieving much for her, but I had to do something! So I went this afternoon to visit a lawyer called Mr Fawcett.'

'Fawcett? I've not heard of him.'

'I'm not surprised.' She sighed. 'I don't imagine he would ever be consulted by someone of your standing. Anyway, I explained what I wanted, but he said he would need payment in advance. There was I, thinking that he'd do the decent thing and take pity on me, but he didn't, and I felt I couldn't give up so…'

'So?'

She spoke very quietly now. 'I don't suppose you remember the little ring we found years ago, when we explored your father's attic?'

'I remember it. Go on.'

'I thought it might have some value, so I offered it to the lawyer as a guarantee of future payment. I didn't realise, though, that it was marked inside with your family crest.'

So *that* was it. That was what had caused the fuss.

'I suppose I did,' he said, 'but I'd forgotten it.'

'Well, unfortunately, Mr Fawcett spotted it immediately and went for the constables. He assumed, you see, that I'd stolen it. So here I am, stuck in Bow

Street, and I am dismayed that I'm causing yet more trouble for you. I shall not forgive Alice for this.'

'Alice is probably your best friend,' he said abruptly. 'Have the men here been rough with you?'

'No. No, not really.' She gazed around that dismal place. 'But I was getting a little nervous because, you see, I couldn't help but hear the constables talking about me and saying things.'

'What kind of things?'

'Oh, what they'd like to do with me, I suppose. It wasn't very nice and I tried not to listen.'

She had raised one hand to push back a stray lock of hair and he suddenly saw the fresh bruises on her wrist. *My God.* His heart was thudding. He growled out, 'Did the villains do *that* to you, Marianne?'

'Yes. You see, I struggled a little when they were bringing me in here.'

'I'll damn well kill them!' He was starting off towards the door.

'No. No, there is no need!'

'There is. They deserve a beating. Shutting you away in here, casting filthy looks at you!'

'Anthony—' she grabbed his hand '—I beg you, please don't do anything foolish.'

Her small fingers felt cold against his and the mere thought of those bastards manhandling her made him sick to his stomach. The scent of her, the sweetness of her in this foul place, seemed so unbelievably wrong that he could think of only one way to make it right.

He pulled her into his arms, and he kissed her.

Her lips were soft and unresisting. As he deepened his caress he thought he felt her tremble slightly, but then he realised that her arms were stealing shyly up around his neck and her mouth was opening to his kiss like a flower to the sun. Feeling his blood pound with desire, he pulled her slender body hard against him until his need to possess her overpowered all his senses.

Then suddenly she was pulling away. She urged, 'Listen!'

Through a haze of thwarted desire, he heard the sound of shouting and curses growing louder out in the main office. Quietly, he went over to the door. What on earth was happening out there?

Marianne provided the answer. 'I think they must be bringing in another prisoner.'

He opened the door a little and when he looked out he saw a big man—a drunken lout from the looks of him—cursing and lashing out at the officers who tried to restrain him.

Anthony closed the door and came back, careful to keep his distance this time. It was best to forget that kiss and, from the way she avoided his eyes, she must feel exactly the same.

'Marianne,' he said, 'I shall get you out of here, but there will be problems. I'm afraid this won't be the end of it.'

'What do you mean?'

He chose his words as carefully as he could, considering his body was still hammering with desire. 'There is already gossip about us. I heard today that people are whispering that I plan to make you my mistress.'

'No!'

'Yes, and I'm afraid there might be even more talk after this adventure of yours. It won't take the constables long to work out who I am and there are muckrakers in the city who will pay them well for the story of your confinement here.'

She looked stricken. 'I'm truly sorry that you've become involved.'

He held up his hand. 'No. You and I were once friends, and I've never forgotten that.' He glanced once more at the door, then back at her. 'My title and wealth may be a liability in some ways, but they are an asset in others. I shall pay the constables to keep quiet about today's episode and we can only hope that the gossip-writers don't get to hear of it.'

* * *

Marianne's heart sank to its lowest ebb yet. Clearly, he felt burdened by his sense of duty towards her. As for that kiss, no doubt he was regretting it bitterly.

All she could say was, 'I'm truly sorry, Anthony, that your life has become tangled with mine again. I really should not have caused you to have to rush here to Bow Street, of all places!'

He smiled. 'Certainly no one could ever claim that an association with you was boring.'

She almost laughed then. But she stopped when he said steadily, 'Nobody dragged me here, Marianne. And believe me, I've faced far worse situations.'

Had he? But of course, he'd had to suffer all the gossip about his dead wife. Marianne guessed that very few people would have dared criticize him to his face, but it must have been hideous for him all the same. Perhaps, like her, he sometimes wished he could return to happier times. Her mind roamed cruelly back to the summer afternoon four years ago at Oakfields, when Anthony had said to her, *There are girls in London who imagine they are beautiful, but they aren't. Not compared to you.*

He looked at her enquiringly and it was as if he'd read her mind because he said quietly, 'Marianne, I have never apologised properly for what happened on the day of your brother's birthday all that time ago. I am truly sorry.'

She forced a smile. 'Do you mean the day you left us so rapidly before poor Simon's party had even begun? I think you might have found the party rather dull after London, so I shall forgive you for that slight misdemeanour. In fact, I will be forever in your debt if you can just get me out of here.'

'Very well,' he said. He was still looking at her as if he was searching for something else to say, but after a slight nod he left her and went to speak to the constables.

Getting her out was an easy task for him. He told the officer in charge that the ring had once belonged to his family but now was indeed Marianne's and the officer, realising Anthony was a man of rank, grovelled.

'My lord,' he whined. 'We did not understand. We made a foolish error.'

'You're damned right you did,' said Anthony, 'and you're lucky that I don't haul you in yourselves on a charge of assaulting an innocent lady. She is leaving with me, and you will give me the ring immediately.'

He slipped it into his pocket and once they were outside he handed it to Marianne. 'Considering your stepfather's lack of generosity,' he said, 'I would have thought you might have sold it to buy a new gown or two.'

'Oh,' she answered, 'I always did suffer from occasional bouts of sentimentality. Quite foolish of me.'

She spoke lightly, but she still looked fragile. Anthony was about to say something else when he noticed a man on the other side of the street, leaning against a wall with his hands in his pockets. After a moment the man turned and walked swiftly away but he'd been watching them, Anthony felt sure of it. Who was paying him—and why?

He hailed a passing cab and ordered it to head for Bloomsbury. During their journey his mind was too occupied for conversation and Marianne was silent too, but when they reached Edgar's home he helped her down and pressed her hand briefly. 'Say nothing of this to anyone, do you understand? Tell Alice to be silent also. I'll see what I can do to keep all this quiet. In the meantime, you must promise me—absolutely promise—that you'll stay out of trouble and avoid any company for at least a few days.'

'Sir Edgar has confined me to the house,' she said. 'I will take heed of him and, believe me, I shall be going absolutely nowhere.'

Alice opened the door to her. 'My goodness,' she said in her businesslike way, 'you had better come inside and get up to your room quickly, before you're spotted. Honestly, the things you get up to.'

Trust Alice to put her in her place. Marianne handed over her cloak and asked, 'Has anyone realised I've been out?'

Alice hung up her cloak and began hustling her up to her room. 'No, because I've told them you're taking a rest in your bedchamber. Edgar has finally come back from his lunch with his charity friends and now he's got your mother trapped in the drawing room, telling her all about it.' She opened the bedroom door and glanced at Marianne swiftly. 'So he got you out of trouble then, your duke?'

'He did indeed.' Marianne managed to say it calmly. 'Though I'm sure it's not an experience he would ever wish to repeat. And Alice, he's not *my* duke. He is the Duke of Cleveland.'

'Not your duke,' Alice murmured. 'Is that right? You should have seen the look on his face when I told him where you'd landed yourself. That man would do anything for you, I swear. Anything.'

Marianne shook her head. 'He came to my rescue most reluctantly, Alice, and it was only because we were friends when we were young. Nothing more.'

'Just friends? Ha! I don't think so.'

With that, Alice left and Marianne looked rather despairingly around her bedroom.

This was awful. Anthony had, yet again, saved

her from trouble and she knew she should be grateful. But she didn't want him to feel a sense of duty towards her and she didn't want his pity. Though, if she was honest, she wanted him in plenty of other ways.

That kiss. Why had he done it? Why? It had disturbed her badly.

When Max had assaulted her at that party, she had felt nothing but revulsion at his hot, wet kisses and the way he used his hands to maul her breasts. She had loathed him for gaining pleasure from forcing himself on her. Anthony had desired her too, she knew that for sure, because male desire was impossible to hide.

But when he had kissed her this afternoon, the merest touch of his lips had sent a strange, tingling warmth curling itself all through her body, making wicked suggestions to those private places she didn't allow herself to think about. In fact, she had been ready to fall into his arms and he would have known it. He must be looking back on it all now and thinking her a trollop, as Jonathan did.

What a mess. He had claimed he wanted to protect her, but he certainly had the power to hurt her immeasurably. And he had his secrets too. The mystery of his marriage, the hints of deep gambling and the sudden death of his poor, lonely young wife—all of these should have been huge warning signals to her, just as he was wary of her and her past.

It was up to her now. She must endeavour to stay out of his way, which shouldn't be difficult since her stepfather had confined her to the house. She must make her own life, maybe find a job so she could live away from London and away from him—as a governess, perhaps, or a lady's companion.

But marriage? That was no longer an option. For she knew now, with a sense of utter despair, that she could never give her heart to any other man—because Anthony, the Rogue Duke, had captured it long ago.

Chapter Six

The next day Marianne went down extremely late to breakfast. After that she returned to her bedchamber after explaining to a curious Eleanor that she really needed to finish an excellent book, and she even ate her lunch alone up there.

But shortly afterwards, Sir Edgar summoned her to the drawing room. Well, actually, Edgar himself didn't, it was Perkins the butler. She went reluctantly down to the drawing room, only to find that Eleanor and Sybil were there too. Her stepfather was sitting in a large armchair studying something that looked like an invitation card, but he looked up when she arrived.

'Ah, Marianne,' he said. 'Now, I know I suggested you should remain confined to the house for a while, in order to curb your propensity for mischief.'

Oh, if only you knew, thought Marianne.

'But,' continued Sir Edgar, 'I really feel that with

your mother and myself there to keep an eye on you, there will be no harm in you attending a private party tonight at the home of Lord Thomas Duxbury. We have all, you see, received an invitation.' He was waving a heavily embossed card.

Sir Edgar was clearly delighted but she wasn't, because she knew that Tom was Anthony's best friend. Which meant that Anthony would be there too—and he would be dismayed to see her there. Yesterday he had made her swear to avoid any company for a while yet instead, the very day after the Bow Street debacle, she would be appearing at a party which half the *ton* would attend. Her heart sank.

'I don't want to go, Sir Edgar!' she burst out. 'I mean… I think you were quite right to forbid me to leave the house, and you really should keep to your promise! After all—' and she looked rather wildly at Eleanor and Sybil '—you don't want me there with your daughters, do you? You don't want them following my example!'

Her stepfather was frowning. 'Sometimes, Marianne, I just do not understand you. I've already dispatched a note to Lord Duxbury saying we would all attend. We should, after all, create an impression of strong family unity.'

Eleanor and Sybil were scowling. She guessed they didn't want her at the party, just as much as she didn't want to be there. *One last try.* 'Sir Edgar, please, I fear I am developing a headache!'

'No, no,' he said, 'that I cannot believe. We shall all leave the house together this evening, at seven o'clock precisely.'

Marianne left the room in what she truly hoped was a dignified manner then headed for the parlour, where Lady Hermione sat on the sofa with Cuthbert at her side. Marianne heaved Cuthbert onto her lap and sat down too. 'Mother,' she said, 'I really do not want to go to this party tonight.'

'Neither do I,' declared Lady Hermione. 'I like Tom Duxbury very much, but I would rather stay here than go to a party with Sir Edgar and his daughters.' She sighed a little then brightened. 'But I have had some very good news! I've heard that Simon's ship is due to arrive in Portsmouth any day now, and won't it be wonderful to see him safely home again?'

'Of course,' said Marianne quickly. But this could pose yet another problem, for Simon didn't like Sir Edgar any more than she did. Simon did not like Anthony either; in fact, from what she'd gathered, the two men had argued fiercely around the time of Anthony's marriage and hadn't spoken since.

Her mother was talking again. 'I was thinking, darling. Tom Duxbury is Anthony's very good friend, isn't he? And—'

'Mother,' Marianne broke in, 'as I keep telling you, there is no prospect at all of him paying court to me. We have both grown out of our youthful friendship.' *And if he is at the party,* she thought to herself, *I would guess he will do his utmost to avoid me.*

Lady Hermione looked crestfallen. 'I can't see this evening being a great success for either of us, can you? I suppose I could pretend I have a headache.'

'I've already tried that,' said Marianne.

'And Sir Edgar wouldn't believe you?' She sighed. 'I really believe there must have been something wrong with my brain when I agreed to marry him. He is so overbearing towards me, he is positively unpleasant to you and I am deeply weary of spending my days in London. But what can I do, Marianne?'

Anthony, thought Marianne rather desperately. *Anthony provided an answer, by offering to buy Oakfields and let us use it.*

But she had refused outright, and he would surely never make the offer again.

'I know,' she said cheerfully. 'I'll find someone else to get betrothed to for the third time, shall I? Even if he breaks it off—or I do—I could become a celebrity, write a book even. People will ask, "Is she the most-often betrothed debutante in England?" Just think, I could probably make a great deal of money out of my awful reputation!'

'Marianne,' said her mother, 'do not jest like that, I beg you. I cannot bear it! I do declare, I feel quite faint.'

'Then you must rest.' Marianne put her arm around her mother's shoulders. 'Go upstairs and lie on your bed for a while. Trust me, I shall find a solution somehow.'

But what? After that, she went rather wearily to her own bedchamber. She felt like lying down herself. But every time she closed her eyes she couldn't help thinking about Anthony, and the way her body had tingled at the touch of his lips…

She should not have let it happen. She had not *wanted* it to happen and she felt desperately, desperately low. Although she had joked to her mother about her plans, she had no intention whatsoever of trying to find another husband, and she also knew that the chances of her obtaining a job as a governess or companion were practically nil, because she was too young and too pretty.

Even the news that her brother would be home at any time failed to lift her spirits because what could he do to solve these problems? Besides, his enmity with Anthony could only make matters worse.

Her heart sank further as the evening approached.

In the big house in Mayfair, Anthony too was restless because Marianne was back in his life and, dear God, she was causing him all kinds of trouble. Not the fun kind of trouble they'd had together when young, careering around the countryside with Simon, exploring the vastness of Cleveland Hall when his father was away and challenging each other into daring tricks. No, everything was far more serious now and he feared very much that, despite the bribes he had handed out to the constables yesterday, the tale of her brief captivity in Bow Street was bound to emerge sooner or later.

Perhaps what disturbed him most of all was that she had grown into an exquisite woman. Even in that dismal court building, her beauty had somehow lit up the grim surroundings and he had yearned to protect her from all of London life's treachery. Had she realised this when he kissed her? Had she realised how his desire for her had pounded almost painfully as their bodies and their lips met together in that agonisingly brief embrace?

He nearly groaned aloud. Yes, Marianne was back in his life and everywhere he went, he found himself thinking of the warmth in her smile and the amazing expressiveness of her brown eyes, framed by those oh-so-thick lashes. He couldn't stop himself imagining her long hair spread in copper-coloured tresses across the pillows of his big bed as he kissed not just her silky-soft lips, but every part of her luscious body.

Yes, that embrace in Bow Street had sent a surge of lust through his veins that still rumbled dangerously through his blood. He found himself recollecting the sweet scent and taste of her skin as longingly as if he were a lustful youth. But common sense told him he was mad to have kissed her yesterday. Neither of them needed more scandal attached to their names. Everyone already believed the worst of him, he thought darkly, including Marianne herself, who surely had known him better than that. He had not changed, but of course neither had she. She was still impulsive, still headstrong, and he guessed there was yet more trouble to come.

Tom Duxbury had called at Cleveland House that morning as Anthony was working in his study. Anthony had greeted him then poured him some coffee. 'I take it, Tom,' he'd said, 'that you've come to remind me about your party this evening?'

Tom took a seat and began stirring sugar into his drink. 'We'll come to that in a moment. But first, I have a question.' He looked up at Anthony suddenly. 'Where on earth did you get to yesterday afternoon, when that maidservant dashed up and hauled you away?'

Anthony felt himself tense. 'Come now,' he said. 'A gentleman is allowed some secrets, isn't he?'

'Perhaps.' Tom stared hard at him. 'But I've a feeling that lately you're acquiring a few too many for your own comfort.' He took a gulp of his coffee. 'Anyway, I have indeed called to remind you about my party. But I felt I ought to warn you that I've been obliged to invite Sir Edgar Radlett.'

Anthony was about to sip his own coffee, but he almost spilled it. 'What did you say?'

'I said, Sir Edgar Radlett is coming. I was at my club last night and inviting several other fellows who were there, when Sir Edgar pushed himself forward and somehow managed to assume he'd been invited too. He thanked me heartily. How could I back out?'

Anthony groaned inwardly. 'Do you think he'll turn up?'

'Most definitely, together with his rather terrifying daughters and, I believe, Lady Hermione and Marianne.' Tom hesitated. 'Hopefully, it won't be too awkward for you, will it? I know I told you there have been certain rumours about you and Marianne. But tonight will give you the chance to dispel them, by showing everyone that the two of you are merely friends—just as you were years ago, back in Kent.'

For a moment Anthony couldn't speak. If he backed out of the party now, Tom's suspicions would be put on high alert, but seeing Marianne there tonight was the last thing he wanted. His emotions from yesterday were too raw, too fresh, and there was always the chance that the Bow Street tale might have begun to spread. By himself, he could maybe deal with it—but if Marianne was there, it would be far more difficult.

Tom was already bidding him a cheery farewell—and Anthony decided his only hope was that Sir Edgar would continue to confine Marianne to the house.

The invitation stated that the party began at eight. Marianne knew that no one was actually expected to arrive at eight, but Sir Edgar was adamant they should be there exactly on time. Marianne had started getting ready early and she had looked rather despairingly through all her gowns. She had hardly one that wasn't either out of fashion or too wild and in the end she pulled one out almost at random and said to Alice, 'I shall wear this one.'

'Yellow,' Alice murmured. 'It's bright yellow, with pansies embroidered on the skirt. Are you sure about that?'

Yellow, Lady Hermione's hairdresser had once informed Marianne, was an impossible colour to wear for someone with hair like hers. But she replied,

'I'm quite sure, Alice. Everyone will be staring at me anyway, I guess, for breaking off my betrothal to Jonathan. So help me put it on, will you?'

She was able to console herself that at least Jonathan wouldn't be at the party tonight, because he wasn't a friend of Tom's. But Anthony would be there. *You must promise me,* he had said, *that you'll stay out of trouble and avoid any company for at least a few days.*

Her heart quailed anew at the thought of his displeasure.

After the dress, there was her wayward hair to deal with and Alice had barely time to pin it up when Sir Edgar called out to everyone that they must depart. It was barely half past seven and they would be embarrassingly early. But Marianne quickly grabbed a muslin shawl and hurried downstairs, only to realise that her mother, her stepfather and his daughters were already in his ancient carriage and—thanks to the bulky skirts of Eleanor and Sybil's dresses—there was not enough room left for her.

Her mother looked flustered. 'Eleanor,' she was saying, 'and Sybil, perhaps you can move up, both of you, to make space for Marianne?'

They each shifted along the seat by no more than an inch and Marianne, still standing on the pavement, said, 'What a shame. It seems as if I might have to miss Lord Duxbury's party after all. Never mind. I hope that you all have a lovely time—'

'Nonsense,' broke in Sir Edgar, who was clearly irritated. 'This is an important invitation. We are a family and we must appear together. Eleanor, Sybil, go and change your gowns for ones that take up less space, will you?'

'But Papa!' exclaimed Eleanor. 'That means we have to get ready all over again!'

'No, I am firm about this. Tell your maids to be as speedy as possible and the rest of us will wait in the house for you.'

They all trooped inside again and Marianne sighed. *Please,* she muttered, *don't let Anthony be at the party.*

Anthony arrived shortly before nine at Tom's house in Clarges Street. The guests were all exclaiming in delight as they arrived, for the gardens both front and back were softly illuminated and the ballroom was decorated with festoons of silk drapery. There was music for dancing, the champagne flowed—and, as yet, there was no sign of Sir Edgar's family.

Tom was surprised. 'I thought,' he said to Anthony, 'that Sir Edgar would be here almost before anyone else. Perhaps he's realised I didn't really intend to invite him.'

Anthony doubted that. Sir Edgar was too arrogant to have any such doubts. So far, his other fears had been allayed; there was no hint here that anyone had heard about Bow Street and neither had there been any signs that he was being followed as he'd gone about his daily business earlier.

It was half past nine and there was still no sign of Sir Edgar's family when one of Tom's footmen approached Anthony and said very quietly, 'Your Grace. A word?'

Anthony had been talking with a group of acquaintances but he made his apologies to them and followed the footman swiftly. He knew Tom's staff were trained, like his own, to watch for any signs of trouble at an event like this. 'What is it?' he asked swiftly.

'Your Grace, the other footmen and I have noticed there's a man who possibly shouldn't be here.'

'An intruder?' Anthony spoke sharply. 'Then shouldn't Lord Duxbury himself deal with him?'

'Lord Duxbury is dancing with Kitty Cadogan and people might talk if I interrupted them.' The footman hesitated. 'Besides, the man appears to be only interested in you. He has been watching you for a while.'

Anthony nodded grimly. 'Where is he?'

'Over there, Your Grace.' He pointed. 'Standing by himself, near the door that leads out into the garden.'

Anthony looked. There was indeed a man on his own, who was dressed in evening clothes that fitted him poorly—borrowed, maybe? But the chief thing was that Anthony recognised him. He was the man who had been following him. He said quietly to the footman, 'Leave this to me. No need yet to trouble Lord Duxbury with it.'

He made his way through the chattering throng of guests and faced the man squarely. 'Go outside,' he said. He pointed to the open door leading into the garden. 'Then you can tell me what the hell you're doing here.'

He spoke softly so as not to be heard by those nearby, but the menace in his voice was clear. The man moved quickly and Anthony followed. 'Right,' he said once they were away from the house. 'Now you can tell me. Who sent you here, and why?'

In the garden, the lamps glowed and the air was warm, but no one else was outside. The man answered reluctantly.

'I've a message for you, Your Grace,' he said. His voice was a mixture of surliness and aggression. 'That's why I'm here. You'd best read it.' He reached into the pocket of his coat and handed over a folded sheet of paper.

Anthony tore it open and read the message it contained.

I know about Bow Street. I know what you're up to with that woman. People like you think you can do whatever you like, but I won't stand for it. NG

Anthony crumpled it in his hands. Dear God, it was Ned Gibson who'd ordered this man to trail him—and, thanks to his spying, Gibson knew about Bow Street. For a man who supposedly despised polite society as much as Gibson did, he was certainly desperate to be a player in it, even if he knew he would always have to be a silent one, as far as the *ton* was concerned.

Often in the last few years, Anthony had wondered what would happen if he told people that his father was the gambler and not himself. He had wondered what people would say if they knew Anthony had been forced into marriage with an unfortunate girl who was unsuited in every way to the rank she had acquired.

He had genuinely tried to make her happy. He'd tried to protect her from the life she had been forced into, just as he had endeavoured to protect his weak father from disgrace. *Honour your family, always.*

But sometimes—like now—the burden seemed

almost too heavy to bear. Gibson knew about Bow Street and it was quite likely he had paid the constables enough money to learn about that kiss with Marianne too. There was a threat implicit in that letter. Was Gibson preparing to break his word, and tell the whole story of his father's misdeeds? His father's cheating, even?

The messenger was still standing there, waiting. Anthony knew he had plenty of friends here tonight, who could help him deal with the villain. But, even so, he had never felt more alone in his life. He gripped the man by his shoulders 'You're an intruder,' he said, 'and I could have you slung into gaol for breaking into a private house. Get out of here, or I'll throw you out into the street myself. Preferably into the gutter where you belong.'

The man wrenched himself away. He was scowling. 'Any message for my master?'

'Yes. Tell him I'll be paying him a visit very soon. *Get out.*'

The man left but Anthony did not move. He knew he should go back inside and pretend everything was all right, but he was almost overcome with anger and despair.

'Anthony?'

He whirled round because someone was coming towards him, from that open door that led to the ballroom. Someone in a yellow gown, with her red-gold hair piled loosely on the crown of her head. *Marianne.* Dear God, as if everything wasn't bad enough already.

He stayed where he was and he said, 'I didn't realise you were here.'

'My stepfather insisted that I came,' she said. 'But we were delayed, and—'

He held up his hand for silence and tried to speak calmly. 'Listen to me, Marianne. I want you to turn around and go back into the ballroom now, this very minute. I do not want a single person to know that you've come outside and spoken with me.'

She didn't obey him, which was no surprise at all. Instead, she looked even more troubled. She glanced at the house then at him and said, 'But Anthony. What has happened? We had only just arrived at the party when I noticed you talking to someone. It looked as though you were angry with him and were ordering him outside. He didn't appear to be your friend.'

It was no good. He would have to tell her about this anyway some time soon, and it might as well be now. He led her further from the house and he said, 'Marianne. That man knew about Bow Street. I've sent him packing, but I fear this means trouble for both of us.'

She stood there, very pale and very beautiful in the faint gleam of the outdoor lamps. She said at last, 'Was he making threats against you?'

He nodded. 'His master was threatening us both, I'm sorry to say.'

He suddenly realised that her gown and her delicate shawl were no protection against the chill that had gathered on this clear spring night. She was shivering and he felt quite wretched. Yes, Bow Street was a disaster. But it was even more of a disaster that they had come back into each other's lives, awakening cruel memories of times when life had been simple and dreams were possible.

He put his hands on her shoulders, realising once more how delicate she was, how fragile beneath her accustomed mask of defiance. 'I will do what I can,' he promised. 'Believe me.'

'I'm sorry,' she whispered. 'So very sorry, that I've caused all this trouble for you.'

She sounded almost broken, this brave, spirited girl who had always seemed so fearless.

'You always did cause trouble,' he said softly. 'But we used to have fun together, didn't we?'

She looked up at him almost wonderingly and he smiled and touched her cheek. For once it was just the two of them, out here alone together in peace and away from the crowds. This, he realised, was how it should have been.

'You've always been different,' he said. 'Stubborn. Strong-willed. Remember when you found that old boat by the lake and insisted I come out rowing with you?'

'But the boat turned out to be full of holes!'

'And I had to pull you out of the lake, ruining a pair of extremely good boots.' Oh, indeed he remembered that day, because it belonged to the times when they were friends, with no hint of the dark secrets that would push them apart.

'I remember your boots. They were brand-new and you must have been furious!' But suddenly her voice changed. 'We were happy then, weren't we? You and Simon and I.'

'Yes,' he said quietly. 'We were happy, and we trusted one another.' He hesitated. 'Marianne, I too have made mistakes. You will have heard unfavourable stories about me and no doubt they've disturbed you. I cannot tell you any more, but I can say this. Quite simply, I have been misjudged.'

'Like me, then?' she asked in wonder.

'Like you. Yes.'

She nodded. 'I want to believe in you,' she whispered. 'So badly.'

Drawing her close, he cupped her face in his hands,

letting his long fingers caress her cheeks. And then—he kissed her. It wasn't a kiss expressing urgent desire, but a kiss of yearning, of longing for a lost happiness that maybe should have been theirs. He felt her almost shyly responding. Her arms stayed by her sides, but her mouth was opening sweetly to him, her eyes were closed and just for a moment he tried to forget that Ned Gibson was promising trouble.

He ended the kiss, but still held her tight as she nestled against him. He was tempted to tell her now about why he'd been forced to marry. But could he trust her to keep quiet? She was impetuous, she was sometimes honest to the point of foolishness—and he was also aware that some day soon her brother might return. She and Simon were close; she might tell him all of Anthony's secrets, and that would be a disaster because Simon had made it clear that Anthony was his friend no longer.

His priority was to deal with Gibson. But Gibson, it turned out, wasn't his only problem, because the next instant the peace was shattered by a sudden roar of rage from the direction of the house.

'Marianne! Cleveland! What the devil is going on here?'

Marianne heard Anthony swearing under his breath. He had swung round and she turned also, to see her mother, Sir Edgar and Tom Duxbury emerging from the house—together with Simon.

It was her brother who had called out. He looked furious and no wonder. There was no denying that she and Anthony had been caught in a flagrantly compromising situation.

'Marianne,' Lady Hermione began nervously, 'look, here is Simon! He arrived in London this evening, just in time for the party. Isn't this a surprise?'

Tom intervened, putting his hand on her arm. 'Lady Hermione,' he said, 'perhaps you should take Marianne inside. Anthony, maybe you and I should have a word?'

'A word?' declared Simon. 'A word? I'll speak to Cleveland myself, Duxbury!' He strode up to Anthony. 'What are you up to with my sister, you rogue?'

'So you're back, Simon,' said Anthony. 'It's about time.'

'My ship arrived in Portsmouth two days ago. I reached London earlier this evening and went straight to Sir Edgar's house, where the butler told me my mother and my sister would be here. He didn't tell me that you, Anthony, would be here also, so I'd say that yes, it's clearly about time I made my presence felt.'

Marianne's heart was pounding with anxiety. Yes,

Simon was back after many months in India and he looked absolutely furious.

'Simon,' she began, 'Anthony and I have recently renewed our acquaintance…'

'Acquaintance? Is that what you call it?' Her brother pointed an accusing finger at Anthony. 'Damn you, Cleveland. Can't you find a better target for your liaisons, now that your poor wife has died? Marianne, come here.'

She didn't move. She knew her brother and Anthony hadn't communicated for years, but to actually see Simon's outright hostility was awful. Then Anthony stepped forward.

'Simon,' he said, 'and Lady Hermione, Sir Edgar, Tom—I would like you all to know that tonight I have asked Marianne to do me the great honour of becoming my wife.'

Marianne was stunned. Speechless. He was gazing at her, his grey eyes steely, as if to say, *I mean it. Do not let me down.*

She was utterly dismayed. She knew that this was the only way to avoid a major scandal because they had been seen out here by several people, kissing and embracing, and she knew her already dubious reputation would be in tatters if he hadn't made his offer. But oh, what kind of ending was this to her long-ago fantasies?

She looked at him almost pleadingly, as if to say, *Anthony, you do not have to do this.* She looked at Simon, who was still glaring at Anthony as if he'd like to challenge him to a fight then and there. She looked at her mother, who seemed stunned; at Tom, who appeared concerned, and her stepfather, who was incredulous and probably hoping that his problematic stepdaughter would soon be out of his household and married to a duke. She also realised that more of Tom's guests, already sensing some kind of scandal, were hurrying out onto the terrace to watch and listen in wonder.

This was just awful.

Anthony was moving closer to her side. 'Marianne,' he said quietly. 'You must answer, I'm afraid.'

She wasn't sure she could speak. But then he took her hand and she spoke to them all in a clear, steady voice. 'Yes,' she said. 'Yes, I have agreed to be the Duke of Cleveland's wife. I accept his proposal with pleasure and with gratitude.'

'Well done,' he murmured.

Simon, though, hadn't finished. He took a step forward and said to Anthony, 'You've compromised her, you rogue. You've quite clearly lured her into a situation where she *has* to marry you!'

Anthony met his hostile stare and said steadily, 'Take care, Simon. You are doing your sister and myself a grave injustice.' He lifted Marianne's hand and kissed it. In his eyes, she saw almost tenderness—but she was afraid. Anthony had been forced into yet another marriage that was no choice of his. Surely that meant this marriage would be equally unhappy?

Everything happened very quickly after that. Tom asked all the onlookers to return to the party, though Sir Edgar and Lady Hermione lingered and Simon told Anthony, extremely curtly, that he would escort his sister back to Sir Edgar's house immediately. 'I think Marianne has endured enough for tonight,' her brother said.

'No. Stay a moment.' Anthony turned to Sir Edgar and Lady Hermione. 'I'm sorry this has come as such a surprise to you. May I suggest that I call at your house tomorrow, Sir Edgar? Then we can perhaps begin to make arrangements for the wedding.'

Sir Edgar accepted gladly and Marianne thought she had never seen her mother look so happy. But her own feelings were in turmoil—and she still had Simon to face.

'You do realise,' Simon said as soon as they set off in his carriage, 'that Anthony has forced you into a situation where you had no alternative but to marry him?'

'He did not force me!' she cried out. 'I came out to speak to him. I was distressed and he comforted me.'

'He did a little more than that,' said her brother grimly, 'from what I observed.'

'And do you think I objected? No! Simon, don't you realise we are talking about *Anthony?* He was your friend and mine for many years!'

Simon sighed. 'Listen,' he said. 'I regret the fact that I've been away for so long. I'm sorry I wasn't here to protect you. But I'm here now, and you must remember we were mistaken about Anthony. Apart from the fact that he married purely for money, everyone knows he treated his wife abominably. You absolutely must think about this again.'

Not *more* people telling her what she must or mustn't do! Marianne found her resistance rising with every word he spoke. 'And break off yet another betrothal? Not a good idea, Simon!'

'Marianne—surely you've heard that the man practically murdered his wife?'

All of a sudden she could hardly breathe. She was remembering Eleanor, spiteful Eleanor, calling out to her, 'They say he's the Rogue Duke! They say his poor wife actually *died* because of his coldness to her!'

But—*murder?* She said at last, 'I think you do him a grave injustice, Simon.'

'Do I? The woman was so desperately unhappy, locked away in that great house of his in Kent, that she set off for London one winter's day when snow was already falling to beg him for a divorce. She died when the coach skidded on ice.'

'I have heard this. Of course I have. But it was certainly not murder!'

'There are rumours,' declared her brother grimly, 'that the coach she travelled in was driven by a man no one knew, and afterwards both coach and driver were never traced. But people say that Anthony ordered the coach for her, and he must have known how dangerous any journey was in such conditions. Marianne, the whole business speaks ill of him, so please, I beg you, don't be deceived by him now!'

She felt rocked by yet another scandalous rumour about Anthony's past, but she drew herself up almost proudly. 'Simon,' she said, 'we believed in Anthony's integrity before and I refuse—yes, I absolutely refuse—to believe he has changed. I am willing to trust him again. Why can't you?'

He looked at her in disbelief. 'So you're going ahead with this? You're willing to marry him?'

I have been misjudged, Anthony had told her. She had seen the near-anguish in his hooded eyes and the taut lines of his face and she wanted badly to believe in him. But she was also desperate to understand why he had married so swiftly, and why he allowed those cruel whispers about his past to persist if they were lies.

She said, 'My own reputation is questionable, Simon. I have two broken betrothals behind me—remember? I am grateful that Anthony is willing to offer for me.'

'Grateful?' echoed Simon. 'Is that really a sound basis for marriage?'

She was silent. Even in the face of her brother's hostility, she knew that whatever Anthony had done in the past, whatever secrets he was keeping from her, the thought of losing him now was unbearable. At last she lifted her head proudly and said, 'I am going to marry him.'

'I will find it difficult,' Simon said. 'Attending your wedding. Being civil to him.'

For a moment, Marianne could not speak. But then she said, as calmly as she could, 'Then do not come. Because I will not change my mind, whatever you say or do.'

No more was said. Soon after that the carriage reached Sir Edgar's house and Marianne hurried up to her bedroom before anyone else should return. Alice was waiting for her and when she saw Marianne's expression she murmured, 'Oh, my. Bad news, my dear?'

Marianne burst into tears and flung herself into Alice's arms. 'Anthony,' she sobbed, 'has asked me to marry him!'

'About time too,' said Alice with satisfaction.

Chapter Seven

Back at Tom Duxbury's house, it was almost midnight and the party was as lively as ever. But Tom had led Anthony into his study and had closed the door firmly against all the noise from the ballroom.

'Anthony,' he said. 'Have you gone stark, staring mad?'

Anthony raised his eyebrows a little. 'Meaning?'

Tom spread his hands in exasperation. 'Well, I think you're making a rather grave mistake. I like Marianne, very much. But…'

The 'but' said it all. 'I don't think I've gone mad,' Anthony answered a little wearily. 'And considering the situation we were found in, I actually have little option.'

'Are you sure? She is remarkably pretty. But she has a reputation, Anthony. Society will be aghast!'

'Don't fret, Tom. The *ton* will get over it. But if it

makes you feel better, you can continue telling me that I'm an almighty fool.'

Tom poured them each a glass of brandy, handed Anthony his then sat down again. 'I would never think you a fool,' he said with emphasis. 'But Marianne does seem to attract rather a lot of trouble. You don't need me to remind you that she's been betrothed twice already, and can you really afford to face more gossip?'

'I'm used to it,' said Anthony.

Tom sighed. 'I certainly wish you both every happiness. But if only you'd left it a while, then time might have softened people's memories of your marriage to Cynthia and they might even stop their eternal…'

His voice faded, probably because of the way Anthony was tapping his fingers on the wooden arm of his chair. 'Stop their eternal what, Tom?' said Anthony politely.

But Tom was clearly stuck for words. So Anthony, taking pity on him, bade him goodnight and set off home.

He knew, of course, that Tom was right. By morning the news that he had proposed to Marianne Blake would be all over town. He could imagine what even his friends would be saying about *that*.

Hasn't Anthony already had one disastrous marriage? Wasn't that enough for him?

If she hadn't followed him out into the garden tonight, none of this would have happened—but she hadn't forced him to kiss her. He desired her, there was no doubting it, and he also felt a sense of duty to her. It might appear to others that he'd made a drastic decision, but it had seemed to him the only possible one.

When Anthony got home, he realised that, late though it was, his poor valet was waiting for him in the ducal bedchamber and trying to conceal a sleepy yawn.

'You can go, Travers,' Anthony told him. 'I'm sorry you've had to wait so long. I can manage perfectly well by myself.'

Travers shook his head firmly. 'At least, Your Grace, let me bring you hot water for washing!'

'No,' said Anthony, 'really, cold is fine.' Already he was shrugging off his coat and removing his waistcoat. But Travers, who had started pouring water from the ewer for him, let out a sudden gasp of dismay.

'Your shirt! Your Grace—I can see blood.' Already Travers was rooting around in the medicine chest and bringing out clean dressings before starting to help Anthony to ease off his bloodstained shirt.

Travers was still muttering. 'I thought the wound on your back had healed completely,' he said, 'but clearly it has opened again.' He regarded Anthony suspiciously. 'What have you been up to tonight? You haven't been waltzing, have you?'

Anthony almost had to laugh. Who needed a personal guard, when they had Travers? 'No,' he said, 'I have not been waltzing.'

But he remembered that intruder at Tom's tonight and the force with which he'd gripped the man's shoulders. He'd felt it then, the stab of pain from the long scar between his shoulder blades. He'd guessed it meant trouble and knew he had to avoid dancing for the rest of the night in case it opened again.

Travers had washed the wound and was busy applying salve. 'Only an inch or two of the scar is affected, Your Grace, but you must take care of it to avoid infection. Dr Jenkins always warned you this might happen and you must let me fetch him, first thing in the morning—'

'No.' Anthony spoke more sharply than he'd meant to. 'It's nothing. Just fix a bandage over it for the night, that will do.'

Travers completed his work then reluctantly departed, leaving Anthony resigning himself to the fact that he would have to sleep on his front tonight and would, in all probability, have to call the doctor as Travers suggested. But that was the least of his troubles.

Tonight, he had offered marriage to Marianne. She would be his wife, his Duchess, and though their marriage would astound the *ton*, her name would be protected by his rank. But they were not the youthful friends they had been when he'd first dreamed of such a thing. On the night of their wedding he would have to explain to Marianne exactly why he had a raised and ugly white scar across his back. And worse, he still had that wretch Ned Gibson threatening his and Marianne's future.

At around eleven the next morning Anthony took a cab to Gibson's house in Aylesbury Street. Gibson was in his study looking at some paperwork, but he rose as Anthony entered. Probably he'd been inspecting his finances—with quiet satisfaction, Anthony reckoned, for small and large fortunes were staked at the Clover Club every night and the winner was always Gibson.

Though born in poverty, the man had clawed his way to wealth by establishing his gaming house in Holborn, away from the usual haunts of the gentry, where men like Anthony's father could play for high stakes in relative secrecy. He could, Anthony guessed, have easily afforded to live amongst the many aristocrats whose vast gaming losses were his gain. Instead, he chose to live here in Clerkenwell, amongst shopkeepers and tradesmen—and how Gibson must relish seeing the noblemen who would usually look down on him coming here to plead for more credit or begging, as his own father must have done, for Gibson to keep silent about their terrible debts.

Anthony would never forget his first encounter with him. 'Either your father will face universal scorn for his weaknesses,' Gibson had said, 'or you marry my daughter.'

That had been no choice at all.

Today, Gibson did not make any attempt at a courteous greeting. Instead, he said, 'I've been expecting you, Your Grace.'

'That's no surprise,' replied Anthony. 'You've set your spies after me, haven't you? That's how you knew about Bow Street. Why are you doing this?'

Instead of answering, Gibson sat down and beckoned Anthony to do the same. 'I've heard fresh news that I don't like the sound of,' he said. 'I've heard that you're marrying again.'

Dear God, the rogue knew everything. Anthony ignored the chair Gibson had indicated and said, 'You must realise it's my duty to have heirs.'

'But not with my Cynthia, eh? Not good enough for the likes of you, was she?' Gibson waved a hand dismissively. 'This isn't about heirs at any rate. What rot. You're suffering from an overdose of lust, more like. I've heard you're marrying a hussy who's spread her favours round—for God's sake, Miss Blake may be a pretty morsel but she's been betrothed twice already. No doubt she's thinking of the old saying, *Third time lucky.*'

For a moment Anthony was so angry he could scarcely speak. At last, he said very quietly, 'You're lucky I don't flatten you for that, Gibson. You have no right to speak of Miss Blake in such a way. As for what happened in Bow Street, she had committed no crime and the story has no power now that I am betrothed to her.'

Gibson leaned back in his chair. 'Perhaps. But there's an old saying that the man who has true power is the man who holds the highest cards. I can still ruin your family's good name.'

This time Anthony spoke through gritted teeth. 'Don't try that again, you rogue. I have paid off my father's debts to you in full.'

'Yes, and so far I've kept to my promise to keep quiet about your father's delinquencies—but I expected my daughter to have a long and happy life as your Duchess!' He pointed an accusing finger. 'I expected high society grandchildren, and now what do I have?'

'Cynthia's death,' stated Anthony with deliberate emphasis, 'was not my fault.'

'So you say. But can you also say that her death wasn't a relief to you?' Gibson's voice had grown harsh. 'You honoured the letter of our agreement but hardly the spirit of it. By proposing to marry your lightskirt, you're making a mockery of everything we agreed. I warn you, I'm very tempted to tell people the truth—that your father was not only a gambler, but a damned cheat.'

When Anthony spoke at last, each of his words came out slow and hard, like the hammering of an axe against a rockface. 'You would not dare.'

'Oh, but I would, Your Grace. Because it's true.' He pointed to the papers lying on his desk. 'All the details are there. I was expecting you, so I've been examining them again. Of course, most high-ranking men gamble, but cheating is a completely different matter. Cheating is a disgrace.' Gibson shook his head. 'I'm afraid your father's name would be blackened for ever if I expose the facts.'

He rang the bell to summon a footman. 'I suggest you leave now, to think things over. But I'm expecting to hear no more of this ridiculous decision to marry Miss Blake.' He added, in a softer but no less menacing voice, 'I'm afraid you might regret it otherwise.'

Anthony left, his heart like stone.

That morning, over breakfast, Marianne noticed that her stepfather was stealing a glance at her every so often as if to convince himself that yes, his wayward stepdaughter was indeed going to marry a duke. As for Lady Hermione, she was a little overcome, both by the betrothal and by Simon's sudden and ill-timed arrival.

'It's wonderful news about you and Anthony,' said her mother when they were alone together. Then she added, 'I think, you know, that Simon will approve of the match once he's grown used to it.'

Marianne had strong doubts about that. All she wanted at the moment was some peace, so she retreated to the garden with a book, confident she would not be disturbed. But soon afterwards Eleanor appeared, making her jump.

'Oh,' Eleanor said, 'you're out here! I thought you might be with your mother, studying fashion plates and deciding which *modiste* to employ to make up your bridal trousseau. I suppose that after your wedding I shall have to curtsey and call you "Your Grace" whenever I see you!'

'Only if you choose to,' Marianne coolly answered

and she carried on reading her book until Eleanor disappeared. As for Sir Edgar, she guessed he must have spent the morning reading about the history of the Dukes of Cleveland in *Debrett's Peerage*, because during lunch he could talk about nothing else. In fact, he appeared to have learned Anthony's ancestry off by heart all the way back to the Norman Conquest.

Once lunch was over, Eleanor and Sybil went out for a stroll with their maid, but Sir Edgar decided that he, Marianne and her mother would sit together in the drawing room to discuss the forthcoming wedding. Marianne was sitting by the window and desperately trying to think of some way to escape when she realised that a carriage was pulling up outside the house.

She rose slowly to her feet. The carriage gleamed with navy paintwork and polished brass; the two grooms wore navy and gold livery and on the side was emblazoned the Cleveland ducal crest. 'It's Anthony,' she said quietly.

Sir Edgar hurried out into the hallway, where his butler was already opening the door to their visitor. Sir Edgar led him into the drawing room.

'Your Grace,' he said, 'this is indeed an honour. I must admit that the news last night of your intentions towards Marianne came as a surprise, but I am, of course, delighted.'

Anthony nodded politely. 'That is why I've called, of course. To make sure that both you and Lady Hermione are happy to give Marianne and myself your blessing.' As he spoke, he moved to Marianne's side and took her hand.

'Oh Anthony,' said Lady Hermione. 'How can you doubt it?'

Sir Edgar was nodding. 'Indeed, Your Grace. I echo my wife's feelings. I shall order my butler to bring champagne, so we may celebrate in style!'

'If you wish. But first, I have something to discuss with you that also concerns both my future wife and her mother. My lawyer, Sir Edgar, has recently been looking into your transactions concerning Oakfields. He has pointed out to me that by selling the house and its land, you have acted illegally.'

Edgar looked startled. 'But Your Grace. It became mine when I married Lady Hermione.'

'You did indeed have the right to take over all Lady Hermione's possessions, including Oakfields. But you were not allowed, by law, to sell her separate estate without her consent. I understand that at present the house is on the market again and my lawyer suggests that you buy it back and convey it to Marianne in a legal settlement that means it remain hers even when she and I marry.'

This time it was clear that Sir Edgar could think of nothing to say.

'Well,' said Anthony casually, 'no doubt we shall be meeting again soon, to finalise the matter. I shall leave you now, since I have business in the city. Good day to you, Sir Edgar, Lady Hermione. Marianne—may I have a word with you?'

Taking advantage of both her mother and her stepfather's silence, Marianne followed him out into the hallway. 'Do you really mean that Oakfields will be mine?' she asked.

'I do.'

'Then that is wonderful news. But why not my mother?'

'Because then it would become Sir Edgar's property once more.'

'Oh, I *see*. The law—it is such a complicated beast, isn't it?'

He smiled. 'Absolutely. But this time we can make it work in your favour. Your stepfather will be most annoyed and considerably out of pocket, but it will be yours, Marianne—which means that you and your mother, Simon too, will be able to make use of it whenever you wish.'

'My mother will be overjoyed,' she said. 'Thank

you.' She hesitated. 'As for my brother, I hope that in time he will become reconciled to our marriage.'

Anthony's expression changed. 'Where is Simon staying? Do you know?'

'My mother tells me he's taken lodgings in Albany.' She hesitated. 'I'm afraid he's rather angry with you, and I *know* he's being unfair. I fear he's listened to too much gossip.'

'Doesn't everyone?'

His voice was so bitter that her heart missed a beat. *Now is the time*, she thought. *Now, when we are completely alone.*

'Anthony,' she said, 'I've heard stories that I don't for one minute believe—but I have been hoping that some time soon you might tell me a little more about your marriage to Cynthia. Please can't you see the damage you are doing to yourself by letting it become a topic of evil gossip without speaking out to defend yourself?'

He was silent a moment. His eyes had grown dark, which was always a danger sign. He said, at last, 'Maybe all the stories are true. Maybe I did marry for money. Haven't you heard the old saying that the richer a man is, the more wealth he wants?'

She shook her head stubbornly. 'I do not believe that of you, nor should anyone else! You are marrying me, yet I have nothing. But Anthony, people will keep talking. I want to understand what really happened, and now that we are to marry, could you not tell me a little more about Cynthia?'

The silence that descended after her words were spoken was so heavy as to be almost unbearable. At last, he said, very quietly, 'There is only one condition that I must impose on our marriage, Marianne. I prefer not to talk about my life with Cynthia, ever.'

Marianne realised that Perkins was appearing. Sir Edgar must have summoned him to show their visitor out. As the butler bowed and held open the door, Anthony took her hand for a moment. He murmured to her, 'No more scrapes. No more adventures. Please?'

Before she could reply, he was gone.

She stood there with her heart aching. He was being kind to her. He was getting Oakfields back for her. But at the moment it seemed to her that the man she was about to marry was a stranger.

After leaving Sir Edgar's house, Anthony went to call on Simon Blake at his lodgings in Albany. Dispensing with any trivialities, he said, 'Simon. Your sister and I will be marrying soon. I hope you will walk her down the aisle?'

Simon had greeted him without warmth. 'Walk her down the aisle? I cannot be such a hypocrite.'

'You mean you would feel like a hypocrite to

approve of our wedding? I cannot comment on that.' Anthony spoke very quietly. 'But Marianne grieved bitterly when she lost her father, and now she feels she is losing you. Your sister loves you, you know. Whatever your opinion of me, please think of her!'

Simon's look was still stony. 'Just tell me. Why are you marrying her? She has nothing to offer you. She has no title, no money.'

Anthony was silent a moment. Then he said, 'I want, very much, to make your sister happy.'

Simon paced the room, then he stopped. 'Presumably the wedding will be soon?'

'Indeed. I shall obtain a special licence.'

'Very well, then.' Simon nodded. 'For the sake of my family, I shall come.'

But he did not offer to shake Anthony's hand.

Chapter Eight

A wedding, Marianne knew, was supposed to be a very special day when all of a girl's dreams came true. Didn't the story books say so? But as her own wedding day approached, she feared it was highly unlikely in her case.

For a start, the weather was abysmal and every morning she woke to leaden skies. Also, she felt sick with nerves. Her brother hadn't helped because two days ago he had called at Sir Edgar's house to tell Marianne, very grudgingly, that he would attend the ceremony and give her away. But at the same time he had made his disapproval all too plain.

Lady Hermione was upset with him. 'Simon, Anthony is our friend! Also—' and she glanced at Marianne '—he has got Oakfields back for us.'

'What?'

'Mother,' said Marianne a little wearily, 'I told you I would explain this to my brother myself. Simon, when Sir Edgar took possession of Oakfields, we all thought nothing could be done. But apparently Sir Edgar had no right to sell it without our mother's approval. Anthony has discovered that the new owners never moved in and the house is on the market again, so his lawyers are arranging with Sir Edgar that he buy it back and give it to me.'

Simon looked incredulous. 'What?'

'It's true, it's to be mine. But of course, you—you and my mother—will be able to stay there whenever you wish and for as long as you wish.'

'Aren't you pleased, Simon?' said Lady Hermione a little anxiously. 'We will have our home back and it's all thanks to Anthony.'

Simon was still looking at Marianne and she suddenly guessed what he was thinking. *Is he going to pack you off to the country, as he did his first wife?*

He spoke at last. 'Clearly,' he said, 'Anthony is going to great lengths to ingratiate himself with both of you. But he is no longer a friend of mine.'

He went soon afterwards, leaving Marianne wondering if her brother could ever reconcile himself to her marriage. The thought of the ceremony itself worried her also. It would be a simple affair, Anthony had told her. The service would be held at St George's church in Hanover Square, followed by a wedding breakfast at his house. Then afterwards—

she had always tried to veer away from the thought of *afterwards*—the two of them would leave for Cleveland Hall in Kent.

They would be husband and wife. Anthony would expect everything that marriage meant from her, and she was frightened.

As the wedding day drew near, Alice came up to Marianne's bedroom to help her to fold away some of the garments that had been delivered for her *trousseau*, including two flimsy nightgowns of satin and lace. Alice held them up in admiration.

'Now these,' she said, 'should please His Grace very much indeed.'

Marianne felt herself blushing from head to toe. 'Alice,' she said, 'when people marry, do they always...you know, desire one another?'

Alice stared at her. 'Now, what are you thinking? You don't imagine your Anthony won't want you as his wife in all the usual ways, do you?'

Marianne hesitated. 'I don't know. Sometimes, I'm not exactly sure how he feels about me.'

Alice peered more closely at her. 'I'm guessing you might be fretting about your wedding night.'

'Oh, I suppose I know the basics.' Marianne tried to say it lightly. 'I grew up in the countryside, after all.'

'Exactly. And don't you worry. That man of yours will know just what to do, believe me.'

Marianne was silent, because she couldn't help remembering that awful night with Max. 'You're cold,' Max had sneered at her. 'That's your trouble.'

Certainly, when Max had begun his fumbling attempt at what he'd called making love, she had been both repelled and frightened. Anthony could never be compared to Max, and she adored Anthony's kisses. But would she be able to cope with anything more?

When Anthony had told her on the day they visited Montagu House that Jonathan had said she'd allowed Max inappropriate intimacies, she had denied it fervently. 'Allowed' was completely the wrong word, for she had hated every minute of his assault and she had felt damaged by the experience, without a doubt. She also worried that perhaps she *was* cold.

Suddenly, she realised that Alice was watching her. 'You're worrying again, aren't you? For God's sake, have some faith in the man.'

Marianne nodded. 'You trust him, don't you, Alice?'

'I do indeed, whatever folks whisper about him.' Alice spoke firmly, but then she sighed. 'His trouble is that he won't defend himself. He likes to keep his secrets, I guess.'

Indeed, thought Marianne. He was certainly reluctant to share his secrets with her.

* * *

On the day of their wedding, the clouds lifted and the sun actually shone. Marianne rose early—in fact she had scarcely slept—and soon her mother and Alice arrived to dress her in her bridal gown.

Lady Hermione had confessed to being a little disappointed when they had gone together to Bond Street's most stylish *modiste* to choose it. The style was high-waisted with long sleeves, and it was made of pale blue silk with a white lace overskirt. Marianne thought it was beautiful, but when Alice helped her put it on, her mother sighed a little and said, 'I suppose it is quite stylish, although I feel you should have taken my advice on the finishing touches. Some satin flowers at the neckline would have looked very pretty.'

Marianne had to laugh. 'My wedding gown suits me very well, Mother.'

'Well, it was your choice, of course. But won't you let Alice do a little more than usual with your hair? It looks rather plain like that.'

In fact, Marianne had requested Alice to loosely braid it and pin it to the crown of her head, with a turquoise comb and blue ribbons. 'My hair is fine,' she soothed. 'I'm quite sure Anthony will approve. I'm a bride, not a desperate debutante!'

The only jewellery she wore was a necklet of

pearls that had arrived that morning from Anthony. Her bouquet was a simple one of sweet peas and forget-me-nots, some of which Alice had secured in the clasp that held up her hair, and when Simon arrived in the carriage that was to take her to Hanover Square he actually told her that she looked very pretty.

'Thank you, Simon,' she said. 'And thank you for being here.'

She was indeed grateful to have him at her side as she walked up the aisle of the church, because her stomach was in knots and she was sure her brother would notice that she was trembling. Seeing Anthony waiting for her at the altar, looking dauntingly formal in a black tailcoat and cream breeches, her heart missed a beat. But he turned and smiled at her and she thought to herself, *Please, let me make him happy.*

Anthony had assured her that this would be a simple wedding and she'd been relieved. It had meant, for example, that she was able to resist the pleas of her stepsisters to be bridesmaids. But…simple? She had no doubt that by ducal standards it was, but the church was still packed. Anthony had asked Tom Duxbury to be his best man and Simon too did his duty, speaking up firmly when it was time to give her away.

As for Anthony, she would never forget the way his clear, calm voice rang out when he said, 'I, Anthony, take thee, Marianne, to be my lawful wedded wife, to have and to hold from this day forward, for better for worse, in sickness and in health.'

Soon the ceremony was over and all the guests moved on to Anthony's house for the wedding breakfast. The ballroom had been filled with tables and footmen served the food, which was lavish. There were platters of cold meats and savoury pies, together with fresh-baked rolls and bowls full of peaches and strawberries. Ices and jellies were also brought out and the champagne and conversation flowed, but once the guests had eaten their fill Tom Duxbury clapped his hands for silence and called, 'Lords and ladies, honoured guests! I'm sure that all of us wish His Grace the Duke of Cleveland and his beautiful Duchess every happiness in the world. I just hope the Duke realises what a lucky fellow he is.' Tom raised his glass of champagne. 'To Anthony and Marianne.'

'Speech, speech, Anthony!' all his friends were calling.

Stepping forward, Anthony took Marianne's hand and gazed round at the guests. 'First of all,' he said, 'I want to thank you all for coming to this celebration. As you can imagine, this is a very special day for me and I too would like to propose a toast—to Marianne. Yes, Tom, I'm indeed a lucky man, and I'm sure you all agree.' Stooping a little, he kissed her cheek, to the sound of applause and the thumping of tables.

Everything about the occasion was magnificent, as befitted the marriage of a duke. The gowns of the female guests sparkled in the sunlight that poured through the ballroom windows and musicians played discreetly in the background. But what Marianne remembered afterwards were the little things, such as Lady Hermione weeping a few tears of happiness and Simon taking their mother's hand then teasing her a little over her flamboyant costume, just as he used to.

As for Sir Edgar, of course Anthony had to invite him and he was there with his daughters. Marianne gathered there had been strong words spoken between her stepfather and Anthony over the business of Oakfields, but Sir Edgar appeared to have pushed all that aside, because now he could boast that his stepdaughter was the Duchess of Cleveland. Eleanor and Sybil, who both wore very expensive and very unbecoming gowns, were busy eyeing up any eligible male guests in the vicinity, Simon included, and Marianne and Simon chuckled about it when they had a moment together.

Simon behaved politely if not warmly towards Anthony throughout the meal. But when the opportunity arose he drew Marianne to one side. 'If Anthony should dare to make you unhappy in any way,' he said, 'then you must let me know immediately.'

Simon was civil to Anthony, though it grieved her that her brother made no real effort to repair their old friendship. But her chief memories were of the ceremony and the look in Anthony's eyes when the bishop had declared, 'Those whom God hath joined together, let no man put asunder.'

It had been a look that said, *You are mine now.* Maybe it was her imagination, but after the speeches, as he circulated amongst the guests in his Mayfair house with her at his side, he kept glancing at his pocket watch as if he couldn't wait for his splendid travelling carriage to arrive and take them to Cleveland Hall. Hour by hour, her fragile hopes rose that this marriage could work and they might find happiness with one another.

When the time came at last for them to leave the celebrations and climb inside the coach, everyone gathered outside to wish them well. But Anthony wasted no time in prolonged farewells. He sat beside her and called out to the driver, 'Proceed!' Then he put his arm around her and she leaned into his strong shoulder, breathing in the warmth of him, the scent of him with that tantalising hint of cinnamon. She silently vowed that if any dark thoughts should cast their shadow over this day—doubts about his first wife, his first marriage—she would cast them aside. By the time they left London's busy thoroughfares and were heading for the countryside of Kent she was asleep—and he was still holding her.

For Anthony, there was no chance of sleep because his thoughts were in tumult. Marianne was his wife now and those blue flowers in her hair reminded him of that summer's day four years ago, when the messenger from London had torn his life apart. His arm was still around her shoulders, but he eased it away very carefully so as not to wake her and gazed down at her. She looked vulnerable and young, with her hair already tumbling from its ribbons and curling around the creamy skin of her forehead and cheeks.

For her, growing up with such freedom at Oakfields, every day had presented a fresh adventure, a fresh challenge. But certainly, the next few weeks would be the biggest challenge of all for both of them. He hoped desperately for happiness, but it was going to be difficult.

Probably he should have told her all about the reasons for his first marriage, but since the evening of Tom's fateful party, everything had happened too quickly. Besides, how could he tell her about Ned Gibson, when the man's venom hovered like a dark shadow over his future?

He gazed at her sleeping face. Those flowers in her hair were wilting a little now and her full lips were slightly parted. She stirred and he wondered if she was dreaming, maybe of him. Tonight, they would be together as man and wife, and he wanted her, oh God, yes.

As if aware of his desire, she gave a soft murmur and nestled closer to his side. He couldn't help imagining what it would be like to make love to her, to feel her softness yielding to his strength and to hear her soft moans of pleasure. Fighting down the surge of arousal that engulfed him, he moved away a little. But he found himself almost praying that for the next few days at least, all his worries could be kept at bay.

Marianne woke as the carriage slowed down and she blinked, wondering for a moment where she was. But Anthony's voice came, steady and clear.

'We're almost at Cleveland Hall now,' he said. 'If

you look out of the window, you can see the building through the trees.'

She looked, mainly because it gave her time to collect herself—and time to push aside the wonderful dream she'd had that Anthony was holding her close and murmuring her name. But that was impossible, because now he looked as cool and distant as any proud duke would be on approaching his magnificent country mansion. All the servants were lined up on the broad flight of steps that led to the main doors.

Underwood, the butler, was the first to greet her, then he and the housekeeper, Mrs Manville, introduced each member of staff to her, from the head footman to the boot boy. But Marianne was delighted that she remembered most of their names anyway, from the many times she had visited in her youth.

'Mr Underwood, Mrs Manville,' she said warmly to them both. 'I'm very glad you're still here. And Mrs Bunting, the cook—how I used to love your delicious mince pies at Christmas!'

The staff were all beaming. 'We are very happy to see you here, Your Grace,' said Mrs Manville.

Marianne had wondered if they might be disapproving to find that their Duke had married the girl who used to romp around here in a most unladylike way, tearing up and down the great staircase with

Anthony and Simon or loitering in the stables to chat with the grooms. But now she heaved an inner sigh of relief because they seemed genuinely glad to see her.

After that, Anthony offered to show her round the vast house.

'I do remember it, you know!' she told him lightly. She used to regard all the magnificent rooms and furnishings with awe and still did, though as he led her from room to room she had to remind herself that she was to actually live here.

On their arrival, the butler had informed Anthony that numerous wedding gifts had been delivered to the house. 'I have ordered them to be placed in the orangery, Your Grace,' he had said. 'They are there awaiting your inspection.'

After a brief survey of the main rooms, Anthony turned to Marianne. 'We'll take a look now at those wedding gifts, shall we?'

She was amazed to see just how many items had been sent. A footman was in there, still carefully putting them all on display; there were vases and ornaments, exquisite pieces of silverware and pictures too. Amongst them were paintings of flowers and of horses—and one, set in an elaborate frame, that was a portrait of a young, dark-haired woman.

Marianne didn't get a chance to inspect it more

closely, for already Anthony had taken hold of her arm and was leading her from the room, slamming the door behind him.

'Anthony, what is it?' she asked quietly. 'What has upset you so?'

She had never, ever seen him like this. His mouth was set in a grim line and his grey eyes had darkened almost to black. At last, he said, 'That was a portrait of my late wife.'

She stepped back, her mouth dry. She wanted to ask so much, but it was clear he was going to say no more.

'We shall continue our tour of the house,' he said, and while a maid unpacked Marianne's things in her bedchamber he led her around the other rooms that she remembered so well.

But she couldn't stop thinking about the picture,

She recalled his shock when he'd seen it and she tried desperately to remember more about it. His wife! The young woman looked sweet and she also looked shy, even anxious, as if she hated having her portrait painted. Why on earth would someone send a portrait of her as a wedding gift? It was a cruel trick to play and she guessed Anthony knew the sender but wouldn't tell her. Secrets. Would there always be secrets?

They ate their evening meal in the huge dining

hall; the servants were attentive and the food delicious, but in here, with oil paintings of all the former Dukes gazing solemnly down at them, the atmosphere was dauntingly formal. After watching Marianne picking at her food, Anthony told the footmen to leave and rested his hand on hers.

'Shall I show you up to your bedchamber?' he said quietly. 'One of the maids will attend to you. I shall join you soon.'

She nodded and rose to her feet; he stood too, and then he smiled. Oh, what a smile. It warmed her from her head to her toes and she felt that her heart had lightened. He rested his hands on her shoulders and said, 'I hope you aren't sorry to be here?'

She gazed up at him. 'No,' she said. 'Anthony, I am so very glad to be your wife.'

He nodded, taking her hand and kissing it. 'Good,' he said softly.

Of course, she had a beautiful bedroom and a sitting room of her own, but a doorway linked her to Anthony's even larger suite of private rooms. One of the maids, Elsie, came to help her bathe and change into her night attire, but Marianne didn't know if a duchess was supposed to chatter with a lady's maid as she used to chatter with Alice. She also felt self-conscious as Elsie helped her into her nightgown, which was an insubstantial froth of silk and lace that revealed far more than it hid. The *modiste* had assured her that it was exactly what her husband would expect, but after putting it on Marianne stepped as quickly as she could into the all-concealing satin dressing robe that Elsie held out for her.

Elsie bobbed a curtsey and left. Marianne suspected she was supposed to climb into the big bed and wait, for Elsie had folded back the coverlet and sheet for her. But she was too restless, too anxious, so she went over to the window instead and drew back the curtains a little. Looking in the direction of Oakfields, she could see the familiar darkness of the woodland that lay between the two houses and she thought she could hear the haunting cry of the owls as they searched for their prey. She waited—and then the door opened and Anthony was there.

He was still wearing his shirt and breeches, but he had removed his coat and cravat and he looked gloriously, wonderfully handsome.

'I came to see,' he said, 'if you have everything you need.'

She walked slowly towards him and her heart pounded. *Her husband.* Suddenly she felt a disturbing surge of longing and she put her hands to his chest, feeling the steady beat of his heart. 'I have everything I need,' she whispered, 'now that you are here, Anthony.'

Something changed in his expression then. His jaw tightened, his eyes blazed, then he pressed his mouth to hers and began to kiss her, slowly and tenderly. She found herself opening to his kiss and it was as if all the heartache of the last few years, all her feelings of betrayal, had melted away. As his kiss grew more passionate, she realised his fingers were easing aside her nightrobe and the delicate fabric of her gown, then his hands were cupping her breasts and his lips were moving down to kiss her there…

She let out a low cry and backed away.

He stood very still. He said, 'Is something wrong, Marianne?'

She closed her eyes in despair. It was still there. The horror, the shame that she had felt when Max had assaulted her. She had tried to forget it, she really had. She had told herself, *This is Anthony. This will be different.*

But the minute she'd felt his hands on her breasts, her entire body had flinched and tightened. The old fear remained—and Anthony's face had darkened as he waited for her to explain.

She pulled her nightrobe across her body once more. 'I'm sorry,' she blurted out. 'Truly, I'm sorry.'

He was still watching her. 'Has this got something to do with your first fiancé, I wonder? The "inappropriate intimacies" that Moseley told me you allowed the man?'

Shame engulfed her. 'It wasn't like that. I didn't want… I didn't realise…'

After a moment that seemed endless, he said softly, 'Did the brute rape you?'

She looked up at him swiftly. 'No. Oh, no! I managed to stop him, but I was so frightened.' She added, very quietly, 'I was hoping that the bad memories would go away.'

'But they haven't. Have they?' He shook his head almost wearily, as if he was saying goodbye to a forlorn hope. 'I think that we had best take things slowly for the time being. I don't want to push you into anything. I never would. I hope you sleep well, Marianne.'

Anthony left, to return to his own bedchamber. Once in his room, he summoned Travers and if his loyal valet was surprised to see his master alone in here on his wedding night, he gave no sign of it. 'Your Grace?'

'I think the scar on my back might need your attention again, Travers, if you please.'

'Is it bleeding again, Your Grace?'

'I don't think so, but it's paining me a little. Some of your salve and a dressing on it would be welcome.'

Perhaps, thought Anthony as his valet began his work, Travers will think that it's because of my troublesome scar that I'm not with my new bride tonight. It was certainly wise to let the rumour persist, for he knew there would be gossip amongst the servants, and it was best they hear Travers's version rather than spread the truth—that his new wife was terrified of intimacy.

It was because of her terrible experience with her first fiancé, clearly. But it saddened him to have such a harsh reminder of how different things were between them than they had been in their youth, when she'd trusted him implicitly. So much had happened since then that could not be undone, for both of them. Would they ever get past it all and find any kind of happiness?

He knew he wouldn't sleep for long tonight, if at all. After Travers had bowed and left, he went downstairs and into the orangery, where moonlight glistened on the finery of all the assembled gifts. He pulled out the portrait of his first wife, Cynthia, then he carried it to his study and locked it away at the back of a tall oak cabinet, along with other reminders of his past.

He knew, of course, who had sent that cruel gift. It had to be Cynthia's father, Ned Gibson.

Chapter Nine

Marianne found the next few days at Cleveland Hall some of the most difficult of her life. They were newlyweds and of course every day there were callers, with the local gentry arriving one after another in their eagerness to congratulate the married couple.

Anthony was always courteous to his guests, but he must know, as she did, that their visitors' good wishes could very easily be a lie. She feared that the minute they left they might be whispering, *So the Rogue Duke has married again—and his new bride is almost as much a surprise as his first! Miss Blake from Oakfields is hardly suitable to be a duchess!*

Even when there were no visitors, Marianne and Anthony were rarely alone together since the Hall employed many servants and at mealtimes there were always at least six footmen to serve the various dishes and wines. Every day Marianne grew more despondent. She knew, of course, that Anthony had been obliged to marry her—how could he do otherwise, when they had been discovered embracing in Tom Duxbury's garden?

Even so, she had hoped they might be able to find some happiness here, away from the London gossip—but nothing had changed. Anthony was still keeping secrets from her and, as for her, she had shocked him, repelled him even, with her behaviour on their wedding night. Clearly, he had been prepared to forget all their mistakes and misunderstandings in the past and had appeared full of desire for her. He'd been ready to make love to her, but she had been blinded by her memories of Max's cruel assault and she had heard Max's voice in her head, felt Max's hands on her skin.

Since then, Anthony had been polite but distant and she was finding it almost impossible to bear.

On the fourth evening, during dinner, with the footmen present as usual, Anthony asked her if she would perhaps care to visit Oakfields the next day. She nodded and said, 'Yes. That would be pleasant.' But the prospect weighed her down, because the thought of seeing their house with all its happy memories in the company of Anthony, who was now so cool to her, was all but unbearable.

That night she could not get to sleep. Anthony had bid her goodnight at ten then left her as usual, and her heart was aching with an almost physical pain. At around eleven she rose from the bed, realising that the full moon was casting enough silvery light through the curtains for her to put on her cream silk dressing robe. She walked towards the inner door that linked her bedchamber with Anthony's then hesitated. There was no sound from within.

Had he even come upstairs yet?

She pushed open the door and walked through his unlit bedroom, past the oak four-poster bed draped with elaborate silk curtains. But then she saw that the door to his sitting room was ajar; candlelight glimmered through the gap and she could hear voices. Carefully, she tiptoed closer.

Her husband was in there and so was his valet. Anthony had removed his shirt and Travers, using a large bowl of water and a gauze cloth, was bathing Anthony's back.

She stood there almost frozen with shock—because the cloth was bloodstained. Had Anthony been injured? But how?

She must have let out a gasp, because Travers looked sharply towards the door and said, 'Your Grace. Your wife is here.'

Anthony turned to look at her then said, 'Leave us, Travers, will you?'

The valet hesitated a moment. 'But your wound,

Your Grace. I was going to treat it with the usual salve…'

'Leave us. Please.'

Travers bowed then silently vanished through the door.

Marianne walked towards her husband. She had seen that on Anthony's back was a raised scar around four or five inches long. It looked old, but it must have recently been bleeding.

'Anthony,' she said. 'Oh, Anthony. Whatever happened to you?'

For a moment she thought he wasn't going to reply. He was quickly pulling on a fresh shirt and Marianne could see that his strong features had tightened and his eyes were expressionless. All of a sudden, she could bear it no more.

Almost compelling him to look at her, she said, 'Anthony, *please*. I know you find it difficult to accept my past mistakes, but I am your wife now, and I have tried to be open with you. If we are to cling to any chance of happiness in the future, you must do the same for me, because this secrecy of yours—about your first marriage and now that scar on your back—just cannot go on!'

He held up his right hand to halt her flow of words. 'Marianne,' he said. 'The scar came from a wound inflicted by my father.'

* * *

He saw the colour drain from her face and heard her whisper, 'No. Oh, no.' Then she was moving closer, wrapping her arms around his waist and laying her cheek against his chest, murmuring, 'Anthony. My love. My dearest love.'

He could feel her hot tears dampening his shirt, could smell the scent of her glorious hair, and he held her as if he was clinging to the very last remnants of hope. At last, she pulled away, just a little, and looked up at him. He saw she was smiling through her tears.

'I think it's time you told me everything,' she said softly. 'Don't you?'

She took his hand in hers and led him to the sofa by the fire. He sat close to her and began. First, he explained how he had learned that his father was addicted to gambling; how his father had got himself into terrible debt and drank far too much to deaden his worries and his guilt.

Her expression said it all. Her pity. Her indignation. Her sadness. 'So it wasn't you,' she said at last, 'who was the gambler? I should have known. I always found it hard to believe. But Anthony, why did you allow those stories to circulate?'

'It was complicated,' he said. But finally, he let it all pour out.

He told her that mere weeks after they'd last parted at Oakfields he had to move permanently to the family's London house—not because he enjoyed London society, but because he was trying to stop his father's ruinous addiction to gaming. Her grip on his hand became tighter.

'One night,' Anthony said, 'my father was frustrated and drunk. He wanted to go out to a gambling club, but I told him he mustn't. I went to bolt the door but, before I knew it, he had snatched at an old cavalry sword that hung on the wall and struck me across the back. I wasn't wearing a coat, so it sliced through my shirt and led to my injury. Travers helped me with it. No one else knows anything about it, either in London or here.'

He saw that she could barely speak.

'I can hardly believe that your own father did this to you.'

'I think he regretted it instantly and the wound wasn't deep. In fact, I thought it had healed, but every so often it opens a little and recently the same thing happened. As ever, Travers has been tending it for me.'

'All this time,' she whispered. 'All this time, when Simon and I believed you were enjoying life in London, you had to endure this tragedy.'

He nodded. 'I'm sorry, Marianne. I have made a poor start to our marriage.'

'No,' she said. '*No.* Much of the fault is mine.' She faced him resolutely. 'But are you saying that you had to marry into money to repay your father's debts, not your own? Did he really owe so much?'

'Yes,' he said. 'He did.'

She was frowning now. 'And that picture. The portrait of your wife. Why would somebody send that to you?'

He tried to keep his voice level. 'It was someone's idea of a joke, I think, to send it to me on our wedding day.'

He guessed she wanted to ask more, but instead she said, 'Then it's a cruel joke. A sick joke.' She had risen to her feet. 'And now—because I am your wife—I am going to tend to your scar myself.'

He rose too, saying, 'Really, I think Travers has done all that is needed.'

'I don't, because I know that I interrupted whatever he was doing. Take your shirt off again, will you? I remember Travers saying that the wound needs some salve on it.'

'Very well.' He was smiling now at her decisive tone. 'I know when to admit defeat.' Already he was beginning to pull his shirt off again while Marianne went over to the bowl of warm water, dipped the cloth that Travers had left and began, very carefully, to bathe away the small amount of blood that had seeped again from his scar.

It twisted her heart, to be doing this for him. She could imagine only too well not only the pain this injury must have caused, but the sense of anger, the sense of injustice. She also knew now that Anthony had been forced to marry unjustly, in order to pay for his father's gambling debts.

She had rarely met Anthony's father because everyone knew the man much preferred to spend his time in London. He was clearly selfish and weak, yet Anthony was still determined to protect him. How Anthony had suffered, in more ways than one, and her feelings for him were tumultuous. She longed to tell him how much she cared for him, how much she wanted him.

The trouble was that he was still keeping secrets from her. He had told her hardly anything about Cynthia—why she had lived in Kent, away from her husband. Why she had felt forced to make that final, treacherous journey.

But she didn't ask, she couldn't ask, because she remembered only too well those chilling words he had spoken to her after their betrothal. *There is only one condition that I must impose on our marriage,*

Marianne. I prefer not to talk about my life with Cynthia, ever.

Or, presumably, to talk about Cynthia's death.

The room was growing cold now; she was growing cold, so she finally put aside the cloth and said, 'Now where, I wonder, is the salve Travers spoke of?'

'Over there.' He pointed. 'It's on top of the medicine chest.'

She went to fetch it and as she opened the jar, she immediately recognised the scent. It was cinnamon! Yes, that was the faint but alluring aroma she had noticed whenever she was close to Anthony.

She hesitated a moment and Anthony cautioned, 'Only a little.'

She nodded. 'Of course.' She used her index finger to scoop out a small amount; it was almost waxy in texture and melted swiftly into the skin, but she took her time in working it gently into and around the raised scar, marvelling at how this cruel imperfection could fill her with such a need to soothe him, kiss him, love him. To try again. A huge surge of longing suddenly engulfed her and her heart ached as if it would burst.

'Anthony…' she said.

'Mm?' He was turning around to look at her. 'What is it?'

'A confession,' she blurted out. 'It's my turn for a confession. Anthony, I must talk about what happened the other night. Maybe I shouldn't have mentioned Max, but I felt I had to explain!'

His expression was unreadable but she blundered on. 'Of course, I know I was unforgivably foolish to go to that party with him. I was rebelling against my stepfather, I suppose, but I hated every minute of it until I managed to fight him off and get away.'

Her voice was trembling now. Anthony said, 'Marianne, there is no need to explain.'

'But there is! I still have nightmares about it all, but I need to tell you that everything is different with you, Anthony—so very different.'

She couldn't say any more. Her throat was dry and her heart pounded. She was frightened, yes, but this time she was afraid of being emotionally hurt, of finding herself desperately in love with a man who had only offered her marriage out of his sense of duty.

And might she not sorely disappoint him? Max had labelled her cold and unnatural. *You're supposed to enjoy this*, he had growled. *You led me on. You're nothing but a man-teaser.*

Whereas when Anthony kissed her, she felt a surge of desire that made her desperate to overcome the barriers that she herself had created.

'I am so ashamed,' she whispered.

'There is no need to be. The shame is his. If he was still around, I would kill him for you. But there is something I can do.' As she looked up at him questioningly, he drew her towards him and gently kissed her forehead. 'Marianne,' he said quietly, 'let me help you. Let me show you what loving should be like.'

He pulled her closer until she was completely enfolded in his embrace. His scent enfolded her too—the scent of fresh-washed skin and, poignantly, the faintly medicinal aroma of that salve on his poor, scarred back. He pressed his forehead to hers and she knew that he was going to kiss her; her body knew it too, for her stomach tightened and she was aware of her blood pounding through her veins, filling her with sensations that were exciting and thrillingly new.

She had thought she might be frightened of this. Instead, she was thinking, *I will die if he moves away from me now.*

He didn't move away. He murmured, 'Marianne, I want to kiss you properly. May I?'

'Yes,' she whispered.

He cupped the back of her head with one hand while his other clasped her waist, then he lowered his head until his mouth met hers and she closed her eyes at the sheer delight of it. He was a strong man with a powerful body, yet his lips were so soft, like silk almost.

Yes, their kiss was whisper-soft but dangerous too, because she was so transfixed that she scarcely registered the moment when his tongue eased its way into her mouth, subtly as if weaving a spell, conjuring up a wicked warmth inside her and, dear heaven, she wanted more.

'Anthony.' Her voice was a low murmur and it wasn't of protest, oh no. By now he had lowered his head so his lips could move down to her throat, kissing and licking her there while his strong arms held her and soothed her. She leaned into him, clasping him around his waist, feeling the heat of his skin. Then his mouth moved back to her lips and this time she let his tongue delve into her mouth more fully, sliding it against her tongue and stroking it in such an intimate caress that she felt an urgent pulse begin to beat in the pit of her stomach, creating a surge of need that became more acute with every second.

This was nothing like Max's swift, brutal attempt at lovemaking. Max had frightened her, thrusting his tongue down her throat and clutching at her breasts until she'd wanted to retch. This was something else entirely. During the last few days she had begun to fear that Anthony must bitterly regret their marriage. But dear heaven, was *this* pity?

She gave a little gasp as he pulled her closer still and his mouth devoured hers even more hungrily. Her frivolous nightgown offered no protection at all against the thrill of contact with his half-naked body, and the pressure of his muscled chest pushing against her tender breasts made them ache almost unbearably. She uttered a faint moan of longing and Anthony said a little unsteadily, 'Your room. Your bed. *Now.*'

She felt sudden dismay. 'You mean…on my own?'

'Are you joking?' He laughed, a delicious sound. 'Come here.'

He pulled her into his arms again. This lovely woman was thinking he wanted her to leave, when his blood was on fire for her and his erection was pounding like mad? 'Marianne,' he said, 'I meant that we must both go to your bed.' He whispered in her ear, 'We shall both be far more comfortable there.'

His hips were pressing against her abdomen and she must have felt his arousal, because she blushed an even more delightful pink. 'Yes,' she whispered. 'Yes, indeed.'

He nodded. He took her hand and led her through to her bedchamber, then he locked the door and turned to face her.

She looked shy, he thought, almost uncertain, but unbelievably desirable in that flimsy nothingness she was wearing. Already her silk dressing gown had almost slipped from her shoulders and he loved the way her almost see-through silk and lace night-dress clung delightfully to her figure, allowing him to glimpse the slender shapeliness of her waist and hips, the gorgeous swell of her breasts and the darker shading of her nipples.

'You,' he said to her softly, 'are very beautiful.'

He drew her close and kissed her again, drinking in the sweetness of her lips and mouth. Thank God, he thought, that he had some measure of control over himself because he was hard and heavy with need and the way she was responding to his kiss, letting her tongue delicately dance against his, was driving him crazy with desire.

Carefully, she stepped away from him and out of her nightgown. She pointed and said softly, 'I think, Your Grace, that you are a little overdressed still?'

Her instruction was so delightfully coquettish that he was almost clumsy in pulling off his boots and breeches. At last, he was entirely naked and when he saw her gasp a little on seeing his rigid desire, he said, 'I won't hurt you. I swear it.'

'I know,' she answered, with an expression of such trust that he really had to pull her into his arms and kiss her again. She smelled delicious, like those flowers she used to love in the garden at Oakfields.

'I do not want to hurt you,' he repeated steadily. 'I shall try to take this slowly—and if, at any stage, you want me to stop, just tell me.'

Almost proudly, she raised her eyes to his. 'I am your wife,' she said. 'And Anthony, I do want you, so badly.'

He thought, just for a moment, that she added in a whisper, *I always have*. But he couldn't be sure and then the moment was lost, because her expression had become one of concern. 'But what,' she said, 'about your poor back? Might I be in danger of hurting you?'

With a husky chuckle, he lowered her to the bed. 'You won't,' he assured her. 'Just do as I say.'

He joined her there and as they lay facing one another, side by side, he twined his heavily-muscled legs with hers, feeling how smooth, how shapely they were. Then he kissed her breasts and carefully reached to stroke her inner thighs, easing his hand upwards until he could stroke her *there* and hear her gasps of delight. At last, he eased himself above her and settled himself between her spread thighs, taking his weight on his elbows so he could see her flushed cheeks and shining eyes. She was gripping his body almost fiercely. ‘Please, Anthony. Don’t stop.’

‘Trust me, I won’t,’ he assured her.

She gave a little sigh of ecstasy as he moved downwards to kiss her left breast then—oh, dear God, he was drawing her nipple into his mouth and licking it, sucking it! Was this right?

She was crying out now, in a mixture of pleasure and desperation; she found herself reaching for his hips, as if to anchor herself. Then—*then*, then she felt something hard but silky-smooth nudging against the very place between her thighs where he had been caressing her. *‘Anthony...’*

He went still. ‘Am I hurting you?’

‘No. No.’

He was being careful, she realised, and tender. He could have crushed her, so delicate was she compared to his male strength, but instead he continued to take his weight on his forearms and he was kissing her everywhere, on her mouth, her throat, her breasts. Then he reached carefully down to tease her again with his fingers, even as the blunt head of his manhood was nudging against her opening, and moments later he eased himself into her until she felt all of his hard, heavy length stretching her, making her gasp.

She wanted more. She was arching her hips, trying to get closer to him, and suddenly he started moving harder, moving rhythmically, while his hand still caressed the tiny bud of sensation at the heart of her that was tingling, flowering…

'Oh!' Suddenly she was clutching his hips and her whole body had tightened as she felt waves of delight starting to flow through her. Her world exploded around her as she cried out his name and, as if from a distance, she heard Anthony let out a groan as he spasmed his own release inside her.

Afterwards, he smoothed some stray tendrils of hair from her cheek before kissing her and she kissed him back.

She curled herself in his arms and together they slept until dawn.

There were moments she would always remember about the rest of their time together that summer at Cleveland Hall. There were times of happiness, like the day when the Hall's head gardener, Harris, showed them around the spectacular summer flowerbeds and talked to Anthony about the next season's plantings. Watching her husband, with his face bronzed by the sun and his mind seemingly devoid of cares as he listened to the head gardener's plans, she thought, *I do believe we could be happy.*

Darker times came when she was alone with her worries. Who had sent that portrait of Anthony's first wife, and why? Had Anthony really been unkind to her, so unkind that she'd made a desperate bid to escape her loneliness?

At least there was no question of separate bedrooms now. Every night he came to her and one evening, just when she had thought that Anthony had kissed her everywhere he possibly could, he moved down between her thighs and began using his mouth and tongue to caress her there.

She must have gasped aloud, because he raised his head to look up at her. 'Too much?'

'Yes—I mean no! No, Anthony, it's not too much, it's marvellous, and please don't stop!'

'As my Duchess commands,' he said wickedly, and continued with his work until she was almost arching herself off the bed in her joy.

'Can I do something like that for you?' she asked him shyly when she'd recovered, and he told her that yes, she most certainly could.

'In fact,' he added, 'if you don't do something very soon, I shall be forced to desperate measures.'

It made her feel powerful, to give this strong man such pleasure. Every night she tended his scar and realised that it was healing up again, as she hoped—hoped desperately—that his heart would in time heal from all the shadows that had been cast over his life. Several times they drove along the country lanes to Oakfields, where Anthony had managed to find and rehire many of the old staff whom Sir Edgar had dismissed. Mrs Thurlby the housekeeper was in charge again and both she and Mrs Hinchcliffe, the cook, greeted them with delight.

'I knew, Your Grace,' Mrs Hinchcliffe said to Anthony, 'that you'd be back some day soon for my shortbread.'

He grinned. 'I loved it,' he said, and he was promptly served with a whole plateful.

Their visits there were always happy ones and the weather remained glorious. Together, they spent a good deal of time in the Hall's grounds, and one afternoon when they were sitting in the shade of a wisteria-clad pergola, an elderly gardener came up to them and bowed before silently handing Marianne a bunch of pink roses.

'Why, thank you!' she exclaimed. She'd risen to her feet. 'These are perfect.'

The man still said nothing but he bowed again and a smile creased his face. She looked questioningly at Anthony, who had also risen. 'I think,' he said to her, 'that you may have met Daniel in the past. He looks after the rose beds and his are the best in the county.' He raised his voice a little. 'Isn't that right, Daniel?'

Suddenly, she did remember him, from years ago when she and Simon used to roam the gardens here with Anthony. He was older now of course, and rather stooped and he had always had difficulty in hearing what people said. Probably because of that, he was a man of few words. He was known as Silent Daniel and though everyone was kind to him, he led a solitary life.

She spoke very clearly to him. 'I remember you, Daniel, and I've often admired the roses here. I love them.'

He nodded, his face glowing with pride.

She indicated the roses he had given her. 'Will you show me where they grow?'

He pointed and, leaving Anthony behind, she followed him towards a tall rose bush that filled the air with the heady scent of its flowers. 'Gorgeous,' she told him. 'Just gorgeous.'

She turned then, to go back to Anthony. But Daniel touched her arm and she stopped, because he was saying quietly, 'He is a good man, your husband.'

With that, he left her and went to continue with his work. When she returned to Anthony he was smiling. 'It looks,' he said, 'as if you have yet another admirer.'

She said nothing of what Daniel had told her. The rest of the day passed pleasantly, but Marianne couldn't stop thinking of the gardener's words. She knew that all of Anthony's staff must be aware of the whispers about their master. They would all have known his first wife, and once again all the questions she longed to ask about Cynthia arose in her mind. Had it truly been Cynthia's choice to stay here, while Anthony lived in London? Had she been happy on her own? Wouldn't she rather have been with him?

The next day Anthony spent many hours in his study with his steward, going over the accounts of the Kent estate, and she wondered what life would be like when they returned to London, no doubt to face the city's poisonous talk once more.

She ate her evening meal alone, because Anthony hadn't yet concluded his business with his steward and the two of them had taken supper in his study. But later that night, when she was up in her bedroom preparing for her usual bath, Anthony entered and dismissed her maid before handing Marianne an elaborately wrapped parcel. He had a mysterious look on his face and she realised why when she opened it, because the parcel contained the most exquisite silk lingerie. There was a pale green chemise with ribbons for shoulder-straps, a pair of finest French stockings and also a pair of lacy garters adorned with tiny pink rosettes.

She thrilled to the mere touch of the delicate fabrics against her palms. 'These are perfect.' She stood on tiptoe to kiss him. 'Just perfect.'

He kissed her back. 'They will look,' he murmured, 'even more perfect once you're wearing them.' His lips lingered against her mouth. 'I'm sorry I've had to neglect you today. After you've taken your bath, you must send your maid away and put these on—these and nothing else.'

'Anthony!' She laughed. 'I shall only be taking them off again!'

'Correction.' His expression now was positively wicked. 'I shall be taking them off. I shall come up in half an hour precisely. Be ready.'

Chapter Ten

It was late the next morning before Anthony managed to drag himself away from Marianne's bed. He moved carefully to avoid waking her and didn't open the curtains, though even in the half-light he could see that her glorious red-gold hair lay in wild tresses around her shoulders and there was a little smile on her lips.

He gazed at her a moment longer then started to pull on his clothes. His wife was beautiful, he had always known that. But now he was noticing qualities in her that he'd never realised before, like how she concentrated on little things that would make him happy: pouring his coffee just as he liked it, or asking Cook to prepare his favourite cake for their afternoon tea. She knew too how to gently massage his shoulders to ease the nagging ache the scar still caused and she had swiftly learned how to make sure she didn't hurt him when they made love.

As one week had gone by, then another, he'd realised there were moments when he dared to feel happy, although the usual shadows always lurked. Since that portrait had arrived, the wickedest wedding gift he could think of, he had heard nothing more from Gibson, but he knew the man's silence wouldn't last. He knew also that the gossip about him still lingered, even here, well away from London.

Of course, they were regularly invited to local social events and although Anthony often declined, he did agree to attend a party at the nearby home of a viscount with whom he'd kept on neighbourly terms. Anthony warned Marianne beforehand that she might hear the occasional comment about his first marriage. 'Ignore it,' he advised her quietly. 'That's what I have learned to do.' But he still worried about her impulsive actions and her lack of caution when she felt driven to speak the truth.

All eyes were on his wife when they arrived at the viscount's house that evening and it was, he thought, no surprise because Marianne looked wonderful in a sage-green muslin gown that made her hair, which was loosely bound up in a green ribbon, glow like molten copper. She was never short of partners for the dancing, and he was pleased to see that all the gentlemen there were treating her with courtesy.

But during the break for refreshments he was separated from her by a crowd of acquaintances and was unable for several minutes to find her again. In fact, it was she who eventually made her way to his side and her brown eyes were ablaze with indignation.

'Anthony,' she said, 'I have just heard some horrid women talking about you.'

His heart sank. 'What were they saying, exactly?'

'They were discussing your first wife, even though they must have known I could hear them. I longed to be rude to them, but I know it's not my place. How can you bear it? Why will you not defend yourself and tell people that you had to marry because of your father's gambling?'

Her feelings were clearly running high and they argued. He couldn't remember afterwards what exactly was said and it was difficult anyway because there was no privacy, but he knew that at one point he declared, 'Let them all say what they like, Marianne. I do not care.'

'But I *do* care!' she burst out. 'I hurt for you. I know these horrible people are wrong, but I can't say anything to silence them, because you have ordered me not to!'

He took her hand then. 'Come with me,' he said. 'Please.'

He led her outside into the gardens that surrounded the house. It was dark by now and stars sparkled overhead in the velvety night sky. A slightly chill breeze meant that no other guests had ventured out and Anthony put his hands on her shoulders.

'Don't pull away from me, please,' he said. 'I'm sorry, Marianne, that I spoke to you sharply just now. But there are good reasons why it would not help me in the least to raise any more conversations about Cynthia. Can you accept that? I thought I'd made that plain.'

She was silent a moment. Then she said, 'You made it plain, yes. But I'm your wife now, Anthony. Can't you trust me with the truth about your first marriage? I know you were obliged to marry, but I cannot believe that you treated her badly, as people love to say.'

He felt the blackness of the past descend again. He said in a low voice, 'I was always kind to her, Marianne. It was her choice to live in Kent; in fact, she hated London life, because she hadn't been brought up to it. She was very shy and she also felt she wasn't worthy of me. I told her it wasn't true, but we agreed she should stay at Cleveland Hall and I visited her often. She hoped,' he added softly, 'that one day she would have children and so did I. But then, she died.'

In that fatal journey, thought Marianne. That was something else those awful gossips had whispered about. *Poor woman*, she'd heard them say. *Setting off in that awful weather, desperate to get to London to beg her husband for a divorce.*

Was that a lie too? But why hadn't he made more effort to quell the gossips? Why had his wife gone on that fatal journey? Surely he knew?

She felt weary. 'Anthony,' she said, 'please can we go home now?'

His face was expressionless. 'Our hosts will be surprised.'

She put her arms around his waist and let her head rest against his chest, so she was able to hear the steady beating of his heart. Then she looked up and murmured, 'No, they won't. We're newlyweds. Remember?'

Then she put her arms around his neck and pulled his face down so she could kiss him.

For Anthony, desire always lurked when she was close. He took her home and straight upstairs, dismissing the servants then helping her to undress. He joined her, then he brushed some tendrils of hair away from her face and kissed her. It was easy to free her breasts from her light summer gown and he kissed each of them in turn, adoring her fevered response. He caressed her and stroked her until at last he entered her with a deep thrust that made her cry out his name and he held her on the edge until her pleasure peaked. He kissed her once more, then at last he gave way to his own earth-shattering release.

She opened her eyes almost dazedly. For a moment he feared she was going to ask him more questions, but instead she gave him a secret little smile.

'Delicious,' she murmured. She reached to touch his face. '*You* are delicious.'

Then she went to sleep in his arms.

The next afternoon they went again to Oakfields. The staff, as usual, greeted them warmly and everything there appeared to be going well. Marianne said as much to Anthony as he drove them back to Cleveland Hall in his curricle.

He agreed but he added, 'Oakfields, remember, is your property now, Marianne. My Kent steward has been looking after everything there for you; I asked him to do so on your behalf, because it seemed the best temporary solution. But if you can think of anyone you would prefer to manage it, just tell me.'

Simon, she thought suddenly. Simon used to run Oakfields for their mother, both the house and its tenanted farms. She knew that he had only joined the army because, on her mother's marriage to Sir Edgar, he had lost not only his home, but the job he had loved.

Probably it was best to put her idea on one side

for now. Simon and Anthony were barely on speaking terms and soon Simon might be posted abroad again. But she did say, 'Thank you, Anthony. I'll bear it in mind.'

She told herself to be patient, just as she told herself she had to be patient over the fact that Anthony had secrets he was still hiding, not only from her but from everyone. Some day he might even tell her the reason why poor Cynthia had set off that winter's day to her tragic death. But it was hard to remain silent, especially when she realised that Anthony was no longer accepting any of the many invitations that arrived and was spending more time each day in his study. She feared that his past still weighed on him heavily.

Each morning, a housemaid left a tray of tea things for them outside her bedroom door and Marianne was usually awake by then, but one morning she was sleeping so soundly that she only stirred when she heard the rattle of the tray. Anthony told her that he would fetch it. 'Stay there,' he said, pressing a kiss to her cheek, and she watched as he climbed from the bed, still naked.

She didn't find his scar repellent and she'd told him so. If anything, it only heightened his essential masculinity. But how could his father have done that to him? She felt her heart hurt anew for her husband as she watched him put on his dressing robe then go to bring the tea in while she eased herself up against the pillows.

She saw, when Anthony returned, that he was holding the letters that had arrived that morning. 'One for you,' he said, 'and one for me.'

Hers, she realised, was yet another from her mother, who was a frequent correspondent. It would be full of news, she knew, about what was going on in London. But she didn't read it because she could see that Anthony was reading his letter—and his expression was suddenly tense.

She said, as lightly as she could, 'My letter is from my mother. What is yours about, Anthony?'

Instantly, she saw him frown. 'It's just something that has cropped up,' he said at last. 'In London.'

She hesitated. 'So do we need to return?'

'We can perhaps have another two or three days here. But then we should get back, yes.'

She said nothing as he put the letter down then came over to place a cup of tea on her bedside table. Then he sat on the bed at her side and asked gently, 'Did you sleep well?'

She made the effort to push aside her anxiety. 'Indeed. I had delicious dreams.'

He grinned, smoothing back a wisp of hair from her face. 'Dreaming of me?'

'Of course. You vain creature, who else?' She put her hand on his forearm. 'I hope we can make the most of our last days here?'

Her voice faded as she saw how his eyes darkened a little. 'Sweetheart,' he said, 'there's a great deal I must attend to before we go back to London and this morning I've planned to go out with my estate manager and visit some of the farms.'

'I shall miss you.'

'For a few hours? Really?'

'Yes. Every minute of them.' She spoke softly. 'I mean it, Anthony.'

He'd started to reach for his clothes but now he came back to take a curling strand of her hair and twist it gently in his fingers. He said softly, 'So you've not forgotten your childhood friend, then?'

'You mean more than that to me now,' she whispered. 'Much more.'

He pressed a light kiss to her forehead. 'I had better be on my way, or else I'll be far, far too tempted to get back into bed with you.' Swiftly, he pulled on his clothes. 'I'll be back by lunchtime, no later,' he called as he left.

He sounded cheerful. But she hadn't failed to notice that before he went he thrust the letter that had arrived deep into the pocket of his breeches, as if it had disturbed him.

She told herself she was imagining too much. *Just something that has cropped up in London*, he'd said. But she guessed it was more than that. She was sure he was not telling her the truth and, after Elsie had helped her to dress, she went straight down to his study.

Swiftly, she leafed through all the documents on his desk, dismissing them because they were either bills or legal documents. Eventually, she was about to give up, when she spotted a little key—and it opened a drawer in the desk.

In it was just one letter. It had to be the one that had arrived this morning, because she'd noticed how Anthony had crumpled it in his fist before putting it into his pocket. It had been smoothed out, though it still bore creases. The handwriting was rough, the letters ill-formed, but the tone of its message was clear.

I am sorry, Your Grace, that you have broken your word to me. I am disappointed. You must understand that there will be repercussions. You had best not delay your return.

There was a scrawled signature. *Ned Gibson, Clerkenwell.*

She felt shaky, almost ill. Finding the nearest chair,

she sat down. Someone was threatening her husband. This was far, far worse than all the whispers.

When he returned later that morning, he told her he'd decided they should return to London that afternoon. 'I'm sorry,' he said. 'I had hoped we would have at least a few more days here. Do you mind very much?'

She summoned a smile. 'Of course not.'

But she was sure that this was about the letter from the man called Gibson, and she prepared to leave Cleveland Hall with a heavy heart. As they set off, those ominous words echoed again and again in her head: *there will be repercussions.*

By the time they reached London, dusk was falling. Anthony told Marianne he had sent word ahead to his Mayfair staff that they would be arriving, but he had said little else to her during their journey. When he told her that he would be spending most of the next day catching up with business, her heart sank again. Something was clearly wrong, but she did her best to conceal her concern.

'I shall visit my mother tomorrow,' Marianne said as they finished their evening meal. 'I've gathered from her letters that Sir Edgar's mood has improved greatly while we've been away, because Eleanor has received a marriage proposal at last.'

'Her fiancé has my heartfelt sympathy, whoever he is,' said Anthony. Then he smiled and took her hand. 'Tell Lady Hermione that I'll visit her as soon as I can.'

The next day, after lunch, one of the grooms drove Marianne to Bloomsbury, where her mother was delighted, if somewhat startled, to see her. 'Darling! I wasn't expecting you back from Kent yet. Goodness, don't you look well! I have a number of ladies here for the afternoon, taking tea in the drawing room. But Alice and the other maids are serving them refreshments and none of my friends will miss me. So come into the parlour, where we can talk.'

Marianne had already handed her cherry-pink pelisse and bonnet to Perkins, who had bowed obsequiously on letting her in. Obediently, she followed Lady Hermione to the parlour.

'I shan't keep you long, Mother,' she said. She settled herself on the settee, where Cuthbert opened one eye to look at her then went back to sleep.

Lady Hermione shook her head. 'No, no. Stay as long as you want! How was Kent?'

'We've had a wonderful time.' She stroked Cuthbert and heard him purr. 'Anthony sends his regards, but he has business to attend to.'

'Of course. He must be such a busy man.' Lady Hermione sighed a little. 'I've been busy too, of course, now that Eleanor is betrothed. I go shopping with her most days and I have to attend various social events with her and her husband-to-be. As does Sir Edgar, of course.'

'Who is her fiancé?' enquired Marianne.

'Edgar's future son-in-law lacks a title, but he is a young man of respectable birth and a reasonable amount of wealth. I will only say that I wish him well.'

'Meaning?'

'I fear,' said her mother, 'that Eleanor will rule him with a rod of iron.'

'Oh, dear. At least Sir Edgar must be happy.'

'Indeed. He is very happy.'

'And you, Mother?' Marianne spoke softly. 'You sound a little weary of London life. Why don't you take a trip to Oakfields? I can't tell you how wonderful it was to see it again.'

'I would love nothing more. But…to stay there on my own?' Lady Hermione shook her head. 'It just would not be the same without my family.'

'I'm sure that Anthony and I will be going to Kent again soon. Meanwhile, you would have all the old servants there for company, and of course you could take Alice. It really needs to be lived in!' She paused. 'Is Simon still in London? You said in one of your letters that he might be going abroad again soon and I should dearly love to see him before he leaves.'

She noticed how her mother's expression suddenly changed. 'Darling,' Lady Hermione said a little awkwardly, 'your brother was here yesterday. I'm afraid he is still not happy about your marriage.'

Oh, no, she thought. *No.* Surely her brother could try, for her sake, to heal his rift with her husband? Aloud, she said, 'Not happy? Even though Anthony has been so very generous in taking action to get Oakfields back for us?'

'Simon still believes what people whisper about your husband, I fear. And I gather that his regiment is due to be posted abroad again some time soon.'

Marianne nodded. She felt angry. She felt indignant. But she said calmly, 'I will try to see him before he leaves. Now, you go back to your guests. I'm sure they will be missing you.'

'You wouldn't like to come and meet them yourself? No—a foolish question. I saw immediately how your face fell and I don't blame you. Do call again soon. And look after that husband of yours, won't you?'

'I'll do my best,' promised Marianne with a smile.

Lady Hermione left to rejoin her guests, but Marianne didn't leave immediately. Instead, she sat alone in the parlour with Cuthbert, who had woken now and was preparing to settle on her lap. Gently, Marianne eased him away, whispering, 'I'm sorry, I have to go now. But I would guess you'd very much like to return to Oakfields, wouldn't you? Just like my mother.'

She saw Alice before she left, and the maid helped her into her pelisse. 'I can see a certain look in your eye,' said Alice. 'I hope you're not planning to do any meddling again, are you?'

'Trust me, Alice,' said Marianne lightly, 'I shan't end up in Bow Street, if that's what you're worried about.'

Anthony's coachman took her back to the big house in Grosvenor Square. But all the time she just couldn't stop worrying about that note from the man called Ned Gibson, because it had been a threat—there was no doubt of that.

During the next few days, Anthony was still busy. She realised, of course, that with his vast estate there were many meetings and financial affairs to attend to. At night, he came always to her bed and their lovemaking was passionate, but she still worried that her husband felt he couldn't confide in her, couldn't trust her, and it hurt her bitterly.

Her mother called round and twice they went shopping in Bond Street together, which was a delight because Marianne was able to treat her to all kinds of things.

'This is to make up for Sir Edgar's penny-pinching ways,' Marianne assured her when Lady Hermione protested about the price of yet another new gown.

'Edgar is a little more generous,' her mother said doubtfully, 'now that you are a duchess. I think he's frightened that Anthony will have something to say if he's unkind to me.'

'He's right,' said Marianne. 'Now, I think you need another bonnet or two. Don't you?'

But her spirits were still low. Simon made no attempt to contact her and Marianne was upset by his continued hostility. The next afternoon, when Anthony had told her he would be out yet again, she could bear it no longer.

I have to do something, she told herself. Surely, if she knew a little more, she might be able to help her husband, somehow. So she put on her plainest cloak and bonnet—ones she usually used for walks in the countryside—and told Elsie that she was going to visit a friend.

'Won't you require a carriage, Your Grace?'

'No, I shall walk, Elsie. It's really not far.'

The maid was startled by her dull attire, she knew, but Marianne took no notice and headed off down the street. She wasn't going to visit a friend. Instead, she headed straight to the cab stand in nearby Mount Street, where she approached a driver and said, 'To Clerkenwell, if you please.'

The driver looked startled. 'Clerkenwell?' he repeated. 'Are you sure about that, ma'am?'

She knew it was an area to the east of Bloomsbury, guessed too that few residents of Mayfair would head there. But she said, 'I'm sure,' and climbed in. As the cab set off, she could almost hear Alice's voice. *Meddling again. Always meddling.*

Gradually, they left behind the more prosperous parts of the town until they came at last to an area of narrow streets filled with tradesmen and shopkeepers. The driver pulled his horse to a stop and called to her, 'This is Clerkenwell Green, ma'am.'

Marianne climbed out and looked around. Just a few paces away was a fruit stall—surely its owner would know the area well? She went quickly up to him. 'Do you know of a man called Ned Gibson? I believe he has a house in this area.'

He immediately looked wary. 'Well, I—'

She held out some coins. 'Gibson,' she repeated.

He spoke reluctantly. 'I know of Gibson. But he's not the kind of man you would wish to deal with, miss.'

Her heart skipped a beat but she held out another coin. The man took it and said, 'He lives in Aylesbury Street.' He pointed. 'That's over to the right there, see? You'll spot it easily enough, because his house is bigger than the rest.'

Marianne went back swiftly to her cab driver. 'Wait here for me,' she said, 'and there'll be more money for you.'

He nodded and pocketed the coins.

Aylesbury Street was thronged with pedestrians and passing vehicles, so she trusted she was inconspicuous in her grey cloak. She walked on until she came to a private residence that was larger than the surrounding buildings; it looked secretive too, for it had a massive front door and all the shutters across its windows were closed.

Was this Gibson's dwelling? Was anyone even living there? She hesitated. Maybe this was enough for today. She had learned where Gibson's house was, she had gathered that people were frightened of him and that maybe she should be too. Her dream of somehow being able to help Anthony was swiftly vanishing.

She had just begun to make her way back to the cab when two burly men dressed in black coats and breeches appeared in front of her. The first said, 'What's your business here, lady? Why the interest in Mr Gibson's house?'

Her heart sank. They must have been watching

her and she was trapped. She also guessed from the way people were hurrying past and averting their eyes that no one would come to her rescue. Before she could begin to think of an answer, one of the two moved closer to say, 'Now, Mr Gibson has been watching you and, as it happens, he would rather like to be introduced. So you'd best come inside and make his acquaintance—without any fuss, mind.'

The men led her inside, then marched her all the way through the house to a room where a middle-aged man dressed in a brown serge coat sat behind a desk. She saw that his features were coarse, his manners too because he didn't even rise to his feet. Did he know who she was? Dear God, she was in trouble this time.

'Well,' Gibson said, 'you're not the kind of visitor we usually get here. Who, in the name of all that's holy, are you?'

He lounged back in his chair, gazing at her insolently. *So he didn't know.* He didn't know anything about her, and that maybe gave her a chance to get herself out of this mess. Marianne lifted her chin and replied, 'I would rather not say at this point, Mr Gibson.'

'Ha!' He folded his arms across his broad chest. 'Then I'll guess. You're just another foolish woman come to beg me to take pity on her spendthrift husband.'

She listened, quite bewildered. But as he spoke further, understanding dawned.

'You'd be surprised,' he was continuing, 'how often I get visits from pretty ladies like you, whose husbands have become a little too fond of my gambling tables. I think you've come to beg me to cancel your husband's debts, but it's no use, because I won't. I never do—though, believe me, I've been offered all kinds of inducements. Personal favours, even.'

He leered at her openly. The man was rough, he was hateful, but she managed somehow to keep her voice steady. She knew now what his business was. He ran a gambling club—and to judge by the fruit-seller's warning and those watchful men on guard, it was a serious and secretive business. Anthony's father once had widespread gambling debts. Had he perhaps owed money to this man?

Her chief business now was to get out of here without him realising who she was. Then suddenly, she had an idea. She said, 'Do ladies ever come to gamble at your club, Mr Gibson?'

He looked a little surprised. 'Why do you want to know that?' But he gestured towards the chair that faced his desk and she sat down, forcing herself to smile.

'You see,' she said, 'I must confess that I have a secret. I adore gambling.'

'Is that so?' he mused. But she could see that he had relaxed a little.

'It is indeed. But my husband has forbidden it and I miss it terribly. I was wondering, Mr Gibson, if I could maybe visit your club one night.'

'Well,' he said, stroking his chin. 'We do get the occasional lady of quality visiting our gaming tables. Discretion is our byword, of course, and—'

He broke off as the door opened and one of those black-clad men came in. 'Mr Gibson, sir. A word?'

Gibson rose immediately. He said to Marianne, 'I trust you will excuse me a moment? In the meantime, I will see that you are served with some tea.'

Marianne smiled her thanks, but that smile vanished the moment he'd gone. How long would her cab driver wait for her? Maybe she had fended off Gibson's suspicions for now, but the man was evil, she realised, and full of contempt for those whose weakness had made him wealthy. Yes, wealthy—the neighbourhood might be shabby, but this house was not. The furnishings were of the highest quality, there were magnificent pieces of silverware on display and on the walls were some beautiful gilt-framed paintings…

Paintings. She rose to her feet, because one in

particular had caught her eye. It was a portrait of a young woman and as she drew closer to it, she put her hand to her mouth. *'No,'* she whispered. 'No. It cannot be.'

Just then a maid came in with the tea tray. She put the tray down and turned to go, but Marianne stopped her. 'Wait, please. Who is that lady in the picture?'

'Her, miss? She's the master's daughter. But she's—'

Before she could finish, Gibson was entering the room again and the maid fled. Marianne saw immediately that he looked totally different. His expression was angry, even threatening. 'I suggest, madam,' he said grimly, 'that you leave, right now.'

Marianne met his gaze as steadily as she could. 'Mr Gibson, you appear to have changed your mind. Why is that?'

He was pointing to the open door. 'My men will show you out.'

They did and clearly they relished the task. What had happened? Why had Gibson become hostile towards her so suddenly?

She didn't know. But she did know now that the lady in that painting was the same as the one in the portrait that had been sent to Anthony as a wedding gift.

Cynthia was the daughter of Ned Gibson—the

author of that letter to Anthony warning, *there will be repercussions*. Gibson still, somehow, had power over her husband. Yes, Anthony was keeping yet more secrets from her—and she really did not think she could bear it any longer.

Chapter Eleven

Anthony's day had been a long one. He had spent most of the morning and a further two hours this afternoon with his lawyer and then with various men of business, but as soon as he returned to Grosvenor Square at four he asked his butler, 'Is my wife in the house?'

'No, Your Grace,' answered Simmons. 'One of the maids told me that the Duchess went out earlier to visit a friend, and she has not yet returned.'

Anthony went to his study and poured himself a drink. These last few days back in London had been tense for him because he had feared that Gibson might already have begun his campaign of retribution, perhaps by distributing bundles of news sheets, or just ensuring that scurrilous gossip spread by word of mouth.

But as the days went by, he was beginning to wonder if perhaps everything would be all right after all. Perhaps Gibson had thought better of the threat he'd made in that letter. Maybe it was time for Anthony to relax.

But he'd taken only one sip of his brandy when Simmons came in and Anthony immediately felt a sense of premonition.

'You have a visitor, Your Grace,' said Simmons a little hesitantly.

From the expression on his butler's face, it didn't look as if he approved of this visitor one bit. 'What is his name?'

'He refuses to give it. He also says he's not leaving, Your Grace, until he has spoken with you. I left him in the hallway.'

Anthony headed straight there, knowing already that his optimism had been a foolish delusion. He faced Ned Gibson and said, 'What the *hell* do you think you're doing here?'

Gibson lifted his eyebrows. 'Now, Your Grace, is that the way to address the man you once called your father-in-law? I've already had a cold reception from your butler, so might I suggest that we settle ourselves comfortably in one of your fine rooms? Then we could enjoy a nice, cosy chat.'

'Be damned to that.' Anthony didn't move. 'You have broken your word to me. I thought we had decided that once I'd married your daughter, you would never contact me again.'

'So we did,' answered Gibson. 'But you also made a promise to me, remember? And I don't find my-self very satisfied with the result.'

Anthony looked around. There were none of his staff in sight, but he knew that in houses like his, the very walls had ears.

'This way,' he said curtly to Gibson and led him to his study, where he firmly shut the door. Then he said, 'It was not my fault that Cynthia died.'

Gibson looked around the room before settling himself in a comfortable leather chair. 'Wasn't it? Your Grace, I'm sure you're well aware some say that you paid that unknown coachman to deliberately cause the accident which ended my poor girl's life.'

'That is a lie!'

'Is it? Have you proof?' Gibson pursed his lips. 'I could easily resurrect the story. In fact, I think I might, because you've been a fool. I thought at first you had sense enough never to breathe a word about our arrangement, but you haven't kept quiet, have you? You've gone and told your wife.'

'What?' Anthony was truly bewildered now. 'Never!'

'Believe me, I understand your dilemma.' Gib-son shook his head sympathetically. 'It's no wonder your brain has been weakened by her, because she's as tasty a bit of muslin as I've seen—' He broke off as Anthony took a threatening step forward. 'Now, now, Your Grace,' Gibson said, 'there's no need for fisticuffs. I did warn you that I was mighty angry about your new marriage. I cannot forget, you see, that you treated my Cynthia abominably.'

'I did not treat her badly,' said Anthony in a low voice, 'and well you know it. As for Marianne, I forbid you from ever speaking of her again in such a way.'

'Do you, now?' Gibson rose from the leather chair and gazed around the room, looking thoughtful. Then he turned back to Anthony and said, 'Did you know that she has just been to visit me?'

Anthony felt it like a blow to the stomach. *What, in hell's name...?* He was winded. Stunned.

'Yes,' Gibson went on, 'she paid me a visit this afternoon in Clerkenwell and very pretty she looked too. I can only guess that you maybe blabbed my name to her when you were enjoying a delicious moment of intimacy. After all, we men are always at our most vulnerable then, aren't we?'

Anthony was struggling to understand. At last, he said, 'Tell me the facts.'

Gibson shrugged. 'Two of my men found her nosing around outside my house and they hauled her in.

She came up with some ridiculous story about wanting to join in the play one night at the Clover Club.'

Anthony was reeling. Why had Marianne done this? What had she hoped to achieve? How could she possibly have known Gibson's name and whereabouts?

The man was still talking, damn him. 'I hope you remember, Your Grace,' he was saying, 'that I sacrificed my sweet and precious daughter to you in exchange for cancelling your father's debts. After the marriage I kept myself out of your way, just as I promised. Yet what happened to my poor girl? She's lying cold in her grave, thanks to your neglect!'

Somehow, Anthony held himself steady. He said, 'I shall speak to my wife and make it clear that she was wrong to visit you. I don't know how she traced you, but it was certainly not through me. I hope this settles the matter.'

'It certainly does not, as far as I'm concerned.' Gibson's voice was menacing now. 'I'm an angry man, and for some time I've felt like letting people know your father was not only a gambler but a cheat into the bargain. How would you like that?'

Anthony clenched his fists. 'I've told you, Gibson. I shall swear my wife to silence.'

'I'm afraid it's too late. You have failed me and

my daughter in all kinds of ways, Your Grace, and I want retribution.'

He was about to set off for the door, but Anthony was blocking his way. 'I absolutely forbid you to speak out against my dead father!'

This time Gibson's voice was harsh. 'I don't think you're in any position to dictate what I do or don't do. Don't push me too far, or I might also decide to spread the story of how this afternoon your pretty little wife used her flirtatious ways on me like a woman of the streets. Come to think of it, her reputation isn't too sound anyway, is it? How many men was she betrothed to before she finally caught you?'

Anthony felt a wave of anger and helplessness surging through his veins. *Calm. Keep calm.* Aloud, he rapped out the question, 'How much money do you want?'

'So you're offering a bribe now? You certainly are devoted to your father's memory—either that, or devoted to your own pride. My answer is, I don't want your money, since I'm rich enough already. I just enjoy being in a position to tell dukes what to do—and you can't buy that, unfortunately for you.'

He left and for a few moments Anthony didn't move. Then he went to gaze out of the window, only to see that it had begun to rain and the grey sky couldn't have better matched his mood. Dear God, what had Marianne done? All his work. All his sacrifices, to protect his father's name. *Honora familia tua semper.* All of it was now for nothing.

What form would Gibson's revenge take? When would it begin? Since returning to London, Anthony had been seeking to find some weakness somewhere, some criminal act maybe, that would enable him to place pressure on his enemy. Gibson was a crook, of that Anthony had no doubt, but neither his lawyer nor his man of business could find anything definite to pin on him. Anthony was a powerful man with friends in high places but he had no means to tackle Gibson, for the man was now armed with enough weaponry against him to be quite deadly.

After what seemed like a lifetime, he heard Marianne arriving and he walked out into the hallway to meet her. Already a maid had come to take her cloak and he saw that beneath it she wore a simple cream gown that fitted her slim figure perfectly. She looked so very pretty, he thought. So beguiling. But all he said was, 'Marianne. Come into my study, will you?'

Something in his voice must have alerted her, for as she followed him she was starting to look anxious.

'Anthony?' she said. 'Is everything all right?'

He closed the door. He knew that she would be longing to hear him say that everything was fine, knew that she would want him to take her in his arms and kiss away her uncertainty. But instead, he stayed exactly where he was.

'Marianne,' he said in a level voice, 'have you any idea at all what you've done today?'

Marianne felt as if the ground was giving way beneath her feet. Was he talking about her visit to Clerkenwell? But how could he possibly know about it?

She tried hard to keep her voice steady. 'I'm not quite sure what you mean, Anthony.'

His response was swift. 'Do I really have to spell it out? You've been talking to Cynthia's father, haven't you?'

So he did know. How, she had no idea—but he knew, and he was furious.

'Yes!' she cried. 'All I wanted was to find out more about him, and do you know why? It was because I needed to find out the truth about your marriage, Anthony! Why didn't you *tell* me that Cynthia was actually the daughter of the man to whom your father owed all that money? I'm your wife, so surely you could have trusted me enough!'

'It seems plain now,' he said, 'that I couldn't.'

Oh, that hurt. She said at last, in a low voice, 'I never actually called at Gibson's house. I never intended to speak to him. Unfortunately, two of his men must have noticed me and they took me inside—but I swear, I never gave Gibson my name! So he could have had no idea who I was—'

'Of course he knew who you were,' Anthony cut in with scorn. 'He has spies everywhere.'

Suddenly she remembered that moment when Gibson had been called out of the room. She remembered how afterwards, Gibson had changed utterly in the way he looked at her, spoke to her. She found she couldn't reply.

Anthony was still speaking, but he sounded very weary now. 'How you managed to find out about Gibson and where he lived, I've no idea. But I know you visited him, because he came here.'

'Gibson did?'

'Yes, a short while ago—and he is absolutely furious. Listen, Marianne.' His voice was hard as ice. 'My father, among his many debts, lost a vast sum at Gibson's gambling tables and it was Gibson's demand that I marry his daughter as his price for cancelling that debt. It was also Gibson's demand that I should never, ever reveal the reason for that marriage, or speak of his daughter's true parentage. But today, you have undone all my efforts to keep my family's name untainted by scandal. Gibson thinks I've told you everything. He is a vengeful man, and he won't hesitate to take action.'

Marianne's heart was pounding so painfully that she felt it might burst through her ribs. Dear God, this was awful.

'Anthony,' she said, 'I'm truly sorry. But, as I've said before, this is your father's fault, not yours! Why did you feel that you had to make such a sacrifice? Surely you could have found some other way to raise the money to pay off your father's debts?'

Anthony waited for her to finish. Then he said, in a voice as cold as she'd ever heard, 'My father, as it happens, did something far worse than gambling. He cheated, Marianne—and Ned Gibson caught him at it.'

She felt as if her throat had closed up. Cheating, she knew, was an unforgivable crime in upper-class circles. It broke every code of honour. She said slowly at last, 'But Anthony, this does not alter what I've just said—that your father's misdeeds were not your fault.'

He was shaking his head. 'Even so, it was my duty as heir to deal with the potential scandal and I thought I had done so. It was part of my agreement with Gibson that he would stay out of my life for good, as long as I never told anyone at all that Cynthia was his daughter. I think Gibson felt a huge sense of personal victory that Cynthia would one day be a duchess, that his grandchildren, his legacy, would belong to a world he could never penetrate himself, but then she died and he was angry. He was even angrier when he learned I was to marry again. He came here to warn me that he intends, as revenge, to reveal my father's wrongdoings. As a matter of fact, I think he'll rather relish it.'

Anthony was speaking in weary tones that chilled her almost more than his anger and Marianne felt sick inside. This had to be a nightmare, but there was no way she could wake out of it.

'But you are a duke,' she whispered. 'He would not dare speak out against you, and besides, you couldn't have been kinder to poor Cynthia. Her death was not your fault. You had no idea she was setting off on her journey that day!'

'You know already,' he said, 'that rather a lot of people believe that I was personally responsible for her journey. I wasn't, of course. Rumour has it that she hired a carriage so she could travel to London and beg me for a divorce. But that cannot be true, because she was happy in Kent and besides, she had the use of my carriage there, and my grooms, whenever she wished. So why hire one? But the evil story has spread and now that she's dead, there is no way of denying it. Gibson is a bitter man, Marianne. I have no doubt that if he fulfils his threat and tells the world about my father's conduct, he will also reinforce the myth that I was cruel to his daughter.'

Somehow, Marianne kept her voice steady. 'There were surely witnesses. Maybe the driver of the coach could be found.'

He shook his head. 'Do you think I haven't tried to question the passers-by who found her? I have and I've got nowhere. The coach driver vanished from the scene and has never been identified—he could be at the other end of the country by now. I am saying no more on the subject, and that's the end of it. I will have to live with this and hope that some day the gossip will die away.' Tiredly, he rubbed his hand against his forehead as if to ease his inner tension. 'Marianne, I have only one more question for you. How, exactly, did you learn about my connection with Gibson?'

Oh, this was too awful. The shame of it washed through her until she could barely speak. At last, she said in a low voice, 'I found that letter he wrote to you. The one you received when we were in Kent.'

'You went into my study?' He looked incredulous. 'You actually unlocked my desk?'

'Yes.' She looked up at him. 'How can I make this better, Anthony? I beg you to tell me!'

Anthony saw the distress that clouded her eyes and he struggled, because he had begun to believe that, in spite of everything, they could be happy. She had always been headstrong, always passionate about what she believed in, and often he'd admired her for it. But, dear God, she had got him into bad trouble this time. He said at last, 'How can you make this better? I'm afraid I can't tell you, because at the moment I don't know.'

She nodded. 'It's no good my repeating how sorry I am. It's probably too late for that anyway. But remember, none of this is your fault! You have borne a truly heavy burden, and if Gibson does reveal your father's mistakes, then anyone with an ounce of decency in them will realise that you are completely innocent of any wrongdoing!'

'My friends will stand by me, I've no doubt of that. But I shall have to prepare for the worst.'

She lifted her head. He glimpsed tears sparkling in her eyes, but even so there was still that familiar defiance, that spirit to fight against what she saw as injustice.

'Prepare for the *worst?*' she said slowly. 'Why? Anthony, have you ever thought that you are perhaps too conscious of your duty and your rank? You are too proud! Oh, how I wish you hadn't kept all these secrets from me! You are sacrificing yourself with your continual silence. You must tell your friends everything now, before Gibson does!'

'But Gibson will still talk,' he said sharply. 'And

he will have more to add now. He will be able to tell everyone that my wife visited his house and he'll be able to use your foolish action today as yet another weapon against me. So to suggest that I should make everything public at this point…' He rubbed his hand across his forehead again. 'Marianne, have you lost your senses?'

There was a long silence. 'No,' she said very quietly at last. 'I don't think so. But Anthony, I fear that you truly lost yours when you asked me to marry you.'

She went straight to her bedchamber and he made no attempt to follow her.

During the next few days they lived, outwardly at least, like a normal married couple. The servants were always around, of course, and Anthony conversed with her civilly during mealtimes. But they slept separately. In fact, Marianne scarcely slept at all.

Every night, when Anthony bade her a polite goodnight and went to his own bedchamber, she lay awake missing him. Every morning when the mail arrived, she saw how tensely he grasped each letter—waiting, she guessed, for a fresh threat from Gibson.

Then, one afternoon, when Anthony had gone to

his club, Lady Hermione called. She chatted a little about this and that. Then she told Marianne her chief news—that Eleanor's betrothal was over.

'There will be no marriage.' She said it with a sigh. 'Eleanor has decided they are not suited, so Sir Edgar is in the blackest of moods, all the wedding plans have had to be cancelled and Marianne, I have had enough of the lot of them. I would love to go to Oakfields!'

'Then do,' urged Marianne. 'I've told you, the house is all ready for you and they would love to see you. Alice will go with you, won't she? And I'm sure that Anthony will let you use his travelling carriage!'

'Oh, no,' said Lady Hermione. 'I think Sir Edgar wants to arrange my journey himself. You see, we really are not getting on very well at the moment.'

She looked around then added quietly, 'Anthony is out, isn't he? I do hope you and he are happy, my dear?'

'Of course,' said Marianne quickly.

But she wasn't and every day her heart ached more and more.

Anthony too felt wretched. During these last few days Marianne had grown quieter and quieter, speaking to him only when she had to. She was repentant, he was sure, and also upset—but dear God, so was he, because she had caused him real trouble this time. For the moment Anthony was biding his time, waiting and watching in the hope that Gibson's threats would die away, but he knew the chances of that were small.

He and Marianne usually took their meals together, and so one morning he was surprised to find that she had not come down yet for breakfast. He ate only a little himself, then pushed his half-finished plate aside and went upstairs to knock on the door of her bedchamber.

There was no reply, so after a moment's hesitation he went in. She had risen and was dressed in a dark blue day-gown that enhanced her creamy complexion and vivid hair. Just for a moment he thought, *If I go to her now and try to repair things, will she listen?*

But then he saw that there was a large, half-packed valise on her bed, and beside it was a pile of neatly folded clothes.

'Marianne, what are you doing?' he managed to ask at last.

'I've decided,' she said, 'to go to your house in Kent—with your permission, of course. My mother told me recently that she was hoping to spend some time at Oakfields, and this morning I received a letter from her to say she has arrived. If I went to Cleveland Hall, I would be able to check that everything is in order for her.' She met his gaze almost defiantly. 'I would like to leave here as soon as you can arrange a carriage for me.'

'And when will you return?'

She answered quietly, 'I am not sure.'

He had to steady himself before saying, 'Are you telling me, Marianne, that our marriage is over?'

She hesitated. 'I realise that our marriage was a bad mistake for you, Anthony. I truly wanted to help you, but it was unforgivably foolish of me to go anywhere near Gibson and I'm not sure at the moment that there's any way back from this. By leaving for Cleveland Hall, I shall give us both some space.'

For a moment he found it impossible to speak. 'Marianne,' he said at last, 'please, for just once, take time to think about your actions. Don't you realise this will probably make things even worse for me? Don't you realise this will look like a repeat of what happened with Cynthia? People will claim that I've driven you away too.'

She shook her head. 'No one will blame you, Anthony. Not with my reputation. Besides, you can tell them I've gone to Kent to keep my mother company, and you can visit me to keep up appearances.' Her voice suddenly dropped to a whisper. 'I'm afraid our marriage was always a risk for both of us, wasn't it? A gamble, if you like. After all, you only proposed to me because you were forced into it.'

Anthony closed his eyes. Did she mean that those wonderful kisses were forced? Their rapturous lovemaking, night after night? Perhaps she did. He looked at her valise on the bed and said, 'I had better leave you to get on with your packing. I shall start making arrangements for your journey straight away.'

After Anthony had gone, grief surged through her so fiercely that she found it hard to breathe. Had she hoped that perhaps he had come upstairs to forgive her that disastrous encounter with Gibson, maybe tell her that she wasn't to worry and he would make everything all right?

He must have known their marriage was a risk, yet during their time together in Kent she had begun to believe that she had made her husband happy. The passion of their nights together had overwhelmed her doubts and she had thought, *We belong together, we can find happiness together and in time maybe the world will forget its cruel rumours about Anthony's first wife...*

But that hadn't been enough for her. Instead, in her usual fashion, she had pushed her way along a dangerous path she should never, ever have taken. She had delved into dark secrets and, in doing so, she had discovered that Anthony was even more noble than she had thought, sacrificing his own reputation in order to save his unworthy father from disgrace.

A sacrifice that would be in vain if Gibson decided to reveal that Anthony's father was a cheat.

She sank onto the bed beside her half-packed clothes, feeling as if a great weight was crushing all her dreams. For the last few days Anthony had been polite to her, but it was a cool politeness that she could no longer bear and she had to go. She didn't know how long for, she couldn't think that far ahead, but her mother's presence at Oakfields gave her a valid reason to leave and to have time to decide what to do next.

She realised now that Anthony's sense of duty had almost stifled his capacity for any other emotion, ruining his chances of opening himself to love. She had sometimes thought he hadn't changed over the years, but he had. He was no longer the person she had once known, her friend and her dear companion, because he had built up an iron-hard barrier around himself that allowed no one, not even her, to get through.

Too proud. Too proud. She swallowed down the

great lump in her throat, then after a moment she rose, took a deep breath and started packing again.

She saw Anthony just before eleven, when he came to tell her that his carriage would be ready for her at one. 'Your maid Elsie is happy to travel with you,' he said. 'I have also informed all my staff that you are going to Cleveland Hall in order to be near your mother at Oakfields for a while.'

That was all. What, exactly, had she hoped might happen? That he would perhaps hurl aside her valise, take her in his arms and say, *I can't bear for you to go. Please stay, Marianne, and we can endure whatever is to come together.*

No. That was pure fantasy. He showed no emotion in their parting and, besides, Elsie was waiting by the carriage and the senior staff were there also, curtsying to Marianne as she prepared to leave. She and Anthony spoke polite words of farewell to one another, but he didn't even give her a light kiss.

Anthony watched until the vehicle vanished from sight. But just as he was about to go back inside, he noticed that a pink silk scarf lay on the pavement close to his feet. It was Marianne's, he realised; she must have dropped it and as he stooped to pick it up, he noticed that it still bore her scent. It reminded him of their lovemaking. Of her.

He would keep up the pretence that theirs was a brief parting only. He would keep up the pretence that nothing at all was wrong with their marriage, but as he turned to go back into the house he was overwhelmed by a huge sense of loss. Perhaps he should have stopped the carriage and said to her, *To hell with Gibson. Together, we can get over any scandal.*

But he hadn't, and whether or not Gibson carried out his threat, this could well be the end of their marriage.

Chapter Twelve

When Marianne arrived at Cleveland Hall later that day, the staff couldn't have made her more welcome. But they were surprised she was on her own, though they did their best to hide it, and she made haste to explain that she had come to visit her mother at Oakfields.

The huge house seemed empty, almost desolate, without Anthony. She tried hard to appear cheerful, and if the housekeeper and the maids noticed she was a little subdued, Marianne hoped they would put it down to her slight tiredness after the journey. The next morning after breakfast, the head groom told her that he would drive her over to Oakfields whenever she wished, but she shook her head.

'My thanks,' she told him, 'but I really think I would prefer to walk.'

He was startled and so was Elsie, but she had made up her mind and very soon she was setting off by herself along the familiar footpath to Oakfields. But that was a mistake too, because memories flooded back of her happy childhood and her friendship with Anthony that had developed into something far more.

Don't, she told herself fiercely. *Don't torment yourself.*

At Oakfields, her spirits lifted a little because, as she drew closer, she saw that Lady Hermione was out in her beloved flower garden wearing a pink and blue-striped gown, which she most certainly wouldn't have worn if she was unhappy. Marianne had to smile too to see that Cuthbert, who must have travelled with her, had already found his favourite place to laze in the sunshine.

'Mother!' she said.

Lady Hermione glanced up and her joy was unmistakable. 'My darling!' she cried. 'What a lovely surprise!'

Marianne hugged her. 'I thought I would make sure you have settled in.'

'Oh, it's wonderful to be here again. And the servants are fussing over me endlessly…' Suddenly she looked around. 'But where is Anthony? Hasn't he come with you?'

Marianne felt her emotions welling up again but

she kept her voice calm. 'I'm afraid he has a good deal of business to attend to in London.'

'Of course. He will miss you. Now, I shall ask Alice to bring out some tea for us, shall I?'

Marianne spent the rest of the afternoon there and after that she visited Oakfields almost every day. It would always feel like home to her, and it was good to see how happy her mother was. Not one of the staff, either there or at Cleveland Hall, made any mention of Anthony and, as for Cynthia, it was almost as if she had never existed.

But to Marianne it was as if her ghost still haunted the great house. She couldn't help thinking of Anthony's first wife living here on her own, and that feeling became more vivid when one day she found, in a cupboard in the sewing room, an ebony box containing several beautifully made gentlemen's handkerchiefs. Each one was exquisitely hemmed with tiny, almost invisible stitches and embroidered with Anthony's name; this must be Cynthia's work, she was sure of it.

Only one, she realised, was unfinished. The first few letters of the name were yet to be completed and the needle and thread lay loose in the box. She found herself wondering if maybe she had last worked on it only the day before she'd died.

She held it up to the light, thinking, *She must have*

loved Anthony very much, and he must have cared for her. Otherwise, she would never have made these for him. She was still gazing at it when Elsie came in, but the maid halted and began to retreat.

'Your Grace, I came here to fetch a needle and some thread. But I can come back later...'

'No, Elsie, please stop! Tell me, did the Duke's first wife sew these?'

'Indeed, Your Grace!' Elsie almost blurted it out. 'The poor lady, she loved him so much and he came to see her often.'

At last. At last, thought Marianne, someone was prepared to speak.

'Do you know why his wife set off on her own that day?'

The maid shook her head. 'No. None of us could understand. Such awful weather it was, what with the snow and ice.'

'Did no one try to stop her, Elsie?'

'How could they? We didn't even know she was leaving the house! Also, no one could see the carriage from here, because it was waiting for her, down at the far end of the drive. She must have put on her hat and cloak and hurried off to it before any of us knew it.'

Marianne asked her next question very carefully. 'How do you know where the carriage was?'

Elsie looked nervous. 'Like I said, Your Grace. I saw none of it myself. All we learned later that day was that there had been a terrible accident—the poor lady died and the carriage drove off. But there's an elderly gardener whom nobody speaks to much but I talk to him sometimes, and he told me he'd seen that carriage. He saw the Duke's wife get into it too, in all that awful weather. But he's never mentioned it again. Maybe he imagined it.'

Daniel, thought Marianne. Elsie must be talking about Daniel.

That afternoon and the next, Marianne went out into the gardens but there was no sign of him. She knew Daniel was quiet and rather deaf; she knew too he generally avoided company. But on the third afternoon, she saw him working with a spade in the rose beds, preparing to put in some new plants.

She greeted him, speaking very clearly. 'How good to see you, Daniel! The roses look beautiful, as ever.'

'I will send you some for the house,' he said. She waited, wondering if he would say any more. *Silent Daniel*, the other gardeners called him, though it wasn't an insult because everyone admired his skills and his dedication. Other gardeners came to see his work from far and wide.

Marianne nodded. ‘That’s kind of you. You like working here, Daniel, don’t you?’

‘I do. The Duke is a good man,’ Daniel replied, ‘whatever people say.’

‘And his first wife?’

‘She was a sweet lady. Awful thing, what happened to her.’

Marianne felt her heart skip a beat. ‘Did you see much of her, Daniel?’

‘I did. She liked to come out to see my roses—loved them, she did. I… I watched when she drove off in the carriage that very last time. Terrible, it was.’

‘Because of the bad weather?’

‘No. Because I saw that she didn’t want to go.’

Marianne stood very still as his words sank in. At last she said, ‘Daniel. How do you know that she didn’t want to go?’

He leaned on the handle of his spade. ‘I was bringing in logs for my fire. It was a bitter day, coldest I’ve known. The carriage stopped on the drive where I could see it and she came hurrying out from the big house, all wrapped up in a cloak and hood like she wanted no one in there to see her.’ He looked at Marianne. ‘She was unhappy. I would swear it. She and the driver—they argued.’

Marianne felt her own pulse thumping. 'Do you think that maybe she didn't want to go to London?'

For a moment Daniel looked confused. 'But she wasn't going to London. Not in that carriage. It was old and in a bad way. It would never have got that far, never.'

She said, as slowly and clearly as she could, 'Daniel, this is important. Have you ever told anyone about this? Hasn't anyone asked you about what you saw?'

He shook his head. 'I keep myself to myself. People mostly speak too quickly for me and I can't hear. They just leave me to my roses. Besides, you don't always know if it's safe to talk.'

What? This time she was reeling with shock. Did he mean he had been threatened?

'Daniel,' she said, 'you are very loyal, I think, to your master, the Duke. Aren't you?'

'He has been good to me,' he repeated. 'Very good.'

'He has been good to many people,' she said, 'and if you have more information about the day of the accident then I believe you can be of great help him. Do you understand? If you fear it's unsafe to talk, he will protect you from any trouble, I promise.'

She saw the old gardener looking round for a moment then back at her. He said at last, 'I know some-one who saw the accident.'

She waited, hardly breathing.

'He worked on a farm nearby,' Daniel said. 'His name's Joseph. He was out with another fellow, checking on the farmer's ewes. He saw that carriage coming by and when it crashed and slipped with one wheel into a ditch, he and his companion carried the poor lady into a nearby barn for shelter.'

'What about the driver of the carriage? Was he hurt?'

'No.' Daniel shook his head emphatically. 'Neither were his horses. Joseph told me that once he'd got the nags to pull the carriage out of the ditch, he drove off again like the devil himself was after him.'

'You say that Joseph worked on a nearby farm. Is he still there, Daniel?'

He shook his head. 'Joseph moved on very soon after, Your Grace. I don't know where.'

Her heart sank. But she said, 'If you find out, will you let me know?'

'I'll do my best.'

'Thank you,' she said. 'Thank you, Daniel.'

She walked slowly back to the house because she needed time to think. Only Daniel, silent Daniel, had seen the mystery carriage depart. Perhaps Anthony already knew this.

But there was something else Daniel had said—something she couldn't forget. *You don't always know if it's safe to talk.*

Maybe his friend Joseph felt the same way. Maybe he'd been threatened even. By the time she reached the house her thoughts were spinning wildly. Should she tell Anthony? Should she try to investigate herself? But, as it happened, any plans of hers had to be cast aside—because as she approached Cleveland Hall she saw that someone was standing there, waiting for her.

It was her brother.

'Simon!' She quickened her pace. 'I wasn't expecting you!'

He embraced her, but then he stepped back a little. 'I imagine not,' he said. 'I arrived at Oakfields an hour ago because I'd decided to visit our mother. She told me you were here. She is anxious for you, Marianne, and so am I. In fact, I'm furious.'

She could hear it in the barely suppressed anger in his voice. 'Simon,' she began, 'let me explain.'

'No,' he said grimly. 'Let me speak first. I cannot believe that Anthony has treated you just like his first wife, packing you off to Kent at the first opportunity.'

'No!' she cried. 'No, Simon, you are quite wrong, believe me!' She looked around. There were no servants out here, but even so they needed absolute privacy and she drew him a little further away to where there were some seats beneath a pergola. 'Let us sit down, and I will explain.'

She did her best. She reminded him that Anthony had done the honourable thing by marrying her, but Simon answered sharply. 'You mean he was caught kissing you at Tom Duxbury's party? But that was his fault, surely!'

'No, Simon. You're wrong again. It was mine.'

'Yours?'

'I had followed him out there,' she explained. 'I might even have kissed him first. We had kissed before, you see.'

Her brother looked shocked, but she carried on. 'It's true, I assure you. Believe me, there were other scandals lurking already, most of them very much of my doing!'

She told him about the Earl of Ware's ball and how Jonathan Moseley had witnessed them alone together, threatening to expose her until Anthony silenced him. She told him about the escapade that resulted in her being taken to Bow Street and by then her brother's expression was indescribable.

'Bow Street?'

'Yes,' she said defiantly, 'I was suspected of theft.

Quite frankly, it could have ruined me, but Anthony rescued me.'

For a moment her brother was lost for words. At last he said, 'I think you're forgetting the fact that his own reputation is atrocious, Marianne. Don't forget that he married his first wife just for her money, and though people don't speak of it because of Anthony's high rank, it must have been because of his gambling debts. He neglected her quite shamefully and treated his own father badly too—'

'Stop!' she cried. She had risen to her feet. 'Stop, Simon. I can bear no more of this. Listen to me, please.'

He said nothing. He listened, he hardly even moved and his expression gradually changed as she told him about Anthony's father, his gambling and his debts.

'And that,' she concluded, 'is why Anthony had to marry, Simon. He had to marry the daughter of the gaming house owner, to whom his father owed a huge amount of money.'

Simon looked astonished. 'But surely,' he said, 'the debts could have been paid off without the drastic step of marrying? The Clevelands are an immensely wealthy family.'

'They could. But the worst of it was that Anthony's father cheated, and Cynthia's father threatened to tell everyone. You see, Anthony was, and still is, desperate to protect his father from dishonour.'

Simon nodded. 'I do see. That's pretty noble of him.'

'Yes.' It was almost a whisper, because she was thinking of the scar on Anthony's back. 'Extremely noble.'

Simon glanced at her. 'Yet you've fallen out with Anthony now?'

'I fear he's displeased with me, yes. I was trying to help him, but by doing so I managed to make things even worse.' Suddenly she felt tears threatening. 'Cynthia's father has now warned Anthony that he'll not only reveal the secret of his father's debts, but he'll also…'

It was no good. She couldn't say any more without breaking down and Simon must have realised it because he was quickly wrapping his arm around her, just as he did when she was much younger.

'Also what?' he said steadily. 'Tell me, Marianne.'

She drew out her handkerchief and dabbed her eyes. 'He's said he will tell everyone that Anthony was responsible for the accident that killed poor Cynthia.'

Her brother was speaking more carefully now. 'You don't think then,' he said, 'that she was unhappy here? Sent here against her will?'

'Not at all. Anthony told me it was her choice to stay here at Cleveland Hall.' She sat down again, because she needed to. 'And before you doubt him again, all the staff here know that Cynthia was happy here. I was happy too, after our wedding. But then…'

She couldn't go on and Simon must have realised, for he was holding her hand. 'Marianne, tell me. I can see that something is badly wrong.'

'It is! Anthony is good and honourable, just as you and I always used to believe. He got Oakfields back for us, Simon! But recently, I have made the most awful mistake. You see, in London, I met with Cynthia's father.'

Simon drew back. 'You did what?'

'I didn't intend to meet him, truly I didn't! I just wanted to see where he lived and maybe find out more about him. But I was seen by his servants. They suspected me of spying, so they took me inside to be questioned by Gibson himself. I believed that I hadn't been recognised, but he realised who I was and almost immediately he contacted Anthony.' She paused for breath. 'Anthony, of course, could barely hide his own anger at my interference, so I came here, because I could not bear what I'd done to him. You see, Cynthia's father—Ned Gibson—is threatening to stir up yet more trouble, over his daughter's death.'

Simon appeared to be thinking hard. 'You say that Anthony was kind to his wife. Why, then, did she make that desperate journey to see him?'

'But that story is all wrong!' she cried. 'There was never any proof she was heading for London, and in fact I don't believe she wanted to go anywhere. I think she was forced by someone.'

Simon was listening intently now. 'How do you know this?'

She managed to speak more steadily. 'I always had my doubts. There is a gardener here whose name is Daniel. He's a solitary man who I think prefers his flowers to people. But he was talking to me earlier, out in the garden, and he just told me something very important. He said to me, *She didn't want to go.*'

'What do you think he meant?'

'He meant that Cynthia didn't want to go on that journey! You see, Daniel's cottage overlooks the driveway, and he saw the carriage pull up close to the main road, out of sight of the Hall. He saw Cynthia hurrying to it, and arguing with the driver.'

'She was probably concerned about the weather.' Simon was frowning. 'Why don't you believe she was going to London?'

'Because Daniel said the carriage was in no condition to make that journey. He also mentioned that two men saw the accident happen and tried to help

Cynthia. One of them told Daniel that the coach driver didn't even wait to see how she was. He just drove off. And Simon, I believe those men—the witnesses—have been threatened. They've been ordered to stay silent.'

Her brother was thinking hard, she could see it. At last, he said, 'Do you think that Daniel might speak to me?'

She shook her head. 'Probably not. I imagine he is frightened too. If he knew that I'd told you, he might not even speak to me again.'

'I see. This sounds as if some threats have certainly been made. But Marianne, I can't understand why Anthony hasn't found out more himself. Surely he questioned these witnesses?'

'I told you. Those men have been warned by someone to keep silent.'

Simon hesitated. Then he said, 'Some might say it was Anthony who wanted the whole business kept quiet.'

'No!' she cried. 'Believe me, Simon, I trust Anthony and so did you, once! He was horrified by the accident. And I think the witnesses were warned not to speak before anyone at all could question them. The one that Daniel knew—his name was Joseph—actually left his job and has moved elsewhere.'

Her brother rose to his feet. 'Let me think about

this. I'll call again soon, but try not to worry. Meanwhile, take care of yourself, won't you? I can tell you're fond of Anthony and I just hope your belief in him hasn't been misplaced.' He hesitated. 'There's something else I need to say before I go. Forgive me, but it's rather personal. Marianne—are you sure you're quite well?'

Her heart missed a beat. 'Of course I am!' She tried to smile. 'But the summer heat does tire me a little.'

He shook his head. 'From what I remember, it never used to trouble you in the least. Listen. You'll probably be annoyed, but I asked your maid when I arrived how you were, and she did mention that you often weren't finishing your meals.' He sighed. 'I guess that you've been worrying about Anthony, haven't you?'

'Yes.' Her voice was scarcely a whisper.

'Well,' said her brother, 'I'd best be on my way. But first, I'll go inside and ask if someone will bring you a cool drink. Like I said, I'll be here again, and I'll be thinking about everything you've told me.'

He kissed her cheek, whispered, 'Look after yourself,' then left. A few minutes later she heard the sound of his horse trotting briskly down the drive,

It wasn't long before Elsie came out with a tray of iced lemonade and biscuits. 'Here you are, Your

Grace,' she said. 'Your brother said you might like these.'

Marianne nodded. 'Thank you, Elsie.'

But she didn't want them. She tried to sip some of her drink then she picked up one of the biscuits, but she put it down again because she wasn't hungry in the least. If any of the servants commented on her lack of appetite, she always said, 'I'm afraid I ate too much earlier.'

Some days, she was fine. If she ever did feel tired and slightly nauseous, she told herself it was indeed because of the heat, and her anxiety over her rift with Anthony. But she guessed the true reason and she dreaded having to face the reality of it. She was almost sure she was pregnant—and she had no idea at all how her husband would react.

As for her brother, did Simon believe her when she'd told him about Daniel and the carriage? Was there any point in trying to do anything, when Anthony himself appeared to have decided long ago to bear the lies told about him in silence?

Perhaps Anthony was right. Perhaps it would never be possible to dispel the gossip, because people always believed what they wanted to believe. Daniel had offered information that could be followed up—but wouldn't Anthony be furious with her, for stirring up trouble once more?

* * *

The next morning, after dressing in a light cotton frock and finding a wide-brimmed sunhat, she went out into the garden again. She still felt lost in the vastness of Cleveland Hall without Anthony there and she had slept badly again last night. Somehow, the garden always comforted her with its scented flowerbeds and winding pathways. She guessed it would be hot later, but at the moment a light breeze refreshed the air, so she wandered as far as the rose beds and was about to return to the shade of the pergola when she saw Daniel.

He was coming towards her and he took off his hat before saying, 'Your Grace, there is someone who wants to speak to you. His name is Joseph.'

As usual, Daniel spoke so quietly that she struggled to catch his words. But… Joseph. Wasn't he one of the men who had seen the accident?

Daniel had already set off along the path and she followed. Clearly, he was heading for his cottage. By the time they drew near, she could see that a tall, thin man stood by the door of Daniel's home, holding his hat in his hands.

He bowed to her, then glanced around as if to check that no one else was in sight. He looked nervous. Frightened, even.

'Joseph,' she said, 'are you here to tell me something about the carriage accident?'

He nodded. 'I am, Your Grace.'

She tried to prompt him. 'I understand that you tried to help the poor woman who was hurt, didn't you?'

He was looking around again. 'I don't want no trouble,' he said. 'No, I do not. I've already lost one job. I've got another now and I don't want to lose that.'

'Why did you lose your job, Joseph?'

He was nervously fumbling with his hat. 'Because we were there!' he said. 'Me and another lad, we were out checking the sheep when we saw the accident. That carriage took a corner too fast. Because of ice, it came off the road and slid partway into a ditch. The door flew open and the young lady was flung out—she was hurt bad, poor thing. We ran to carry her into a nearby barn, to try and keep her from the cold, but she died soon after. The driver didn't even try to help, just got his horses to pull the carriage out of the ditch and left her to die.'

'The carriage,' Marianne said. 'Daniel told me it was old and badly cared for. Was there anything you noticed about it, Joseph?'

'He saw a name,' said Daniel. 'He can read, you see.'

Marianne looked at Joseph. 'There was a name?

On the side of the carriage? Did you tell anyone this?' She had to try hard to control her emotions. 'Weren't you asked about everything you saw?'

Surely, she thought, Anthony had tried his utmost to trace both the driver and his vehicle?

Joseph hung his head. 'I said nothing. You see, I was told my wife and children might come to harm if I blabbed. Like I said, someone's already made sure I lost my job.'

He was looking around again and she feared that any minute he might run. 'I will make sure you are protected, Joseph.' She was almost pleading with him now. 'Please—will you tell me the name on the carriage?'

At first, she feared he was going to refuse. But at last he said, 'It was Wilkes and Sons. That was the name painted on the side.'

'Do you know anything about Wilkes and Sons?'

'They have carriages for hire in Sevenoaks. I know because I work in the town now, at an inn, and I've seen them.'

Sevenoaks.

'Thank you,' she said. 'Thank you. You will be rewarded for this.'

She hurried back to the Hall and went straight to the stables to find a groom. 'I would like you to take me to Oakfields,' she said. 'Now.'

When she got there Lady Hermione was startled to see her, but all Marianne said was, 'Where is my brother?'

'Simon is up in his room. This morning he received a letter from his regiment and I believe he is studying it. Marianne, is something wrong?'

But there was no reply because Marianne was already hurrying up the stairs.

Her brother frowned when he saw her.

'Simon,' she said, 'I need you to come with me to Sevenoaks. Please?'

Simon made her sit down while she told him everything Joseph had told her. 'Please,' she added when she had finished. 'Please, help me with this. Help Anthony.'

At first, he didn't answer and she found the waiting almost unbearable. Then he said, 'Very well. We'll set off for Sevenoaks right now.'

Simon drove the gig and on the way she told him more of what she'd learned. By the time she had got to the name painted on the carriage's side, he was nodding decisively. 'Right. We'll ask at The Chequers—it's the main coaching inn in Sevenoaks. They'll know more.'

It was market day so it took them a while to get through the town's busy streets, but at last they reached The Chequers. The inn's courtyard was crowded, with one carriage after another either arriving and disgorging its passengers or waiting to set off. Simon and Marianne climbed down, Simon paid a young lad to hold their horse and then he headed straight for a group of ostlers.

'Do any of you know of a firm called Wilkes and Sons? Are any of their carriages or drivers here at the moment?'

His strong voice was already attracting attention and Marianne had noticed that people were stopping to stare and listen. She had also seen that one of the coach drivers who loitered by his vehicle, no doubt waiting for customers, had started hurrying off.

'Stop,' she called out to him. 'Stop!'

He was going to outrun her and soon she would lose him in the crowd. So she called out, 'That man who's running away! Stop him! He has stolen my purse!'

Instantly, several men were surrounding the fellow. He kicked and struggled, but they held him firmly. Then Simon was there. 'Thank you, gentlemen,' he said. 'I shall deal with this.'

His air of command did the trick. The prisoner cowered and all the others stepped back. 'Well done,' Simon said softly to his sister. Then he turned back to the prisoner. 'Now,' he said, 'where were you off to in such a hurry?'

* * *

In London, the time went by slowly for Anthony. He had tried to carry on with his life as normal, but...normal? What the hell was he thinking? Nothing was normal.

He had told everyone that Marianne had gone to Kent to visit her mother. But he saw the sideways glances and he knew that his enemies would be busy resurrecting the old slurs. *Do you remember how he banished his first wife to the country? Looks like he's trying the same trick again.*

He missed her, badly. He also expected everywhere he went to see some sign that Gibson was on the warpath again. He had become suspicious of almost everyone, and whenever he thought of that final argument with Marianne his chest would grow tight with despair. At night especially, he was almost overwhelmed by the need to race to Kent and beg her to come back to London with him. With her bold demeanour and her infectious smile, she had broken through the barriers with which he guarded his heart and he had actually started to believe that maybe his life could be filled with the kind of happiness he'd never allowed himself to imagine.

She had left him, though. She had accused him of being too proud and yes, he probably was. Clearly, she regretted trusting him with her heart. Indeed, before she'd left, she had sounded broken almost. Now the pain of missing her tormented every hour of his days and nights. But he hid it and he carried on attending parties and balls, because he knew it was his duty.

Lord Delfont's party that evening was particularly arduous. Perhaps it was Anthony's imagination, but more people than usual seemed to be glancing in his direction then looking away swiftly and whispering to one another. In fact, he was thinking of leaving early when his friends, led by Tom Duxbury, arrived and drew him into their midst, talking cheerily of the horses they'd been inspecting at Tattersalls earlier. It was, he thought, almost as if they were protecting him in the way that soldiers closed ranks around an injured comrade.

So he stayed at Delfont's party and he went to another one the next night. He visited his club often and dealt every day with the affairs of the ducal estate. But everywhere he went he kept expecting to hear Marianne's voice: mischievous, laughing, loving. Since she had gone, he'd hardly slept at all. When he did, he dreamed that she was running away from him and, no matter how hard he tried, he could not catch her.

Everywhere he went in his big, lonely mansion he would catch sight, somewhere, of the family crest and the motto that had been drummed into him since childhood. *Honora familia tua semper.* Honour your family, always.

Then one day he decided—be damned with that. If Ned Gibson chose to do his evil work while he was away, then let him. Anthony knew that he must do something—*anything*—to save his marriage and to heal the wound that Marianne's departure had opened in his heart.

He had to go to Kent.

Chapter Thirteen

On the morning after her visit to Sevenoaks with Simon, Marianne awoke to see that the weather, yet again, was quite perfect. The sun was hot and just a few wisps of white cloud floated high above the glorious landscape. She horrified poor Elsie by choosing, when she'd had her breakfast, to change into a faded blue cotton dress and her brown laced ankle boots, then she tugged her long hair into a knot at the nape of her neck and put on a wide-brimmed sunbonnet with trailing blue ribbons.

'I'm going to walk to Oakfields,' she told Elsie.

Her poor maid protested. 'No! Your Grace, I've told you before that it's not right for you to go out alone, especially dressed like that!'

'Because I'm a duchess, you mean? Elsie, I'm extremely comfortable in this old dress and I'm afraid no one is going to stop me.'

She needed to see her brother. She wanted to talk

with him about what they had discovered yesterday and she wanted his opinion on the best way to tell Anthony. Should she return to her husband in London, or write to him? Would he listen, or would he be angry with her again?

Her anxiety lifted only a little as she followed the familiar footpath across the fields and through the woods. Her intention was to speak with Simon in private, but as she neared Oakfields she spotted her mother out in the garden, sitting under the shade of an old pear tree with Cuthbert beside her. There were, Marianne noted, the remains of a cream-filled sponge cake on the table beside her, alongside a teapot and two cups and saucers.

'Marianne!' exclaimed Lady Hermione, jumping to her feet. 'This is a lovely surprise!'

She looked a little embarrassed, thought Marianne.

'Mother,' she said, 'I suspect you've had company. But it can't have been Simon, because he wouldn't have left that cake unfinished.'

'Oh,' said Lady Hermione, 'Simon has gone off on some errand. But Sir George Willoughby called—you'll remember him, I think?'

'Of course. He lives nearby, doesn't he?—and he is very pleasant.' Marianne sat down and her mother did too.

'Indeed,' said Lady Hermione, 'he is charming. He is a widower now, sadly, since his poor wife died a year ago. He is extremely polite and considerate.'

'He is also clearly making you happy,' Marianne said softly.

Indeed, whether it was caused by her blushes or the way she had styled her hair more softly, her mother, looked extremely pretty.

'I am very happy,' said Lady Hermione, 'because I have Oakfields back and both my son and my daughter with me—for the moment, anyway.' She hesitated then said more quietly, 'All I need now is for you to be happy too, my darling. Do you think Anthony will be coming to join you soon?'

Anthony. Oh God, Marianne realised she missed him desperately. Yesterday, hope had lifted her heart—the hope that she, with Simon's help, might have found a way to free her husband from the shadows that clouded his past. But might that awful man Gibson have acted already? She could imagine only too well the whispers that could be racing around London even now.

Also, at some point she would have to tell him she was expecting his baby, and he might be horrified to learn that he was bound to her still further. Would they have a child whose mother and father were totally estranged?

She would give anything to cancel out that trip to Clerkenwell that had led to her disastrous meeting with Gibson. She would give anything if only she could prove to Anthony just how much she loved him. If only they could start anew! There was no one else for her—there never could be anyone else for her…

'Cuthbert!' Her mother's sudden cry made Marianne jump.

She saw immediately that Cuthbert had gone dashing off in pursuit of a squirrel that was scampering along a wall between their garden and a neighbouring field. Cuthbert took a leap at the high wall, landed on top of it, then lost his balance and vanished over the far side. The squirrel, meanwhile, had run up a nearby oak tree from where it gazed down at them all.

Lady Hermione had already gone to peer over the wall, though she had to stand on tiptoe to do so. She turned round to Marianne. 'I cannot see him anywhere because of all the brambles and nettles over there. What if he has hurt himself?'

Marianne hoisted up her skirt, hung onto her wide-brimmed hat and clambered onto the wall, wriggling in a most unladylike way until her legs dangled over the far side. She gazed around, but of Cuthbert there was no sign.

'Darling,' called her mother suddenly, 'you can come down now because Cuthbert is here. The mischievous creature—he must have got back over the wall by himself, somehow.'

Marianne nodded. But she was a little tense, because as she tried to turn and come back down from the wall she realised that her full skirts had snagged on a jagged stone and she couldn't move.

'You're not stuck, are you?' Lady Hermione was saying anxiously. 'Shall I fetch one of the gardeners to help you?'

'No,' Marianne said a little sharply over her shoulder. The last thing she wanted was to be seen in such a predicament. 'No, I shall manage. It's just that this dratted skirt is caught, and I can't—oh!'

She had unhooked the material at last, thank goodness, but her manoeuvres meant she was now sitting inelegantly astride the wall, with her skirt and her petticoat barely covering her knees. She tugged them down impatiently, only to realise that the breeze had whipped off her hat and sent it flying over into the field.

'Damn,' she muttered. She was finding the ridge of the stone wall exceedingly uncomfortable to sit upon and she wasn't at all sure how to get out of this fix. 'Mother,' she said at last, 'I think I might need some help after all.'

But her mother wasn't listening. She was staring into the distance and Marianne looked too, shading her eyes from the sun. Then her heart missed a beat—several beats, in fact—because now she could see that there was a curricle making swift progress along the track towards Oakfields.

And the curricle was driven by Anthony.

Her heart was thumping wildly. Maybe he came with bad news. Maybe Ned Gibson had done exactly what he had threatened, and was telling everyone that Anthony's father had been a gambler and a cheat, just as Anthony had always dreaded.

Apprehension racked her, but she stayed where she was because she guessed that if she tried again to get down from the wall, she might tumble off it altogether. The curricle had arrived in the courtyard now, and as the Oakfields grooms hurried to take charge of the two beautiful horses she saw Anthony alight and speak to them briefly.

Then he turned. He must have seen both her and her mother straight away, for now he was coming towards them. She realised that he wasn't wearing a coat or a cravat; she saw too that his dark hair was a little unruly and his face was tanned from the sun. But altogether he looked so breathtakingly handsome that all she could think was, *I love him. I love him so much.*

She couldn't speak. Her mother's pleasure, on the other hand, was obvious. 'Anthony! How wonderful to see you! And you could not have arrived at a better time because, as you see, dear Marianne is in a bit of a pickle.'

He was glancing again in her direction. No doubt he'd already noticed how inelegantly she was perched astride the wall. 'So I see,' he murmured.

She felt hot with embarrassment. Since losing her hat, her hair had escaped from its ribbon and fallen loose to her shoulders. She was still trying to pull her dress and petticoat down over her stockings when she realised that Anthony was coming purposefully towards her. He looked her up and down and murmured, 'Well, Marianne. This is just like old times, wouldn't you say?'

She didn't know how to reply. Was he amused or merely exasperated with her?

'It was Cuthbert,' she explained a little weakly. 'He jumped up here then disappeared, so I offered to fetch him. Only the wall was a bit higher than I thought and my hat blew off, and…'

'And you're stuck.' He was rapidly assessing the situation. 'Right. Is your skirt free? Then I'll hold you while you get ready to jump down.'

He put his hands firmly on her waist. He appeared oblivious to the awkward way in which she had to manoeuvre her right leg so it was on the same side as her left, and after that it was easy for her to jump down to the ground with his support. But the thing was that afterwards…he didn't let go of her.

Instead, he just kept holding her and gazing into her eyes until at last they heard Lady Hermione's voice.

'Do you know, Anthony,' she was saying, 'I have just remembered that Mrs Hinchcliffe was baking one of her chocolate cakes earlier—the kind that you always enjoyed.' She was addressing her son-in-law as if she was completely oblivious to the fact that he was looking at her daughter as if he would much prefer her to any cake. 'I shall go inside and ask her if it's ready yet, because I am sure you would like some, wouldn't you?'

'Hmm?' Anthony was still gazing at Marianne, but then he looked over his shoulder and said, 'Yes, of course, Lady Hermione. Delighted.'

He waited until Lady Hermione left, then at last he let Marianne go.

She smoothed down her hair. She tried to straighten her faded, crumpled dress. Then she took a deep breath and said to him, 'You've found me in a bit of a mess, I fear. As usual.'

He shook his head. 'I wouldn't quite say that. I see

that you've quickly got back into your old ways, but I will be rather cross if you apologise.'

He spoke the words with such tenderness that her heart almost bumped to a stop. But she braced herself, she drew a deep breath and she said, 'Anthony, ever since I left London I've been longing to tell you how very sorry I am, for interfering as I did. And now there is something I really must tell you…'

He held up a hand for silence. 'No more,' he said. 'Let me speak first. I've come because obviously we must resolve this situation we find ourselves in.'

Situation? Her heart couldn't help but sink at the cold-blooded word. 'Yes, indeed.' She tried to stay calm. 'I did warn you that you should have chosen someone more suitable to be your Duchess. Someone who wouldn't drag you to Bow Street and get herself stuck climbing walls. And Anthony, since I've been here I've found out—*oh!*'

She hurried over to the garden bench because, all of a sudden, the nausea of her pregnancy was overwhelming her again. *Not now*, she was begging under her breath. *Please don't let me be like this right now! When I have so much to tell him.*

But it was no good. She had to sit and close her eyes until the wave of sickness had passed, which meant that she didn't realise Anthony had sat next to her until she felt his hand on her arm.

'Marianne.' He spoke gently. 'Marianne, what is wrong? Are you unwell?'

She opened her eyes and shook her head. 'No, not at all,' she tried to say lightly. 'I just needed to sit down after the excitement of my wall-climbing escapade. Truly, I'm fine now.'

He was still gazing at her. 'You look very pale,' he said quietly.

She drew a deep breath, fighting back another wave of dizziness. Perhaps it was as well if he knew the truth now, before they discussed anything else.

'Yes,' she said. 'That's because I'm fairly sure that I'm pregnant. But Anthony, listen. This need not make things any different between us, so if you wish us to live separately—'

'If I *what?* I never, ever wanted us to live separately!' He sounded almost angry. 'Marianne, you are carrying my child. Why didn't you tell me?'

'Because I hardly knew it myself!' she cried. 'And I did not want to force you into staying with me, since I've been nothing but a disaster for you!'

He was shaking his head. 'No,' he said quietly. 'Just the opposite.' She looked up at him in disbelief as he added, 'I've never been so happy as I was during our honeymoon at Cleveland Hall.'

Oh. She felt truly dizzy now. 'But my visit to Ned Gibson's house spoiled everything, didn't it?'

He shook his head. 'I'm to blame entirely, for not trusting you with the truth.' He lifted one curling strand of her hair and twined it around his fingertips. 'I've realised that I've ruined everything between us, and it's all because of my wretched pride. Can you ever forgive me?'

His words lit up her aching heart with a sense of unexpected, unbelievable hope and suddenly she was in his arms. Who had moved first she wasn't sure, but he was holding her tightly and she leaned into him, pressing her cheek against his strong shoulder, inhaling the scent of his crisp linen shirt and the faint cinnamon odour of the balsam he used on his scarred back. She ran her hands over his muscled shoulders, thrilling to the familiar strength of him through his clothing, then she twisted her fingers in his dark hair and pulled his head down because she desperately wanted more of him.

He obliged by kissing her so thoroughly that she couldn't help but respond and she ached for more, she longed for more.

'Have I told you,' he said, 'how glorious your hair looks when it glows in the sunshine?' He was tenderly stroking her cheek. 'And you have two freckles. I adore freckles.'

She looked up at him wonderingly.

'You're still worried about Gibson,' he said, 'aren't

you? Forget about him and his mean tricks, because whatever he tries to do, we'll cope.' He put his arm around her. 'And besides—'

Then he broke off and swung round, because someone was calling out his name and coming towards them. It was Simon.

Anthony felt himself grow tense. He kept his arm around Marianne, feeling both wary and protective, guessing that Simon's presence here could only mean trouble.

But as Simon approached, he nodded to Anthony then said to his sister, 'Have you told him yet, Marianne? About everything we found out yesterday?'

Anthony was puzzled because Simon, instead of reacting to his presence with barely concealed hostility, looked almost cheerful. Anthony turned to Marianne and raised his eyebrows slightly. 'Well?' he said quietly. 'Are you going to tell me?'

So she did.

She told him about the gardener, Daniel, and how he had seen Cynthia reluctantly approach the waiting carriage on that cold winter's morning. She told him also about Joseph, who had witnessed the accident with a colleague.

Anthony listened to all this. 'But those men were questioned about the accident afterwards,' he said.

'I know they did what they could to help, but they also swore that the coach and its driver disappeared and they could give no details.'

'They gave my sister details,' said Simon. 'Tell him, Marianne.'

So she did. 'One of them,' she said, 'could read and he had noticed the name of the cab company painted on the side. He knew too that the firm was based in Sevenoaks. Simon and I went there yesterday, and we found out that the driver was paid to fetch poor Cynthia from Cleveland Hall and drive her to Sevenoaks, not London, as everyone thought.' She nodded towards her brother. 'Simon encouraged the man to talk. He told us that Cynthia had not wanted to meet the person who sent for her. In fact, she was frightened of him.'

Anthony listened in silence. He was remembering all his efforts after the accident, to find out exactly why she had left the safety of the Hall on that bleak day to set off in some hired carriage that no one seemed able to identify.

Everywhere he had gone, every question he'd asked, he had met with either blank denials or the barest minimum of information. He had already suspected himself that people had either been paid or frightened into absolute silence. But now it appeared that Marianne, with Simon's help, had succeeded where he had failed. These friends of his childhood were still, it appeared, his staunchest allies.

He said quietly, 'The man behind all this was Ned Gibson, wasn't it?'

Marianne grasped his hand. 'So you had guessed?'

'I had suspected it often. But I had no witnesses, no proof.'

Simon was nodding. 'It all makes sense now. But Anthony, why do you think he told her to make that journey, and in such awful weather?'

'I can only imagine that maybe Gibson feared she was about to denounce him at any time. You see, Cynthia had told me that she hated the way her father made money from other people's weaknesses. She told me too that she knew he rigged the odds at his gaming tables, by using marked cards and loaded dice. I always advised her to leave the matter alone, because I feared it could only make things worse for her. She was happy living in Cleveland Hall and confronting her father would only have brought more trouble. But I guess Gibson was still afraid she might say too much and so he took action. He probably intended to warn her, but it ended in tragedy.'

Marianne was shaking her head in disbelief. 'I thought he loved his daughter. I thought he believed that nothing was too good for her.'

'I'm afraid he was a harsh father,' said Anthony,

'and he just wanted to use her for a stake in the Duchy of Cleveland.'

They stood in silence for a moment, then Simon spoke. 'Anthony,' he said. 'Marianne has told me all about the reasons for your first marriage. I just want to say that I'm sorry, for not believing in you as I should have done. What will you do now, about Gibson?'

'I intend to tell him that his game is up,' said Anthony. 'He'll hardly want this story exposed. By forcing his daughter to travel that day, he and he alone was responsible for the accident that killed her.'

Marianne looked anxious still, yet so unbelievably beautiful that all he wanted was to take her to Cleveland Hall and up to his bedroom right now. Simon must have guessed because he was noisily clearing his throat.

'I think,' he said, 'that I had better join my mother in the house, before she wonders what's going on… Ah. Too late.' For Lady Hermione was already emerging from the house, with a trio of maids bearing trays of sandwiches and cakes.

Simon turned to Anthony and Marianne and said softly, 'If I were you, I'd make my escape now. Agreed?'

'Agreed,' said Anthony. 'And Simon, please accept my hearty thanks.'

The two men shook hands. 'I did very little.' Simon was smiling. 'I just provided a bit of back-up for my enterprising sister, that's all.'

Marianne's heart was full as she watched her brother and Anthony together. After that, Simon headed swiftly towards their mother, to lead her and the maids back into the house. Anthony was still beside her, but she couldn't think what to say.

This was the moment when surely all the shadows that had haunted both their pasts should be melting away in the sunlight. But she was still afraid. Afraid that if she opened herself up to him by sharing his life and his bed, she would be vulnerable again, terribly so, because she loved him so much.

Then he said, 'Marianne, do you want to spend a little more time with your mother and Simon? I can always go back to Cleveland Hall and come for you later.'

She gazed up at him and she said, 'No. Please don't leave me.' *Ever. Don't leave me, ever.*

'You mean it?'

'Yes. Oh, yes!'

He held her tightly then. 'Marianne,' he said, 'I'm here for you. You have not deserved all these awful things that have happened to you—including the ways I've let you down. No, don't protest. If you're still worrying about your past betrothals, I've already told you that if your wretched army captain wasn't already dead, I would happily have dealt with him for you. As for Moseley, I've thumped him and threatened him with ruin—and I'll do exactly the same for anyone else who makes you unhappy.'

This time she really felt as if she was going to cry. But she found she was smiling a little as well. 'Thump them, you mean? Please don't, Anthony! You know it wouldn't really help!'

'No?' He brushed a stray strand of hair away from her forehead. 'What would help?'

'You're helping me now.' She leaned into his embrace, resting her cheek against his shoulder. 'By being here. By believing in me.'

'Always,' he said quietly. 'I mean it.'

She was silent a moment. Then she said, 'Do you really believe you can keep Gibson quiet now, about the past and your father?'

'I do,' he said steadily. 'Thanks to you. After Cynthia died I tried my best to find out what really happened that day, but you have succeeded where I failed. I shall never forget what I owe you. I owe you my love, for ever.'

He kissed her, and her heart was full.

Anthony led Marianne to the curricle, keeping his arm around her. He realised she still looked a little overwhelmed by all that had happened, but he loved her all the more for it. Yes, he was ridiculously, madly in love with her and there was no hiding it.

He helped her up so she could sit next to him on the driver's bench. But before he reached for the reins he took her hand and said, 'I've missed you. I've missed you more than I would have believed possible. I left London at first light this morning because I realised that it didn't matter what malicious lies Gibson might try to spread; in fact, nothing mattered, as long as I had you.'

'I've missed you too, darling Anthony,' she murmured. 'Please, take me home.'

He gathered up the reins and nodded. 'Home.'

That night was like their first night together all over again. They ate supper in the parlour rather than the vast dining room, and afterwards Anthony took her by the hand and led her up the stairs to her bedroom.

There they kissed again—Anthony had quite lost count of how many times they had kissed already this evening—but he managed to ease himself away to say, 'Marianne, you are the most precious thing in my life and I don't want to lose you again. I don't want, ever, to hurt you again.' He hesitated. 'Is it all right if I share your bed tonight?'

She gave him her beguiling smile. 'Now that I'm pregnant, you mean? Of course it is.' She reached up to caress his face, her fingertips lingering a little over the shadowy stubble already darkening his jaw. 'Besides, how can I possibly bear another night without you?'

He helped her to undress, tossing away the final scraps of her underwear and kissing her everywhere until she was desperate with longing. He gave a husky chuckle at her impatience, he teased her a little more with his kisses, but finally he urged her to the very peak of pleasure and with his own release it felt as if they were as one. He gathered her tightly in his arms and for a while they lay together in silence, needing no words.

But at last she stirred a little and whispered, 'So you don't hate me, for telling you that you were too proud, and for meddling in your business?'

'No,' he said. 'Because you were right. Absolutely right.'

'And you don't mind that I still like climbing walls in the countryside and getting myself in a mess?'

He eased himself up on one elbow so he could gaze down into her velvety-brown eyes that were filled with a mixture of hope and trust.

He said, 'I don't mind. In fact, I insist that you stay exactly as you are—brave, adventurous and loyal.

Those are just some of the things that I love about you. My Duchess. My redemption.'

His redemption? Yes, it was true. Because Marianne, without realising it, had saved him from himself. He had become cynical in the last few years, both about life and about the people who surrounded him, and in his bleakest moments he had even resolved that if he were to marry again, it would be a marriage of practicality, not love.

But then Marianne had come back into his life and during the turbulent weeks that followed he had sometimes been amused by her, sometimes exasperated. But always he had known, from the depths of his soul, that she truly was the only woman for him.

He loved her and now he was able to love her openly and honestly, without a care as to what people thought. He guessed that even with Gibson silenced, some people would still mutter about his first marriage and her two betrothals. Probably Marianne would get into still more scrapes, because she was impulsive and forthright. But the girl who had been his friend for years was now his wife and he would be by her side always, not just for her sake but for his. He needed her. He loved her. Without her, his life was incomplete.

They were to have a child and hopefully there would be more. Together, they were at the start of a great adventure, and through it all he needed her to light up his life and share the good and bad things that happened to everyone. He wanted her as his Duchess, his partner and his wife, every day for the rest of his life.

Epilogue

Two weeks later, five men rode up to the large house of Ned Gibson in Clerkenwell. As they dismounted, Gibson's two black-clad henchmen emerged. 'Stop right there,' growled one of them. 'What's your business?'

Anthony was the leader of those horsemen and Simon was by his side. The other three were Simon's army friends.

'My business,' answered Anthony, 'is with Gibson, not you.' He turned to Simon and his colleagues. 'Stay here, will you? I won't be long.'

Simon nodded. 'We'll be waiting.'

Anthony's confrontation with Ned Gibson was brief but lethal. 'I know what you did to your daughter, Gibson,' Anthony told him. 'You sent that carriage for her, so that you could order her to keep quiet about the tricks you use in your gambling den.

You certainly succeeded in silencing her, you rogue, didn't you?'

Gibson tried to speak, but Anthony held up his hand to stop him. 'Listen to me. You can carry on with your sordid money-making if you choose. After all, many businesses like yours use the same tricks. But don't ever dare to say a word about my father or Marianne. Because I'm warning you that if people were to learn you were responsible for Cynthia's last, fatal journey, not even the most desperate gambler will want to give you their custom.'

He left before Gibson could utter a word.

Within the month Gibson had closed down the Clover Club in Holborn and his big house in Clerkenwell lay empty. It was said that he had moved to Paris to set up a new gaming club, but Anthony never enquired and no one heard anything more of him.

In February the following year, Marianne gave birth to a baby girl and Anthony was besotted with her, as were they all. Anthony decided to hold a party at Cleveland Hall to celebrate, inviting their friends from London. Lady Hermione had taken up permanent residence at Oakfields now, and so had Simon—for soon after the incident with Gibson he had come to consult Marianne and Anthony.

'I've decided,' he said, 'to resign from the army

and stay with Mother at Oakfields, just for a while. I thought that I could spend some months restoring the estate and helping the local farmers to get the most from their land, just as I used to before Mother's marriage to Sir Edgar. That is, if you approve, Marianne?'

She had approved warmly, and the arrangement was working out well. But she longed to do more for her brother, and on the night of the christening party, two hours before their guests were due to arrive at the Hall, she approached Anthony in his dressing room, where Travers was bringing out a selection of cravats for him to choose from.

'Anthony…' she said cajolingly.

Her husband nodded to Travers. 'Leave us for a few moments, will you?'

'Certainly, Your Grace.'

As soon as he'd gone, Anthony went up to his wife and put one finger under her chin so he could tilt up her face towards his. 'I know that voice,' he teased. 'It means there's trouble in store.'

'No! Not really, Anthony! It's just that I've had an idea.'

He pretended to groan.

'Listen,' she went on. 'Truly, this is important. I know that Oakfields is mine, but I would very much like to give it to Simon. He is running it so well and, besides, some day he is bound to get married and it would be a wonderful family home.' She stopped, a little breathless. 'What do you think?'

'I think,' said Anthony, 'that it's a wonderful idea. Simon deserves it. And your father would have approved, I'm sure.'

She wrapped her arms around his waist. 'I think,' she said softly, 'that you must be the kindest and best man in the world.'

He gave her that lopsided smile that she loved. 'High praise indeed. Might you be overdoing it a little?'

This time she looked up at him stubbornly. 'No, not in the least. Kiss me, will you?'

Very gladly, he obliged until she broke away with a gasp.

'The party!' she exclaimed. 'We must get ready for the party!'

'That,' he said, 'is exactly what I was trying to do.'

She kissed him one more time then ran off to her own room, where Elsie was waiting to help her on with her finery.

Lady Hermione and Simon had already arrived from Oakfields. Marianne had left her mother down in the nursery, and when Marianne and Anthony went there at last, they found her mother reciting nursery rhymes to her baby granddaughter while Simon watched in amusement.

'Look, Marianne,' said Lady Hermione. 'She is

smiling at me. I'm sure she understands every word, and she is going to be a most intelligent child. My first grandchild, and not my last, I trust. Tell me her name again, will you, Anthony dear?'

'In full, Lady Hermione?'

'Indeed, yes. All of it.'

'Very well.' Anthony cleared his throat. 'Her name is Lady Philippa Mary Isabel Georgina Cleveland,' he pronounced.

'Oh my, how wonderful! And so delightful for me, because I am, after all the daughter of…'

'The daughter of an earl!' they all chorused.

Yes, Lady Philippa had a long and indeed a slightly formidable name. But really, Anthony and Marianne preferred to call their beloved baby just—Pippa.

* * * * *

If you enjoyed this story, why not check out one of Lucy Ashford's other captivating reads

The Master of Calverley Hall
Unbuttoning Miss Matilda
The Widow's Scandalous Affair
The Viscount's New Housekeeper
Challenging the Brooding Earl
Lord Lambourne's Forbidden Debutante

MILLS & BOON®

Coming next month

DARING TO FALL FOR THE PRINCE
Heba Helmy

Their banter was easy, natural, but then Saleem raised the coffee to his lips and it took all of Elise's strength *not* to gape at how their fullness overwhelmed the thin-lined golden rim of the demitasse. Tried to ignore the tightening in her chest as she imagined those lips on hers.

Saleem mused, 'There is such a thing as a late-morning start.'

'Do you have them often?' Elise hadn't *entirely* meant to imply anything untoward, but Saleem took it that way.

He answered mischievously, 'Late nights lead to late mornings. The best fun to be had is in the evenings, when the sun isn't there to bear witness. Or chaperons with eyes at the back of their heads.'

Beneath the table cloth, Elise clasped her fingers together. Saleem had the kind of mannerisms that were dangerously disarming. Couple them with his handsomeness and even the most restrained and contained women would lose sight of who they were in his presence.

She was no exception. 'Ah, but, Prince Saleem, you are the sort to bask in the sunlight.'

Were they flirting with one another?

'You've looked into my soul, Miss Elise, and got the mark of me.' Saleem's chuckle came effortlessly. 'Lucky for me, this is Egypt and we get much of it. Even with the latest of mornings, we do not miss out on the sun.'

Then, before she knew what he was doing, he'd taken his fork and lifted a piece of the dessert on it, then held it out to her. 'If you will not drink coffee with me, you must try the *basboosa* at least, infused with rose syrup. My idea. Cook wasn't too sure, so your honest opinion is required.'

She could not say she actually tasted it, but Elise savoured the sensation of it. The fork, having been in Saleem's mouth, on his lips, and now being in hers and on hers felt…dangerous.

Continue reading

DARING TO FALL FOR THE PRINCE
Heba Helmy

Available next month
millsandboon.co.uk

Afterglow Books is a trend-led, trope-filled list of books with diverse, authentic and relatable characters, a wide array of voices and representations, plus real world trials and tribulations. Featuring all the tropes you could possibly want (think small-town settings, fake relationships, grumpy vs sunshine, enemies to lovers) and all with a generous dose of spice in every story.